Elephant

By Natalie Rodriguez

For My Grandma Connie.
Ditto (I love you too).

~~~~~~~~

This story is for those who feel their voice is unheard and for
children, teenagers, and the adults who have never had the chance
to heal from their pain. No one is EVER destined to repeat the
cycle. The cycle can be broken.

If you would like to tell us your story, be sure to message us at
@elephant_bookya on Instagram or tweet us at @Ebookya, using
the hashtag #TheElephantInMyRoom.

Contents

Contents

The New York Times

A tragedy in a family…

For the Smith family, it was a day that would infamously be remembered until the end of time. On the night of August 4th, 1992, sixty-two-year-old LUCIA SMITH had received the worse news of her life, involving the whereabouts of her husband of forty-three years, FRANK, and their only child, JIMMY. The incident that had changed their lives forever.

1.

IT WAS DIFFICULT TO SEE, as though an ice cube had enclosed his body. Frostbite worked its way down his fingertips, turning bluer by the second.

Something was visible. He was visible of the silhouette.

Around 5'8", a silhouette of a man—no taller than the teenage boy—stood in front of him.

"Wait!" The teenage boy called after; his breath vapored out into puffs of clouds.

He pushed forward.

"Come back!"

But the teenage boy was distancing away, not the silhouette. The boy lunged forward and came to an abrupt halt. Somehow, somewhere, in the white frosty air, his feet kept getting sucked into the ground, into the white floor. Winter wonderland.

An invisible force field was among the boy and the unknown man.

"Wait!" his voice now croaked. The boy stretched out his arms, but, starting at the tips of his fingers and working its way down his wrists, forearms, and arms—a blaring light shone.

He squinted as the light traveled through the white cloud storm, forcing him to look away.

* * *

The teenage boy's eyes shot wide open, awakening. He wormed his way up, giving the mattress a few squeaks. The door was closed, and the curtains were concealed with floor length curtains. There was zero amount of light coming into the bedroom. He kept his hand on the chain of the lamp atop the bedside table.

Matthew Jimmy Smith was his name.

Around 5'8", he was a teenager in the midst of puberty with a possibility of another growth spurt, not a boy,

Acne: *great*. Body type: lean-ish. Puberty check: no fucks.

Mood: moody. The childhood paintings on the walls also had a mind of their own, with squiggly letters of his name, **Matt**, and his nickname, **Matty**. A few of them were written in bold as well.

Matt had thick, wavy rock-n-roll-drummer-hair, but now his dark brunette neck length locks decided that they were best to puff out like an inhaled balloon. He had big hair like Dee Snider, one of the too many band posters displayed on his off-white colored walls. Kurt Cobain, Alice Cooper, and Angus Young accompanied the neighboring posters.

Matthew…Matt…Matty (the boy with countless identities) lowered his hand from the bedside lamp. He rubbed the sleep from his eyes. The dirty piles of clothes on the floor were still a bit visible. They brought a God-awful stench into the bedroom, like a fresh pile of cat shit dropped into an indoor litter box with the windows shut. "Gross!"

Matt chucked the camouflage comforter and the matching black-and-blue bedsheets off his body. Immediately, he noticed how his entire body was covered in sweat. He wore his gym shorts; his T-shirt—displaying the IVY HIGH SCHOOL, HOME OF THE POISON logo—clung to his hairless chest like peanut butter smudged across a piece of paper. He sniffed around some more and immediately, his nose was drawn to the blob of sweat underneath his armpit. Nope, that was not the cause of the cat litter shit stench.

Then, he tugged at the centerpiece of his T-shirt and held it to his nose. Oh, it made sense now. That God-awful stench, the case of B.O., was *him*.

'*Jesus*!' He turned his head away and released his T-shirt; it clung back to his skin, and he wiped the last remains of saliva from the corner of his mouth.

Swinging one leg over the full-size bed, the other followed and fell off the mattress. Life could not have been easier, but then his daddy long-legs got caught in the midst of their own storm. "Dammit!" He moved his legs left and right, then right and left. After a few kicks, his legs broke free from the tangled bedsheets. But with his body already too close to the edge of the bed, he toppled over to the floor. He fell with a loud thud. Outside of his bedroom door, the wooden floor gave an eerie haunted house creak.

"What was that?!" said a girl with a husky voice, still in the process of womanhood.

"He's up!" It was a boy's voice, *also* in the process of puberty.

Matt perked up his head, just enough to see over his bed. Shadows huddled closer to the door through its small crack of an opening. The dead giveaway was the twisting and turning of the golden doorknob, rejecting their entry.

"Matt?" It was the same girl, followed by a few knocks.

"Maybe we should let him…"

"Let me do it," the boy interjected to the *other* girl. "Like this."

The door jolted at every bam, bam, bam from the two drumroll-fists that pounded on the door. That definitely did not sound like a pretty picture.

"Derek?"

"What woman?"

"Don't you *ever* call me woman!"

Matt set his chin onto the edge of the bed. He let out a chuckle and thought to himself, '*Typical. Typical Jamie and Derek.*'

He reached for the closest piece of clothing on the floor and found dark gray gym shorts. He was clueless if they were clean or not. Probably not.

"Children," he announced. "Children of the corn. Please don't fight! I'm a comin'!" He gave a thumb ups to the Jimi Hendrix poster. He broke out and got down to the opening verse of "Hear My Train a Comin'."

As he inched closer to the door, the footsteps trampled away, and the shadows vanished from the door's slight gap. "What the...Guys?"

Matt flung the door open to nothingness except for the little amount of light that streamed through the windows along the hallway. They revealed the last bits of another orange, yellow, purple, and pink sky of a summer evening. Truly, it was the definition of beauty. But it was still muggy and hot as a motherfucker.

Matt dabbed at the beads of sweat from the four corners of his face. "This weather."

And then, the lights zapped out, revealing the hint of glow from the corner of his eyes...

An aisle of picture frames lit him a walkway that he motioned down; he discovered the book-lights attached atop the frames rendered the faces visible in the photographs.

Pacing right to left and left to right, it was a walk down memory lane. There were photographs of himself as a toddler with curly, light brown tints of golden locks. In other pictures, he was a young boy with brown, spiky hair that either had burgundy, blue, or green gel at the tips. His soft olive complexion had also gone through its own transition: olive in the earlier days and overly tanned around the middle school days (he frowned in all the baseball headshots and team AKA class-photos). Not to mention his teeth! They had a story of their own as well. He was a metal mouth and gave his best "toothpaste commercial smile" in the sixth and seventh-grade yearbook photos—with red braces that looked like a pool of blood. He caught a glimpse of his present day "tanner" but still so awkward, adolescent self. At least, that was what he had always believed himself awkward as fuck.

Matt was not exactly popular.

Ascending the staircase, the pictures formed a countdown. It all began at picture frame number one, July 1st. The candles on top of the birthday cake in each photograph indicated what year it was and how old he was; all thirteen of them. At two-years-old, he sat in the highchair. At seven, he was crouching like a hidden dragon by the untouched birthday cake

Nine…Ten…Eleven…Twelve…Thirteen…

The trail of photographs came to an end as he arrived at the dining room archway, where it smelled like fresh-out-of-the-oven bakery rolls. *"Happy birthday to you…"*

And there they were, the four of them. His seventy-six-year-old grandmother, Lucia, and his three best friends since childhood, Jamie, Derek, and Lisa. The four of them stood behind the oversized chocolate chip cookie that sat atop the wooden oak dining room table for six. On the birthday "cake" resided two sparkling numerical numbers: **one and four.**

"…Happy…birthday…to…you…"

The chandelier was turned up a notch and added a simple, almost angelic touch as the four of them hit the high note. They were not the best of singers. By the end of the song, Derek's voice cracked a few times and it turned him into Kermit the Frog, only his voice was scratchier. Matt busted up, cry-laughing. He had to. It was typical. Typical Lisa as she sang her heart out. Typical Lucia as she watched the other two, cracking up as well. Typical Derek, as Typical Jamie elbowed him. Jamie's words were readable, as she mouthed to Derek, *"Shut. Da. Hell. Up."*

Only, Derek dropped to his knees and spread his arms out like an eagle ready to fly. *"And many more on channel four…"*

"And a big fat lady on channel eighty," Lisa joined in.

Jamie gave a smile. "Happy birthday, Matty."

"Make a wish, sweetheart," Lucia said and gestured to the cookie cake.

"Remember," Lisa chimed back in, "always keep your wish a secret. Don't jinx that shit."

"Lisa…"

"Sorry, Lucia."

Matt gazed down at the chocolate chip cookie, seamlessly well-designed. An icing cutout of a basketball, outlined in black and white frosting, sat in the center of the cookie itself. From top to bottom, beady stars were scattered everywhere and sketched out in brown frosted lukewarm syrup. Colored sprinkles and M&M's of all sizes aligned with the crust.

Three weeks ago:

A machine sitting underneath the banner, "CLASS OF 2006. CONGRATS GRADS," sputtered out confetti onto the graduates. Matt caught a few of them in his hands. Most were designs of tiny size caps and gowns and the big ol' '06 and 2006. Jamie had a few stuck in her curly hair. She would only curl her hair on special occasions. Matt removed the one piece of confetti that had drifted onto her cheek. It was a red snowflake. She smiled at his intrigued expression and pulled him in for a hug, wrapping her arms around his lower back. He dropped the piece of confetti, as his arms mocked hers…grazing over the small of her back. Skin to skin.

* * *

Back in the dining room, his eyes were already closed. He leaned forward and the calligraphic words at the bottom of the cookie, in sky-blue frosting, HAPPY BIRTHDAY! WE LOVE YOU, was just inches from his T-shirt.

"Here," she said. Then, he felt a whiff of cold air against the side of his body. He knew it was her. That voice. Jamie had pulled back his T-shirt, so the icing would not stain it.

He felt the back of his T-shirt tightening against his lower back. She refused to let go, until he stood up again.

In that moment of darkness (quite literally), his heart picked up tempo as he asked, not stated, "Thanks?" His cheeks grew hot. He clenched his fingers into tiny boxing gloves—the only tick that sped down his pulse. His lips shaped into a perfect 'O', he inhaled and held his breath for an instance. *This* was what he wanted: them; his friends and Lucia. But his world of darkness was also missing something else: *them*.

"Come on, *Matt*!" Derek said. "Matt! Matt!"

His mother, His father, his grandfather, they were no longer with him and Lucia.

Matt exhaled and blew out the burning flames on the candle **one and four**. The dining room exploded into a round of victory as his friend pounded their feet against the wooden floor. Derek even gave a few dog barks. Lisa clapped her hands around in circles. Jamie whistled between the small gaps on her four bottom teeth.

"And he's officially fourteen!" Lucia praised in pitch blackness.

2.

"SO MUCH FOR 'I'M ON A DIET.'"

Derek stuffed another soy sauce-loaded Italian meatball into his mouth.

"Shut up, midget!" Jamie retorted and set another pepperoni sausage olive pizza slice onto her plate.

"That's so rude." Lisa shoved a spoonful of chicken manicotti into her mouth. "You're like calling her fat."

"*She's* the one who's always saying, 'I'm so fat! I'm so fat! Guys do I look fat or *phat*?!'"

"Oh," Lucia chuckled, "neither one of you needs to lose weight. In all honesty, you can all gain a few pounds."

She peered at Jamie, who smiled. "Thanks." It was in the eyes.

"Well." Matt chewed off his last bite of a sweet and spicy boneless chicken wing from the sticky orange sauce on his fingers. "Who's next?"

"Mine." Jamie handed over a sealed envelope. On the front, "MATTY" was handwritten in bold navy blue ink.

"Thanks." As soon as their hands brushed, a shock of electricity ran through his body. "Uh, thanks." It was all he had thought of—that spark between them and taking an extra look at Jamie; her eyes were still on him like a hawk's.

Everyone sat at the edge of their dining chairs. Lucia took a sip from her glass of red wine, as she leveled up the digital camera in the other hand (mad pro skills). Matt glanced at their eager faces, although Derek's big ol' goofy grin held his attention for a moment longer. The boy sure had some crooked ass teeth, to be truthful. It was also unsettling that Derek's grin grew wider like a mannequin in a window display and not the pretty looking ones either, more of the

Stepford wives with clown makeup and pumped lips and cheekbones.

Matt opened the envelope and into his hands spilled two gift cards: Tillys, and iTunes. For some reason, he sighed with relief.

"See." Jamie leaned back in her chair. "I can follow your crazy, 'only gift cards' rule. We all remember *last year*."

Lucia snorted and covered her mouth to prevent the wine from spilling out. But a few splashes sputtered through her nostrils.

"Yeah," Lisa added on, "those clothes were all baggy in the wrong places."

"You looked like a damn hobo!" Derek cackled.

"Thanks, Jam," Matt said with a bit overzealous smile. '*Shit*,' he thought to himself. '*Motherfuckin' shit*.'

He turned away and placed her gift on the small pile: gift cards Derek got him for Chick's Sporting Goods and Best Buy with Target and Starbucks gift cards Lisa got him.

"Thank you…"

"Anytime, Matty." And that time, Jamie smiled back. Holy, moly! She had pretty little teeth too.

"I'm done!" Derek backed up his chair and unbuttoned his Levi's to air out his potbelly. That was when Jamie broke focus with Matt.

"Derek—put that thing away!" she screeched.

"Mini Buddha's belly!" Lisa chanted and wiggled her arms over her head like a gorilla.

"Derek…"

"Sorry, Lucia." He scooted his chair back in, which gave the floor a few squeaks, so the red tablecloth concealed his stomach—his VERY pale, sole patched, Buddha's belly.

"Well, I don't know about you four but I'm *tired*." Lucia swayed to her feet; her fingers went white as she clutched a hold of her glass. Matt eyed that second empty wine glass like it would come alive. "I'll see you all."

"Wait," Derek interjected. "Aren't we supposed to—"

"SHHHHH…"

They had their fingers pressed to their lips. Jamie and Lisa even glowered his way. Matt's eyes broadened with horror, as his head drooped closer to the table. It was done, all over.

Clueless at first, Derek's eyes shot wide open as though struck by lightning. *"OH—"*

"SHHHHH!"

"Matt," Lucia said, her speech troublesome, "is this…"

The pieces of confetti on the table were shinier than ever. Matt rolled one of them between his thumb and middle finger. The confetti was a lustrous blue circle, although it felt like blazing hot fire. The creators of confetti had it all wrong. They should have been red—a mighty, burning passionless red.

"Matt…"

"I want you to…" On that last deep breath, he looked up at his grandma. "We're going to the cemetery—"

"Goodnight, Matt—"

"Why don't you ever want to talk about *it*?!"

Jamie, Derek, and Lisa moved robotically. The lower halves of their bodies went paralyzed, as their eyes rolled side to side to catch glimpses of each other and the Smiths. By now, Matt was on his feet, his fists planted on the table. The tablecloth was scrunched up as he leaned forward, steadying his balance on his elbows. His pulse raced throughout his body, rigid as stone and hot as lava.

"Why can't you let it go," he pleaded unintentionally. "I did."

"Matt, I'm very…" Her back was to them. Lucia lingered in the dining room archway, but by the sniffles and refusal to turn around, it was obvious. She did everything she could to cover up the waterworks; she even tugged at her sleeve (long sleeves shirts were all she ever wore). "I'm very tired. I'll see you in the morning."

Off her glance, she was gone. Her red sea of swimming pool-eyes was no longer in their sight. His sight.

Jamie, Derek, and Lisa averted their attention away from Matt. Suddenly, he felt…funny. Something seemed to boil at the pit of his stomach. Whatever it was, it shot up to his chest and formed a sour taste in the back of his mouth, like he had just eaten something spoiled, weeks after its expiration date.

"Matty…"

Her fingers drifted over his fist like a cloak. Matt's fingers unfolded, but he refused to look at her. It was obvious—the strain and worried look in her eyes, as she caressed his hand. His shoulders shot up, about an inch from touching his earlobes. The twinge of sorrow prolonged in his eyes and strengthened the veins to pop right out; red, so very red from the haggardness and stress, all from another wasted amount of energy from a big waste of time. *'Every year,'* he thought to himself. *'Every year on my birthday.'*

3.

"AND I THOUGHT I WAS JUST tired from practice," Matt said, his words oddly slurred. "Coach has us doing suicide runs at the end of every damn practice. Every single FUCKIN' day!" And up came the flask. "Like grandma…Like grandson." He raised his flask to the royal deep blue sky. "Cheers, bitches!"

Swarms of itty-biddy stars winked at him, as he titled his head back to drink and chug. He sat atop a cleanly shaven tree stump that was attached—or nailed in—to the dirt ground. Who knew! The summer breeze chafed his cold face, and he pulled his hood tighter to his black pull-over sweater.

"Now you look like a serial killer." Jamie yanked back his hood and grabbed the flask from his hand. He was not *too* happy about that.

"Hey!"

Jamie aimed her arm up and chucked the flask. It soared through the air like a bird, swallowed up whole by the night's air. They only heard an off distant *clump*. Matt crossed his arms and pouted. He puffed out some air and his lips vibrated with a motor-like sound. Derek and Lisa sat Indian style from across him and Jamie. It looked like Derek was in the middle of prayer, since his arms rested on his thighs, and his fingers were curled in. Lisa shivered and buried her mouth in her button-down jean jacket.

"Turn it up," Matt said, already getting down, and pointed to Derek's cell phone. "I like this song."

His friend did as he was told. The volume for AC/DC's "Highway to Hell" went up a few notches, and so did Matt's voice as he sang, shouting along with the words. "God! I was born in the wrong era!" He bobbed his head around some more, a total metal head rocking out but without the long hair. *"'I'm on the highway to hell. Highway to hell…'"*

Jamie popped a squat next to him, as he dropped it like it was hot during a play of air-guitar. It took a moment before he looked at her and said, "You didn't have to throw that earlier."

Before she opened her mouth to speak, the music came to an abrupt halt.

"Yo!" Matt tossed his arms up in the air.

The bold digital numbers blinked 9:35 PM on his cell phone. It rang. Derek was consumed by discomfort. "It's Lucia," he said, too afraid to look anywhere else but at the ground. He kicked a nearby pebble. It did not go too far.

"Matty."

But he trudged away from her, away from them.

"Where the hell are you going?" Now the irritation carried the heavy weight of her tone.

"Anywhere but here," he retorted. "I may not stop her from holding a grudge, but I sure as hell won't let her fun my ruin."

"I think he meant, 'Ruin my fun,'" Lisa said.

"Fuck," Jamie spat. "Matt!" She followed him.

"Uh, Lisa…" Derek went wide eye, biting his bottom lip, unsure what to say or do. "Should I—"

She rejected the call for him.

Around the corner, Matt carried his tune without the help of AC/DC's Bon Scott. *"'Some weary clock strikes midnight. And there's a full moon in the sky'…*Oh, shit!"

He rammed his foot into one of the many random rocks that were spread around the dirt, pebbly, and (literally) rocky ground that just screamed for trouble. Tripping over one of the pebbly, dirt rocks, the pressure drove his body forward. Thankfully, he was in luck and grabbed ahold of a nearby tree branch before he ate shit. He laughed, one side of his body rigid as the other half swayed along to end verse of

AC/DC's "Night Prowler". He belted out the lyrics loud and proud. It was his over-the-top grand finale. The blood rushed to his face from his near-death injury and the fact that his voice cracked on that final note. But the fun and games came to a stop when he looked elsewhere and kissed his grin goodbye.

Beyond the gravestones, the miles of grassland stretched on like an endless fantastical battlefield, a scene directly out of the *Lord of the Rings* movies, until he reached a fork in the road. Two choices. Two very different destinations. Fascinated by one of the pebbly dirt patches that bordered the fresh cut green grass, his eyes scoped the area some more, as he got closer to the gate. It was a perfectly symmetrical design.

"Matty!" he heard Jamie call from some ways. "Guys, did you see which direction he went off to?"

"No," both Derek and Lisa said amicably.

His eyes were closed, and he was taking in a whiff of the alpine scent. The sprinklers hissed through his ears like cartoon words. He reopened his eyes to watch the sprinklers sputter around in circles, watering the trees of all sizes. Petite. Gaunt. Sturdy. Trees towered to the sky like skyscrapers. He felt a sudden rush of vertigo and his legs jolted.

"There you are!"

"Shit." His free hand snatched ahold of the same tree branch that kept him on his feet, unable to see Jamie. The tree, his protector, prevented him from collapsing backward onto a small boulder. The tree also held his attention. It was a tall mighty tree. Green leaves and pink feathery toppings drifted off the branches from the touch of the summer breeze. His mind was taken away from the lukewarm sensation that trickled down his hand and down to the dirt.

"Matt." Jamie's voice shot five octaves higher. "You're bleeding!" She pinballed to his side but, in reality, he had not gone far at all. Derek and Lisa were still in the deer hunter's sights.

Matt looked at his hand and there was, indeed, a scratch on his palm. The blood was minor, but Jamie went overboard and tossed one of his arms around her shoulders. "Like she can do the heavy lifting."

"What?" she said.

'*Shit, I said that aloud.*'

"Come on." Lisa nudged Derek's arm and slipped on her neon, winter cotton gloves. "Let's go home."

They met up with Matt and Jamie. Matt blabbered on about how summer's eve looked. "Winter came early this year!" His eye watered up, and its veins were already a deep red and purple. The left lazy eye was a giveaway on how exhausted he felt.

"One of you…" Jamie gritted her teeth. "…a little help."

Derek rushed to the opposite side and yanked Matt's arm, the one holding on for dear life, off the tree branch. "Let's walk it off. Do a little dance. Make a little—"

"Might want to rethink those lyrics, Pal." Jamie tucked in her purple scarf, officially bundled up in her lavender, winter creampuff jacket or as Matt had once called it, 'A Powerpuff Girl.' It was puffy but nowhere close to being fluffy.

"Whoa." Matt already had their undivided attention, only he had eyes for the skeleton design on Derek's black beanie. "I dig that. It's *spooky*!" And out came the spirit fingers, wiggling them individually.

Finally, they headed out. Jamie took one last look over her shoulder.

Each step forward pushed them further away from the miles and miles of flowerbeds that blossomed from the roots of the grass. Behind the tree stump, where Matt sat moments ago, was a portion of fresh cut grass. Sitting atop that specific portion of grass was two flowerpots before two gravestones:

FRANK SMITH   **JAMES "JIMMY" SMITH**
Loving husband   Loving son
Loving father   Loving father
Loving grandfather   Loving friend

The rusty brown iron gates shut behind them. They exited
White Rose Cemetery.

4.

"FAUCK! **SHE'S GOING TO KILL ME** when I show up like this. FAUCK."

Speech: clear...er. Complexion: pinker than red and it was progressing. He was a work in progress.

"Drink up."

"Jamie…"

She pressed the glass against his shoulder. He squirmed from the coldness. "Now."

Groaning, he raised his head up from his hands. He grabbed a hold of the glass during his rant, rather mumble. Jamie's hand swooped back in with two Advil. "Really?" he said.

"Trust me. You'll be thanking me for it tomorrow."

He obeyed and tossed the pills into his mouth and drank until the glass was empty. It was refreshing water, ice-cold. The hairs on his arms started to rise—like a line of assembled, women and men. He puckered his lips and let out an, "Ah!"

It got a chuckle from her. She playfully rolled her eyes and joined him on the opposite end of the couch. There was a big ol' gap between them. It was at that moment her cell phone buzzed and filled the void. "It's Lisa. Just got—"

Beep. Beep.

"'Home,'" Matt read Derek's text message from his cell phone. By the look and gesture, he could care less. He tossed his phone aside; There were three missed calls and voicemails listed. All from Lucia.

His fingers turned white as he gripped onto the glass, making his fingerprints visible through the emptiness. He glanced around the living room. It was well furnished. Everything had a gold and emerald green design, including the curtains. Some areas were a bit over-the-top than others because the shelves and tabletops were crammed with framed pictures. Photographs of Jamie, the only child, were presented in the trip down memory lane with just her and her mother. The marble fireplace-mantle also had a school photograph of Jamie, at least six or seven years old then. The telltale was her two missing front teeth, as though they were knocked out in a boxing match, which did not keep her from smiling. It got him smiling a bit, too.

The Castellanos residence was prettier and bigger than his home (he hated that). After all, Jamie and her mother lived in a gated community neighborhood. There was even a code box outside the tall black iron gates, but nobody ever really used it. Cell phones were used, granting their access to the home. The perk of the Castellano's residence was a short walking distance from the fun side of town. There was an outdoor shopping plaza with restaurants, an indoor mall, and an arcade. All that surrounded Matt, Derek and Lisa's homes were banks and office buildings. Some places were even abandoned. Anything was better than his home. Just about anything was better than his home.

"You can stay here if you want," Jamie said, twiddling her fingers. He noticed that she did that a lot lately. Like a lot. At that moment, she flushed. "You know, just so you can get a break from home." Now, she was all fidgety, crossing one leg over the other and vice versa, and some more vice versa.

Matt remained silent and set his cup down on the glass coffee table. There was a shimmery gold outline forming the table's edges.

"You swapped some from her cabinet earlier. Does she know?"

"Nope," he replied like it was no big deal, but it was. "It's from last time when the four of us were supposed to experiment with drinking." By now, he slouched to his side on the couch, compressed against the black rim framing of the couch. A gold and green striped couch. God, he even chuckled at that. *'Basic bitches.'*

"What's so funny?"

"Nothing." And at that moment, their eyes met. The adrenaline rush started at the bottom of his feet and traveled upward, moving very snake-like from his calves to his thighs and further. Whoa.

He removed his hands from his pockets like that would end the tingling sensation. He felt odd again. There was pressure in the middle of his forehead, and it worked its way inward, closer, and closer to his brain like it was about to snap in half or something. Or something else. Ah!

One thing for sure, it was really *really*—

"Hot," he said and jumped to his feet. He flapped a piece of his pull-over up and down to let in the cool air. It helped. His body was consumed by the chill, putting a stop to the goosebumps.

"Someone needs to *relax*." Jamie ascended to her feet and picked up his empty glass. "I'll get you a blanket and a pill—"

"No! I mean, it's cool. I'm just going to…" And before he ran out—

"Wait!" The sound of her voice paralyzed him in places. He stood underneath a solid white archway, bordered with black lining. Thank goodness. Jamie sighed, something heavy on her shoulders. "This is…I mean…Look, it's just been…"

"Different?"

"Yeah." She sounded relieved. "Ever since…"

"Sandra."

That name. They were already tense, their spinal cords curled up like a snake ready for an attack. They stood there, ten to fifteen feet apart from each other. Strong eye contact. Only the sound of a speeding car passing by disturbed the dead silence and a teenage girl screaming, "Woohoo!"

Jamie gave a small smile, but that did not prevent the tears from welling up in her eyes.

Matt hurried over. "Hey…"

She turned away; He got closer. "I'm sorry—"

"Don't."

"I know we agreed to not talk about it. I feel so stupid."

"I was there, too," he finally said.

The reminder made her turn around. She stared into his eyes and saw the integrity. His eyes were a neon hazel in the light. Her baby doll amber eyes were bluer by the instant because the tears did not stop. She was the first to break focus and dabbed at her eyes. Before he took his cue to leave, she asked, "Can I show you something?"

He felt the slightest jolt pulse through his legs.

"Jamie, this is…." He gazed down at the giant white poster board on the floor, locked in his own bright tunnel of memories.

The poster was covered with photographs of all shapes and sizes from his thirteen—whoa, now after today— fourteen years here on Mother Earth. Although, they had yet to fully celebrate his and her (not until September) fourteenth birthdays. Whatever year it would be. The photos were cut out in designs of squares, triangles, rectangle, or ovals and positioned in opposite directions from the memory next to it. Some pictures were tilted to the right. Others to the left. A few of them were even upside down like seats on a roller-coaster loop. His younger days began at the top left. His later days, all thirteen of them, stopped at the bottom right of the poster. The first photo was taken at the Convention Center that the four of them had attended on an elementary school field trip. Jamie and Lisa's teeth sparkled at the camera from their million-dollar smile—there were a few missing baby teeth. Matt and Derek had their tongues curved out like Gene

Simmons. *"Kiss Army!" they chanted nonstop and even tossed up the devil's horns.*

"Supposed to finish it yesterday," Jamie said, unaware of that she brought Matt back to the present. She pushed aside a few glue sticks and colored sharpies. It was his cue to join her on the beige carpet floor...only, it took him a moment to realize that he was already seated. He leaned on his hand, inching closer to her; like he was not already. Puh-lease! Jamie's bedroom was also nowhere close to making guests claustrophobic, because none of the items matched the light painted pink walls. Every item was a different neon color. Jamie was living in a highlighter bedroom. "But, we all promised your...We promised Lucia that we would help her out with dinner tonight, cutting back on my time to finish this."

"And Scooby Doo on channel two," Matt sang, but it was on the cheerless side.

They scanned the photographs for a few minutes and laughed as their fingers scrolled across the mall photo strip. The four of them were crammed inside of a Hello Kitty theme booth. Everything was bright, pink, and flowery. The sad moments were far gone. Matt and Jamie engaged in chit chats of what their younger selves were possibly talking about prior, during and after each photograph that was captured for eternity, especially in their ritual Hello Kitty photo booth collage photographs. The clothes that they once wore made them crack up. A hideous fashion sense, in their eyes—

"A *skort*?!" Jamie screeched. "How did I ever leave the house in *that*?!"

"I dig the light-up Sketchers though..."

"Shut up!"

But their smiles vanished, as his fingers scrolled to the last row. The second to the last photo of thick moss that Jamie positioned, hovered over—what was supposed to be—two empty flowerpots in front of the gravestones of...

FRANK SMITH   **JAMES "JIMMY" SMITH**

And that was it, the remainder of the gravestones were blank.

Jamie peered away, her fingers clenched together, as her body slouched forward. "It's just that I've always wondered what kind of people they once were. I know you think the same because they mean *a lot*—"

"No memory," Matt nearly whispered, his attention still on the photo. "Started in a picture of rocks. Ended in a picture of rocks. That's all I know them for—a big pile of dirt."

"I'm sorry. I shouldn't…" Her eyes got red again.

"Hey," he said, making a complete one-eighty, changing the subject. "We look pretty sharp."

She followed his finger; it pointed to the last photograph in the snake-like trip down memory lane, and beside it was nothing but blank poster paper of the unfinished collage. The Castellanos backyard garden was what a life at home magazine would use for its cover. In front of shrubs with red, yellow, and pink roses, the photo was snapped less than two months ago, hours before their eighth-grade promotion dance began. A few of the prickly stems peaked outward like feathers of a peacock. In the center of the picture was a miniature waterfall, where two baby angels, carrying their own vases, smiled. The vases were tilted to their sides, so the water could stream out and trickle down into the pond. Matt and Jamie stood side by side in front of the pond. It was a horizontal camera angle of them. Matt had his arm ringed around Jamie's lower back.

* * *

Just inches below the small opening of her black cocktail dress. Her long brown hair dangled down in spiral curls. She was already flashing her teeth at the camera. He gazed at her. She could sense it and looked at him. He felt his heart skyrocket to the moon and back. And by the look in her eyes, the feeling was mutual. Off camera, someone called for their attention. They looked back at the camera and smiled together, his arm tightening around her.

* * *

"I need to lose weight…"

Jamie held that same black cocktail dress against her pear-shaped body. Her displeased expression was visible to herself through the closet mirrors. It was as though her double-mirror reflection took over and knocked down her self-esteem. She huffed and puffed, pouty as she swayed her hips a bit, side to side. Matt watched her, tempted to say something but the words got stuck. He thought girls were batshit crazy for stressing about their bodies with their whole, *"I'm fat! I'm ugly! Oh, my God, a FUCKIN' ZIT!"*

He was in no position to judge anyone. He glanced at his reflection in the mirror for a moment. To him, she was perfect. Jamie had a perfect body—a tiny waist, a slight curve in her hips, and an ass—

'Guess that makes me pretty sexist.'

"Just stop it!" It caught them both off guard, more so for her, as she turned his way. "I think you're perfect. I wish you'd see that." His eyes dropped to their flushed faces in that last photograph. Heat rushed over him, and he patted his forehead with his cotton-made hoodie sleeve. Without a doubt, he knew that his cheeks were a bloody red color. It matched his anxious, awkward eight grader self in the photo, where his smile came off too forced. His fingers curled into miniature boxing gloves, and his heart only pounded faster.

"Of course, you'd say that," Jamie finally said to break the ice. "You're my best friend." The seriousness dispersed as soon as she gave a small smile that created two perfect little circles in her cheeks, an inch or so from her mouth.

'God…I love that.'

But all he could say to calm the nerves and the prickly sensation that tingled from his fingertips was, "Music wasn't as bad as I'd expected—"

'What are you doing?'

"I, uh—"

'UH?! REALLY?!'

"—liked the decorations. The colors of the theme."

'Please stop rambling.'

"'It's Time to Say Goodbye…For Now.'" Jamie chuckled and sat beside him; the dress splayed over her crossed legs. The bottom of the dress was puffy like a cupcake AKA the Powerpuff girl. "I hate clichés."

"Yeah…"

They gazed off into opposite directions, stuck in a trance-like state. Matt re-crossed his legs. Jamie wrapped her arms around her legs and the itchy tutu undergarment fabric of the dress smacked her in the face. It got a laugh out of them. She turned beet red. Matt scanned the room and a sense of discomfort overcame him like it was the first time he had been there. He chewed off his hanging thumbnail, because he been at it from the moment he stepped into the bedroom. Behind the twin-size bed, which had a black and dark purple stripe comforter, resided an eight-by-eleven poster of the *High School Musical* cast. To the right of it were Noah and Allie from *The Notebook*, who were "getting it on" in the downpour of rain.

Matt's eyes bulged out of their sockets, and he immediately looked away. He met Jamie's sight, but it was by accident since there was nowhere else to look. His forehead, chin, and entire face broke out in a red hot sizzle, as though on fire. He went to a scratch all four corners of his face. That only reddened his features like he had been crying on and off for a few hours. Only, she held his gaze, her eyes locked with manic depressant statehood. But he never broke focus either. It was impossible. His heart clouted a million miles against his chest and his hands, feet, and the four corners of his face broke out into a cold sweat. Jamie pursed her lips. Her breathing grew heavier. He touched her rosy cheek—it was warm. She balked at the touch of his cold hand.

"Sorry." Before he drew his hand away, she held it, tightly against her cheek. Their beady eyes...Pre-anxiety attack breathing.

He gulped. They both leaned in, but the sound of a garage door opening forced them to stop midway. "I'll, um," she said, only inches apart from him, "finish your gift this week."

"Sounds good," his tone dropped to a whisper. "I should probably—"

"Good thinking!" She bounced to her feet, and his fingers slowly fell from her cheek.

Downstairs, the front door opened. A woman in her forties stepped inside, her long, big curly hair a shout out to her days as an eighties tween, most likely with a perm. Slowly, she shut the door and removed her knee-length blue trench coat. She wore a little black dress that stopped an inch above her knees to show off the nude-colored stockings. Not to mention, her giant silver hoop earrings glammed her up like fine dine Hollywood royalty. As she kicked off her black, suede five-inch-high heels, there was a creak.

The woman pounced up, aiming one of her heels in midair. She sighed with relief as Jamie and Matt descended the marble staircase. "Jesus, Jamie!" The woman clasped ahold of her chest.

"Mom," Jamie responded wryly. "Are you sneaking in?"

"No! Besides, aren't you supposed to be at a sleepover?" Something dawned on her, as she pecked her daughter's cheek. "Where's the other—"

"Home," Matt said. "With basketball practice every day—"

"Oh, that's right! You certainly need your rest." Then she said to Jamie, "A simple text would've helped, sweetheart." Before she went in for the hug, included, "And happy birthday, sweetie."

"Thank you, Ms. Castellanos." He could hardly breathe with his face smashed against her…bosoms. But it was not his fault. Her DD cups were just so… "up there."

Jamie cringed; Her shoulders were up to her ears. *"Mom."*

"And how's Lucia?" Ms. Castellanos pulled back, but she held onto Matt's muscular arms, a work in progress. It was his damn mind that was stuck in pervert-horny-teenage-boy-land.

"Good," he said, although he sounded unsure. "She's doing…just fine." That nearly killed him.

There was a cricket gap—or maybe he had imagined it. The crickets stopped as soon as Jamie clutched a hold of his hand. Sweat raged throughout his body, ending at his feet. *'Damn hormones!'*

"We'll be out front, Mom."

"Okie dokie!" She watched as Jamie nearly hauled Matt outdoors.

"Bye, Ms. Castellanos!" Matt called out before the front door opened and shut in a blink of an eye.

"Friends, my fat ass." Ms. Castellanos chuckled, shaking her head.

As they meandered down the gravel pathway, Jamie started anxiously, "So, uh, I guess I'll see you tomorrow then." They came to a halt at the start of the sidewalk, already facing each other. "After your practice, of course."

Matt was the first to break eye contact. For whatever reason, he just stared at her house: a massive two-story, three if the small attic counted as a level. There were too many windows. The second story had flowerpots on each windowsill. Everything was so…white, but it was thrown off balance due to the red *American Beauty* front door. *'Of course…'*

His eyes diverted to the second story window at the top left, where a light flickered on through the curtain.

"She can't see us," Jamie said, more as a reminder than a stated fact. "Trust me. She'll be calling Mr. Lover Boy Number Four—or five if you count one-night stands." His pupils dilated to the size of a grasshopper's gleamy eyes, "Yeah…I heard her once."

Matt balked like a callous bug was crawling all over him. It was over-the-top with squeamish, *'Ews'* and worm-like movement. But it got a smile out of her. "At least yo' momma is getting some. Maybe if Lucia—"

'Really? You really want to talk about a penis.'

Now it *really* gave him the heebie-jeebies. He rammed his fingers into his ears. "La, la, la—"

"…Right into her—"

"Okay!" He gradually uncovered his ears. "I get it." It was back to another one-eighty. As they looked at each other, his heart raced at lightning speed again. "So, uh, thank you for the gift…" She took a step toward him. "…the cards…" She paused momentarily. "…just everything…" She leaned in and nearly missed his lips as he muttered, "Thank you."

He was utterly speechless; his lips even did that stupid but silent, "Wha—Wha."

Jamie smiled and swung their hands around a bit. "Later, Matty." She tugged his hands toward her as she walked away. They dropped until she was no longer able to hold onto them. As soon as she reached the front door, "I don't regret her seeing us that day."

"Neither do I," he responded sooner than he would have liked to. "I was waiting for Crazy Sandra to dump me anyway."

"Night, Matty." She smiled, turned on her heel and slipped back into the house.

His cheeks were on fire and scorched from a Scorsese-red to a violent Tarantino-kind. No matter how hard he tried, his body refused to move. He convinced himself that his feet were cemented to the sidewalk, but he remained too petrified to check; He just focused on that red front door. *'What da fuck just happened?'*

5.

"DUDE," DEREK SAID, "WE LOOK LIKE the dudes from Men in Black.*"*

Hair slicked back, the boys were decked out from head to toe in button-down dress shirts, black slacks, socks, and shined shoes. Matt also wore a lavender silk tie. Derek tugged at his emerald cotton tie for the past few minutes.

"Derek," Mrs. Santoso, his mother, admonished.

"But it itches!"

Mrs. Santoso shoved her disposable camera into her husband's hands. Everyone came to a halt in the middle of the gravel pathway that guided them to the red front door of the Castellanos residence. Matt watched Derek huffing and puffing, while his mother hushed him as she straightened out his tie. For whatever reason, he gave the goofiest smile. Lucia wound up her disposable camera and took a snapshot of Matt. It caught him off guard.

"Sorry," she said. "It's just that you look so handsome." They exchanged smiles.

"Ah, Mom!" Locked in her side hug, the camera flash captured Derek and his mother's red painted lips against his cheek. He squinted in their candid moment.

"Thank God I didn't leave you two with these crazies," Mr. Santoso reassured the boys.

"Oh! It's only once in a lifetime when you see your son look like a movie star," his wife joked in return. "Derek, your tie—"

"Mom!"

The front door opened. Matt, Derek, and their guardians stopped at the bottom of the porch stairs, only three steps high. Ms. Castellanos sashayed out in a little pink dress that touched an inch or so above her knees of bare skin. The men saw her matching pink high heels.

221132

22122411213211121

"My! Oh, my!" she said and squeezed her hands together like a child star winning their Oscar. *"Don't you boys look handsome! Like a young Warren Beatty."*

"Wasn't that before your time," Mrs. Santoso said with a smile. *"Unless you just look amazing for someone your age."*

And Ms. Castellanos smiled right back, but one of those, 'Fuck you, too, cunt' smiles.

"Thanks, Jamie's mom." The boys nearly drooled. Derek's mother nudged him.

"I now present," Ms. Castellanos spoke in a chipper tone, her arms gestured out like the host of a game show, *"the two most beautiful gals, who will be at tonight's 'It's Time to Say Goodbye…For Now' dance."* She glided off to the side and swayed her arm out like a ballerina—mid-Black Swan pose—to the front door. *"My daughter and her best galfriend—"*

"Don't need to be so dramatic, Mom."

"I don't mind it," Lisa said.

The girls held onto each other's arms with their French-tipped manicured fingernails, as they wobbled out onto the front porch. They had on two-inch-high heels and cocktail dresses. The lavender dress gave an angelic glow to Jamie's fair complexion. The valiant emerald dress brightened up Lisa's hazel eyes. The small crowd among the girls moved in for a closer look, as though they were strangers,

"Wait for us!" a woman bellowed from inside of the house. An older version of Lisa dashed outdoors with a camera and a husband linked to her arm. *"Couldn't find our camera!"*

The mothers and Lucia nearly deserted the boys.

Click. Click. Click.

The women maneuvered around and took snapshots from different angles of the two mature young ladies. Jamie and Lisa shifted awkwardly and gave real and fake smiles to the camera. Mrs. Peralta and Ms. Castellanos had to pause a few times for those last-minute tweaks to their daughters' spiraled curls, the heavier but *natural toned makeup, and, the fringe and silk material of their dresses.*

"Wow," Derek said as he, his father and Matt remained put. "They look so…"

"Different?" His father snorted.

"Awesome." Derek tossed his fist into the air. "Yeah ladies!" Lisa looked his way and pumped her fist in the air, too. Together, they broke out into their weird alien-like techno-dance routine with the "Unz. Unz. Unz."

Matt was absorbed in his own routine. He watched her, and his heart sped up. His body grew heavy, as though consumed by a tidal wave. Her mother made her turn around for another pose. Now, Jamie faced his direction. She smiled. His legs jostled.

* * *

'*Watermelon*,' was all Matt had thought, as he touched his bottom lip lightly and felt the stickiness of Jamie's lip gloss. Those butterflies remained in the pit of his stomach. Flapping their wings faster and harder, he winced a few times. It was chillier than usual because it was eight-forty-five…or nine…or maybe, it was ten. He was unsure. Those bold digital numbers on his cell phone looked a bit fuzzy. The alcohol still needed to be walked off and sucked away by the night.

He strolled along the sidewalk, reflecting the summer's howling moon. It had been minutes since he left the Castellanos residence, half drunk…half sober…coming in and out of washed over memories. Every few steps—every sidewalk crack—he was swallowed up, as though by the night shadows that cascaded through the leaves of the hallowed trees. For an instant, their branches and leaves towered over him. It was a bit spooky. The leaves that skated across the asphalt and sidewalk did not help.

"Excuse me, Son." A runner zoomed on by.

Another local resident. Seeing a fellow neighbor faded away the tightness in his chest, but it was still weird to see anyone outdoors lately, especially in the recent heat conditions. He never minded the heat. In fact, it helped him lash out any long-running train of thoughts. Heat always won over the anxiety and stress, because the last two times, he got an upset stomach that led to a bad cause of shitting his pants out. Most citizens of La Crosse despised any form of sunlight. It was like living in a town filled with vampires, since one too many of the townspeople used umbrellas in the summertime. The channel five news made recent weather reports of there being two-weeks in the nineties with strong humidity until the temperature would go up to the one-hundreds.

Matt took a deep breath, slowing down his rapid heartbeat. The cool air chafed his cheek and he exhaled, his pulse at a regular, normal beat. He shivered and bundled himself up. It was no more than a few steps before he slowed down and stopped completely at the black iron gates of White Rose Cemetery. So much to process, the memories from earlier.

* * *

Taking down the flask from the top shelf of his closet, stored away in secrecy. His friends. Lisa. Derek. Jamie. Lucia.

He pulled on his black pull-over hoodie. Fast, he walked away.

"And you're sure you don't want to go?" Lucia put the car into park in the drop-off/pick-up zone.

Matt gripped onto the straps of his JanSport backpack, his straight teeth pressed down onto his chubby bottom lip, turning it a ghostly white. He gazed at the passenger window where the sun streaked through and onto his face like soft angel's kisses. A few feet from their gray Honda Accord were a handful of students. Short or tall-ish like Matt. Others were short and round like Derek, who at the time weighed heavier than most children their age (he shed off fifteen pounds from swimming, but he felt still insecure).

"Derek," Matt only heard Jamie's voice echoing in one ear and then out the other. "Why the hell are you wearing a T-shirt?"

The students lingered by the long metal fence, adjacent to the football/cross country field. Most of them were eager to unlock the entrance gates, so they could get through another tedious school day. On his right, Matt pressed his face to the passenger window for a clearer view: a giant banner dangling from the roof of the front office. Imprinted on the white poster in bold neon bubbly letters read, Time to Say Goodbye...For Now, followed by the three different ticket pricings...

Single.
Couple.
Group.

'A and C.'

"If I were you," Lucia spoke up, breaking the silence, "I'd go—"

"Dances are lame," Matt interjected. "Besides it's not like I want to go—"

"Oh, bologna! People who say that are the ones who really want to go. Trust me. I was once—"

"Young."

"Matt, I just don't want you to miss out on the—"

"Fun."

Matt's eyes drooped away from the baby blue sky, where miles of clouds that looked good enough to eat like cotton candy swam around. He inhaled a whiff of fresh summertime air. Something tickled his nasal tissues, he sneezed and coughed at the same time. His attention diverted to the culprits of the strong scent, eighth graders, his fellow classmates but certainly NOT his kind of crowd. They were a lot cooler than him—too cool for school. An eighth grade boy wore skintight jeans, a biker's jacket, and a matching pair of black Harley Davidson boots. The two girls next to him had on puffy black miniskirts and halter tops...pushing the 'no low-cut tops' school policy. The three of them sauntered by the Honda Accord. The boy was in the middle, his arms around the girls' shoulders. Whatever he said or mumbled, his lips barely moved, as though they were attached to each other, and the girls burst out into giggles.

"You are so funny!" The sluttier looking one squeezed the boy's shoulder.

Matt scowled. "Why do people pour the entire bottle of Britney Spears and Axe body spray onto themselves? Idiots!"

Lucia laughed. It forced her to turn off the car. "You certainly get that stubbornness from me, especially when it comes to—"

"What? Jealously? I'm NOT jealous—"

"—or the obvious." They sat in silence, until Lucia's merry smile collapsed into a straight line. "Sweetheart," she said and grabbed a hold of his hand, "it's okay if you're not like Mr. Casanova over there." She bobbed her head to the three eighth graders. "Those girls are probably laughing at him because, well, he looks like a Raggedy Ann doll."

It cracked a smile on him. "I don't get why girls like dudes in tighter pants. Like how does one...Well, you know...His junk—"

"Censor, Matt!" Lucia shook off the heebie-jeebies. Now, it was his turn to laugh. She looked at him. His smile made her smile. "Ask Jamie to the dance."

Silence until, "Grandma, she's my best friend."

"Derek can go with Lisa. Think about it: 'You'll have a better time because neither of you will have to worry about the first date cliché stuff like, 'Do I kiss her/Should I bring a condom—'"

"Okay, this is officially getting weird!" He unbuckled his seatbelt.

"Sorry doll! But your comment grossed me out seconds ago!"

He opened the passenger door but came to an abrupt halt as he felt her reach. She gave him that look where her eyebrows perked up. He only stared back at her. Then, he broke focus and sighed. The temptation to chew on this one a bit longer seemed bogus. "Okay, I want to go to this stupid dance. There. Happy?"

"Ecstatic."

* * *

"Watch it!" an adolescent boy asserted.

Matt screeched to a halt at the edge of the sidewalk, as the navy blue and white stripe Mustang zoomed by and off into the darkness.

"Woohoo!"

Because of the overly tinted Mustang windows, Matt was unable to identify the culprits.

"Jesus Christ!" He hunched over for a moment and held onto his thighs to catch his breath. At one point, he felt dizzy. It was like no air pumped to his head, his brain. The air seemed to be stuck in his chest, tighter than usual. A creature of the night wanted out. A few seconds later, his vision cleared up and his breathing normalized. He picked at the bandage on his hand…and did a double take on it. *'When da FUCK did that get there?'*

"You okay?!" A man in workout attire and a woman in yoga wear ran toward him from across the street. "Some kids are just so stupid these days."

"Yeah…Yeah, I'm okay," Matt said to them. "Just forgot my…inhaler."

The pretty blonde woman was alarmed more than ever. "We should call someone—"

"No! I mean, no. I'm close to home anyway."

It was back and forth until Matt gave a half smile, which could have gone two ways: heartfelt filled with such honesty, or flat out fuckin' clown creepy. The woman and the man huddled close to his mouth. They jogged away, eaten up by the night. Matt watched as the man wrapped his arm around the woman's waist.

He peered away and dug out his cell phone from the front pocket of his hoodie. *'Oh, I still have my hoodie on.'*

With just the right amount of little artificial lighting, he looked like a fuckin' serial killer. A prowler in the nightfall-shadows, his dilated eyes came off as sinister, as one of the lampposts that glowed in a warmer hue, darker than the others' street-halos. He leaned against the 'stop' sign pole and looked up to the sky. The stars were…squinting. He was…squinting. He brought his head down and opened his eyes fully. But they were already fully open. His surroundings returned to blurred shapes and sizes.

He fumbled for his cell phone and nearly lost a hold of it. The time. There it was in bold white digital numbers on the phone screen: 10:00PM.

It was in clear view. *'Get it together man!'*

A click here. A click there. He pulled up his message inbox. Now, he was the worried one because of the multiple unanswered text messages sent from his end.

> To: Grandma
> I'm sorry…
> Just left Jamie's.
> Can we talk later?
> On my way home.
> Can you pick me up somewhere?
> Grandma?
> Grandma?
> Grandma???
> Grandma?????????

The message in progress…

??

"Fuckin' answer me!"

Matt crossed the street after a triple take to see if any other asshole drivers wanted to run him over and chop him up tonight. It was colder now, sucking in air like Dr. Hannibal Lecter on the pursuit of the living. He dialed and waited for the other line to pick up, but it just rang…rang…and *rang*. *'FUCKIN' SHIT. BITCH. PRICK. ASSHOLE. CUNT.'*

As he turned the corner, AT LAST, he found Maple Oak Street, his street.

He walked straighter—the booze already lost in the air. Only seconds later there was something soft in the breeze; a whistle. It echoed through one ear and then out the other. It had a sense of its own, chillier than the actual atmosphere. He shivered and buried himself in his pull-over. Everything decided to tilt left to right, then right to left, as the whistle grew louder.

Matthew.

He came to a stop. Something forced him to stop. Unable to fought it, the same thing effected his body, feeling like string jelly.

Matt…

But as his body tilted right…right…right, a harsh riiiiiiing in his ears resonated. His sight burst into black and white pixels. Next thing, he realized an incredible and powerful force brushed up behind him.

Matt!

Knocked off one foot, his other fell off the sidewalk. Impossible to steal a glance over his shoulder, he saw just yellow and white lines.

He went headfirst on the asphalt.

6.

WINTER WONDERLAND.

'Wait a minute!'

Matt turned around, but all he saw was black. Everything around him was pitch black. His breathing grew harsher and smoked out into white air clouds. White into the black. He spun round and round, but he saw nothing. Swallowed up in a cube of doom, he staggered all around—he must have, because his own footsteps (unless he was barefoot) echoed as they hit the icy ground...or was it tile?

And there it was...

A glow of light fluttered from miles away. It curved one way and then another, shapeshifting into a silhouette. Unlike his white wonderland, the light—whoever it was—floated closer to him. It started at his feet—he was barefoot after all—as the light washed over him. Matt sprinted off—going forward—a pursuit to reach the light. Only, something pulled him back... that force again.

"Stop!" he implored and squirmed around. But as he lunged forward, the faster he went backward. "Wait!"

The light grew brighter.

Blinded by the strong white glow, Matt closed his eyes as he cried, "No!!!"

* * *

"Matt!"

It was Lucia. He was positive because her hot, flushed face pushed through the white, back to normal color room tone. Her breath no longer reeked of Devil's booze, as she wailed, "My baby!"

On "three," he felt another force lift him up—

Paramedics. Four or…maybe there were five of them. It was difficult to tell since his surroundings had yet to arrive in clear focus.

Eyes opened. Eyes closed. Opened… closed… closed… opened…

The gurney was white—the one he was lying on, secured, and strapped in, ready for takeoff. His breathing was visible in the nightfall air; until he had realized that his exhales were boxed in the oxygen mask that covered his nose and mouth. There was also a long yellow tape around his home that prevented entrance of the dozens of unfamiliar faces, who watched from the street. Neighbors. Nosy ones. Terrified ones. Angry ones. Some were even in awe at the sight of blood—human pain must have really got them off. Some appeared to be secret fans of the pleasure of torture. "Gnarly!" one adolescent boy said.

"Really?" the adolescent girl next to him retorted, most likely the shitface's girlfriend.

Here and there, Matt saw the hands of bystanders reach for their own mouths, pale and fragile, like snow, eyes wider than horror itself. They were, obviously, in fear for the lives of their children, more than themselves. A nearby father, who had a firm hold of his little girl, got too close to the front of the line.

"Easy!" A man in uniform used his body as a shield to block him off the Smith property.

Men in black…or blue (his surroundings were still in and out of magnifying focus). There was, at least, a dozen police officers present, armed and uninformed. "Okay, ready," the voice behind him said.

Two men in navy blue uniforms, hovered over him. It scared the living daylights out of Matt; and his pulse jumped into his throat. The paramedics slid the gurney—Matt—into the back of a van, handing him off to their colleagues. It was a matter of seconds before *it* came through one ear and then out the other.

Riiiiiiiing…

He cringed but was too weak to even lift a finger, his hands remained immobile, as though they were also strapped down. "You're…Going…To…Be…Alright," the medic with salt and pepper hair told him in slow motion. Matt only stared at the man, in and out of twilight…

…until he saw blood. He caught a glimpse of it. Beginning—somewhere around the kneecap—and down it went, in a zigzagged roller coaster of hell.

"Hold still."

There was a hole in his jeans, freshly cut. The younger looking medic was already applying pressure to stop the bleeding. Matt watched as his own red hot, sticky, fresh, streams of blood absorbed through the white towel on his mid-thigh, prolonged into a darker and darker blob. By now, it looked purple. The lower half of his body was eaten alive; his shoes were consumed in one sluggish, juicy, bloody gulp.

The nonstop voices, including the random faces, zoomed around him, hard and fast. He overheard something about if he were to live or die; if he was okay; if *she* was okay.

"WAIT!" Lucia barged in—or could have possibly soared into the back of the van, at that rate. "I'm not going anywhere." She was all slobbery in tears and snot.

He wanted to scream, but something stopped it; his throat tightened up, making it difficult to breathe, as he held eye contact with her. "You'll…be…okay," she said; he could not exactly hear her. He only caught her lips moving, but none of the words escaped her lips. It was when he noticed her peach colored blouse was covered in his blood…

Riiiiiiiing…

His head grew heavy and dropped to the side. Hot sticky streams ran down his face. All he saw next was black…pitch black…and then red. His eyes twitched shut from the last visible drops of blood that snuck in—

"MATT!"

7.

MATT WAS DRESSED IN BLACK from head to toe. He pulled on his hood—not the one from his pull-over sweater—and blended into the shadow of the night. The wind whistled through one ear and then out the other, but it all seemed inaudible to him. His focus never diverted away from his home's front door of forest green. The layers of fog suddenly grew thick around him, as he ascended the first step of the brick staircase. All the lights were turned off inside the house. He was positive, since all the curtains covered the windows in black, pitch black, except the left window on the second story, belonging to Lucia.

A dim hue glowed through the pulled down window-shade, visible to the outside world. About three to four steps away from the top of the red brick staircase, Matt already halted, and his eyes remained on the window to Lucia's bedroom. But when the light went off, he felt it.

Something touched his cheek. He put his hands there, until something yanked it away. His hands hit his sides. Someone spun him around, but there was nobody in sight.

He gasped for air like a fish out of water. What seemed like a hand lifted the bottom of his black hoodie. Then, the invisible force hauled him down the staircase.

"STOP," his lips formed, but the words were silent, as he flew over the staircase and went straight toward the empty street. Dead to the world.

The wind grew mightier. Aluminum cans and plastic bottles soared over the curbs and landed onto lawns. Most of the litter collided into trash bins, crashed over from the incredible force. The bins rolled into the streets, were swallowed up whole; and they dispersed into the night like dust. The air whipped through Mother Nature's greens, the flowerbeds torn up and shredded into itty bitty pieces.

The air devoured the oranges and tops of trees. Red petals squeezed into liquid; drops of red splattered all over the sidewalk and asphalt. Most of the trees waved their decorations, greeting Matt, as he inched closer and closer to asphalt. And then, they stopped in unison as soon as his body dropped onto the sidewalk.

His foot reached for the sidewalk, one foot landed just right, but the other bent sideways.

SNAP!

He nearly howled at the moon, as his head flew back. Tonight, a full moon made its way through the gust of fog. He tumbled over the sidewalk—headfirst—and whirled away to prevent further damage. He slammed flat on the left side of his body. His left foot curved up, broken in all the wrong and right places. A hot sensation filled up his eyes—and on the top of his head. Then he felt it all over his nose.

Red.

Rivers of red flowed out of his nostrils. He could smell nothing, his nasal tissues blocked by the nonstop blood that started gushing out. Immediately, he wiped at his nose, first with the centerpiece of his black pull-over. That only worked for so long, until his hands were needed to catch the puddle of liquid red. It began to turn blue…cold baby blue due to the low atmospheric temperature. Splatters of blood remained as an inked, navy blue on his face, as the rest of it splattered into puddles on the ground. Once again, his chest felt–tight. His lips shaped into an oval, he choked back inaudible screams.

Footsteps. They were close. Too close. He looked up and watched it all play out with his own eyes.

Him. Turning onto his street, Maple Oak Street…

"HEY!" he silently screamed. But as he had attempted to move, his body refused.

His eyes went wide with desperation and plea as the force knocked him over. He lay there, paralyzed from the waist up, and waist down. He attempted to scan around, but his eyes prevented him from doing so. Those two pools of black grew wider like a

wildcat's, fierce and angry for answers. Positioned there, now on his
right-side, he saw the perfect view of the night playing itself out fast.

Him. Pulling on his hoodie, bundling into the color of
death.

"STOP!" It was no more than a whisper; his throat bled
from the bottom up.

Him. The sudden heaviness of his body forced him to
stop, forced him to sway left to right.

"PLEASE!"

Left to right. Left to right. Right to left. Right to left.

As Matt (the one on the asphalt) watched himself (the one
from that night) in a hemorrhaging state of body movements,
something brushed against him.

From the corner of his eye, he noticed a piece of black fabric.
The piece of material glided with the breeze, matching the eerie
levitation of the silhouette from That Night.

Him—as his body tilted right…right…right…*Matt*
screamed, and it blared out a hollow riiiiiiing throughout the night.
Forcing the wind to grow thicker than cobwebs. Through the gaps of
ghostly clouds, all he saw was…

Him. His doppelgänger soared over the sidewalk—a
bird without its wings. The silhouette—*someone*—stood
behind him. It collapsed onto the asphalt and his left leg
jolted. His right leg gave a loud *crack* and the gash on his thigh
broadened vertically.

Matt grimaced at the image, as though he was just kicked in
the gut. The white air circled around him, he caught the slightest
glimpse of his unconscious, now past, self.

His past-self was bleeding from the leg gash. Three
medium size rocks were pushed up against his right leg,
sharpening its edges through his black jeans, directly onto his
mid-thigh's skin.

Matt gagged, but the vomit constricted his throat. He snuck
one last look at his doppelgänger, displayed in a distorted freakshow
way.

Flat on his back, one arm straightened out like a STOP sign; the other bent like a scarecrow's dance. His left foot tilted to its side, his right leg twisted halfway around, and his right foot pointed at himself.

A chill crawled up his spine and made him shiver. It was a sickening observation to witness his own body mirroring his doppelgänger's position. Then he remembered who was still present. Matt stared across at the unknown, and who remained on the sidewalk, close to his doppelgänger, no more than thirty feet from him. It was impossible to tell who it was exactly because of the black hoodie that hovered down to the middle of its face. A nose should have been there, skin should have been visible, if not for the long black graduation-like robe that covered its entire body.

The stranger held eye contact with Matt when it stepped toward him. With each step closer, closer to its victim, the white air colored in the last gaps of visibility, blocking off all surroundings from Matt. Trapped, Matt stored himself up in his own white cube, far away from the stranger, nowhere to be seen. Matt stayed safe in his own white wonderland.

* * *

Beep.

Slowly, his vision pushed into the brightness…no sign of red.

Attached to the wall behind him was a glowing fluorescent light. His attention scrolled from the wall to the matching, off-colored, white ceiling that seemed to stretch on for miles and miles.

Beep.

His head sagged to the right, where a machine stood. There were too many numbers on the screen, where a line zigzagged up and down like small tidal waves.

Beep.

Those sleepy eyes of his creaked open and traveled down the heart monitor screen, to the clear tubes inserted into his right-hand...

Beep.

A polka dot gown clothed his naked body, and plain white sheets covered him from the waist down in a bed that was not his own.

Beep.

Suddenly, he felt dizzy as his head did somersaults. He caressed his forehead and saw the reality that sat in front of him. Somehow, he missed it just seconds ago. His left leg was underneath the sheet, but his right leg—

Beep. Beep.

Clammy hands. His heart bumped against his chest. Goosebumps prickled all over his body that burned like fire—

Beep. Beep. Beep.

A bulky cloth, as tall as Mt. Everest, wrapped around his lower right leg and stopped inches from his ankle. It was far from his knee—a kneecap that looked pressed in, almost deformed from the fall.

Beep. Beep. Beep.

There was a groan, but not his own. It came from someone else. Someone was in the room with him. Chest tightened up Matt wheezed for air. All he tasted was cherry medicine. He turned away and coughed up strings of saliva, thicker than glue, which drenched through the bed sheets. Whoever was in the room gasped, "Doctor!"

Beep—Beep—Beep—

His surroundings rocked side to side, including the silhouette that sprung forward—

"MATT!"

He could do was scream and scream some more; his eyes inflamed with tears. As a dark—shadow—hand reached for his wrist, he bounced backward and rolled off the bed. The IV rack tipped forward and smacked down onto the floor.

Matt went headfirst toward the white tile until he collapsed into the burly arms of a man with salt and pepper hair.

"Ramirez!" the man called out, calmer than the first voice.

The second pair of arms assisted the man to pull Matt back onto the bed, followed by a *pinch*—a needle was in his upper left arm. Matt's eyelids were too heavy to find out whose hand it was that injected the clear liquid into his system. As his body grew lighter—slowly numbed away—his eyes twitched and everything around him blotted to black.

He caught a glimpse of Lucia in his clear bubbles of vision. She steered away from the spot on the floor, where the stranger stood just seconds ago…

'Unless there was never a stranger.'

There was not. It was just *her*.

"I… kept… telling… him… it… was… me," Lucia sobbed, as a man in scrubs sat her down on the cheap-Goodwill sofa in the corner of the hospital room. "But, he just looked at me, like I was a…a *stranger*!"

She lost it on that last part.

8.

THE WOMAN WITH FRIZZY gray, shoulder-length hair stopped in the middle of the sidewalk. She scanned the line ahead, where mothers and fathers waited with their children, her eyes dilated like a rat's. She sighed; her lips drooped in an upside down "U". But when those tiny sausage-fingers folded into her long piano hands, it made her smile again. The boy beside her was wider than a rollie pollie. He tugged a hold of her arm.

"You're sad," he said.

"No." She knelt in front of him. "I'm not, sweetie."

"Then, you're about to be."

The boy looked down at the ground; his feet—his Red Power Ranger Velcros—pointed toward each other like a duck's. The woman's eyes turned lukewarm. Her bottom lip trembled. Her lips parted slightly, ready to speak. But the boy wrapped his arms around her legs. "It's okay."

That nearly killed her. Guilt was written all over her face, as she hesitated to hug him back.

"'The wheels on the bus go 'round and 'round, 'round and 'round, 'round and 'round.'" The boy pulled back. "'The wheels on the bus go 'round and 'round, all through the town.'"

"Why you are singing the 'boo-boo' song?" she asked and lowered to his level, matching his height.

"So, I can take your boo-boo's away."

He gave a small smile and so did she. He wiped away her fallen tears that skimmed down her cheeks. She tugged him back into her arms and held on tight. He kissed her cheek and she glided her fingers through his curly light brown locks. "I love you," she whispered much softer. "So much."

"I love you too, Grandma," he whispered into her ear.

* * *

"Vitals are good." The pen scribbled sideways. "No sign of a concussion. You are *incredibly lucky*." The man with short salt and pepper hair flipped to the next page on the metallic clipboard. "Bruises will ease down, over time. In a week or so, you'll apply an ointment onto the cuts. For now, 600mg for the headaches if they become unbearable, as well as for the…"

He did not need to look because it was the elephant in the room: the small cast.

"The cast is temporary. The cut was deep, but not deep enough for permanent damage. Should be off in a few weeks, watch for stitches reopening or infections—but they're rare, just a forewarning."

He tore off two slips of paper, as he turned around, his hand lowered.

"Matt." Lucia approached the bed and sat down at the edge of it, carefully. "Honey, talk to us."

It was an unbearable feeling. There was something sour that boiled in his gut.

Matt only had eyes for the disfigured face that reflected at him on the compact mirror in his hands. A thick, white bandage was wrapped around his forehead—front to back. There was a deep red circle on the center of it; his goddamn head was on its fuckin' period. The fabric of the bandage could not have been much bigger; his goddamn brain took a shit in its own built-in diaper. The multicolored bruises also made his face puffy, especially underneath the eyes, like an addict going through withdrawals…sleepless hours.

"That's enough," Lucia admonished and reached on out. "You're only—"

"I'm a monster."

His tone dwindled away after each letter. Slowly, he lowered the double-sided mirror. A strong sensation stung his eyes and turned them a deep red. Lucia reached for his arm, but he refused; too disgusted to be acknowledged.

"A nasty fall," he whispered. "Are you looking for the...whoever it is—whoever was there that night?" Now, his eyes went up to the man.

The doctor remained in front of the counter, as though he was the fresh face for a business suit advertisement—because of the black slacks and knee-length white coat. Plus, he was easy on the eyes—his eyes were blue, matching his button-down dress shirt. For a moment, Matt saw the doc. for who he once was, most likely the ladies' man who never got told.

"No."

"Well." Mr. Pretty Face said. "Yes and no."

'Should've seen that ONE coming!'

"However," the man proceeded, "for the time being, there will be someone keeping an eye out on your home and the both of you." He looked to Lucia until someone started snickering.

"Sorry," Matt said although the hint of sarcasm was a giveaway, "it's just that...This stuff only happens in the movies! The glitz and glam of old Hollywood. So, when it happens in real life..." His fingers knotted together. For some reason, the same happened to his throat because he had to cough a few times in order to speak up. The result seemed to frighten him. His smile vanished. "I *saw* what I *saw*."

"I understand, Matt—"

"But doesn't that say *enough*? Dreams, nightmares, whatever. There's a reason why I saw this person—or dreamed of them. The nameless in black. The Stranger. Dr. Brown, I know this sounds crazy."

As he stared right at—the man now with a name—Dr. Brown, he felt his grandmother's hand gliding over his back. It made him flinch a bit. His entire body tensed up. It was nothing. Anxiety had its casual toll on him. Before he said more, Dr. Brown intervened, "It's not crazy, Matt. It's possible that, yes, through dreams and even nightmares there are answers given to us. You gave a description. The cops are looking into it."

"Jesus Christ!" Matt peered away, oblivious that his inner thoughts were said aloud. Instead, his eyes settled down upon his interlaced fingers. They turned a mixture of red and white as he *squeezed them.*

"Matt." Lucia rested her hand on his. That sent a wave of relief through Matt. He was comfortable enough to tap his thumb against her palm.

"In case you start feeling overwhelmed," Dr. Brown said, as he dug into his side pocket, "because reactions to and after trauma—"

When she saw what it was, she jumped to her feet and rammed her foot into the bedside table. "Ouch!"

"—including stress—"

"Grandma."

"…and anxiety," Dr. Brown said more to himself, pink in the cheeks. Even the doc. was in some sort of paralyzed daze. They were both lost in their own train of thoughts.

"We'll, uh," Lucia started before Dr. Brown said something first, "be sure to pick these up in a few." Lucia reached for the prescription slips, which snapped him out of his funk.

"Yes, please do that."

"My grandson and I would like to get home now."

Matt glimpsed at her and then her worried eyes surrounded with crease marks. "Of course." Dr. Brown turned to leave until he stopped in the doorway moments later. "Try not to walk too much. Adding too much pressure to the leg could cause blood clots."

But he was already in midair, with his legs spread out, and his hands pressed down onto the bed as though he was ready to takeoff. "Got it." Matt lowered himself and his bottom hit the mattress.

Lucia was halfway to the door. She exchanged a few more words with the doc and appeared not necessarily in a rush anymore to leave. Lucia looked less 'interested' in the conversation. She kept her arms close to her lower abdomen and stole glances with Matt in between inaudible words.

A nurse squeezed by, pushing a wheelchair into the hospital room, Room 402. The longer he stared at his grandmother, all Matt thought was, *'Where were you? Where were you during my accident?'*

9.

"'GO, GO, POWER RANGERS...Go, Go, Power Rangers...Mighty Morphin' Power Rangers...'"

And with one last tug, he tied his white shoelaces into bunny ears. "I did it," he mumbled, his eyeballs engorged with exhilaration. "I DID IT!" He jumped to his feet and scampered out of his Power Ranger-themed bedroom.

His short sausage-size legs slid out into the hallway like Tom Cruise from Risky Business. "Mighty Morphin' Power Rangers," he chanted and pumped his fist into the air. "GRAN'MA! I tied my shoes!"

He turned right and nearly collided with the ajar door. "Gran'ma!" He burst into the bedroom and wrapped around the chestnut bench that stood at the end of the bed. He dropped to the floor and untied his shoelaces. "Look, Gran'ma! Look!" After the loop, swoop and pull—along with an "ARGH"—he hopped back to his feet with the biggest smile. "Did you see that?!"

Strands of gray pooled around her head that rested on the pillow. A lavender cotton robe covered her skin with blobs of moisture due to her wet showered hair. She lay on her right-side, facing his direction, her eyes focused elsewhere, distant.

"It's been three years," she uttered and stole a glance at him. "They're never coming home." She turned onto her other side, away from him.

He watched on, his tiny round face as morose as his hunched shoulders. Without a peep, he walked to the door and took one last look at her.

Lucia hugged the unused pillow beside her. By then, her eyes lowered to the floral comforter. She was immobile, like a stone. Matt sighed and stepped out of the doorframe and into the upstairs hallway. His head slouched forward, like Charlie Brown, as his feet touched the wooden floor outside Lucia's bedroom.

* * *

"*Ouch*!" Matt grimaced as his fingers glided over the white bandage that bulged out of his forehead—it was worse than an unwanted pimple. "*Fucker*," he grunted.

It still throbbed—worse than the shades of green, blue, purple, and black at the corner of his eyes and underneath the pieces of tape that held down the bandage. He pushed the sun-visor mirror back to the roof of his grandmother's white Toyota Corolla. He sank into the passenger seat and stayed there—an endless ship in the deep blue. He resembled a child with its blankie, as he wrapped his arms around the pharmacy bag that sat on his lap.

Lucia kept her eyes on the road less packed than the opposite lanes, where traffic had stopped, and car horns honked every few seconds. The Smiths sat in silence as the morning radio pulsated through the speakers and echoed with the rumble of the tires from the roadway. Matt gazed out the passenger window, where everything passed by like a slideshow, including the twinkle of a stop light.

The sun sat above the horizon at 7:00AM. Birds stroked across the baby blue sky and conducted a sweet symphony with their chirping chorus line. Residents departed their homes in workout gear. Some of them retrieved the newspaper in bathrobes. Decked out in business attire, few local neighbors juggled paperwork and pleather bags to their vehicles.

'*Let's not forget about the cool kids!*'

A few adolescents dressed either in wrinkled or torn up clothes—not on purpose because that was the *new* look. A lot of girls wiggled through cracked windows on the second story of their home (Matt was certain that was their property, their parent's property). As their car passed by five more houses, Matt spied two teenagers with a tight hold of their weakling friend, until the friend lunged forward and barfed all over the front porch of a two-story house with a red front door.

Matt rolled his eyes at *that* one again. But as his attention drifted to the next door's lawn, he saw a black cat chewing through the intestines of a blue jay's ripped open stomach. A boat out in the sea; Matt felt seasick. He peered away and everything through the windshield rocked sideways. Something lukewarm and acid-like rumbled at the pit of his stomach. He caressed his temple and groaned as the sharpness burned up to his chest. The taste of sour apples fizzed at the back of his mouth. He pressed his head against the window and shivered from chills that spiked the hairs on his arms and legs.

"Whoever did this…" Lucia gripped onto the steering wheel. "I should've been awake." There was no sign of why she was passed out in the first place. After a deep intense breath, "Your friends offered us to stay with them. I think it is best—"

"No," he said, surprising himself.

"Matt, last night was—"

"I know. But I want to sleep in my bed."

"You need to be with your friends."

"I want to be alone."

Through the passenger window, he noticed the sapphire diamond on her left ring finger. It gave off a gorgeous lavender-emerald hue as it winked back at him. It blinded him for a second.

Lucia eased her foot off the gas pedal, as a sea of swimming sharks got closer.

"There he is!"

"Where?!"

"OVER THERE!"

"MATT!"

Matt blanched at the sight of multiple red camera-eyes flashing and recording him from the hands of ravenous news reporters. Lucia still sat in the driver's seat, but the car had a mind of its own and crept forward, even when she released her foot off the gas pedal. There stood two men at the hood of the car, they ordered the hungry crowd to back off, police officers on guard. Most of the men and women in black…or blue (the way the sun hit them made it difficult to tell) grabbed their guns, forewarning those who attempted to duck underneath the yellow tape between the Smith and next neighbors' house.

"Get back NOW!" a woman officer asserted to one nearby brown-noser.

Before the Smith vehicle pulled into the driveway, the yellow tape that read, **Police Line Do Not Cross**, got lifted by another group of local officers. The tape immediately dropped back down as soon as the vehicle crawled up. Lucia had to press the gas pedal a bit into the park. The driver and passenger doors yanked open right away.

"I'm Officer Riley," the tall and lanky one said.

"And I'm Officer Franco." The one with a seventies porn star mustache took a hold of Matt's arm.

"We're here to keep you safe!" A meatball-sized officer dashed to the driver's door.

The Smiths became puppets, under complete control of their masterful puppeteers. They nearly hauled the Smiths out of the vehicle, although Matt needed further assistance, a pair of crutches rushed over to him. Showtime.

"Is it true," they heard a reporter asking, somewhere amidst the sea of swimming sharks. It was extremely difficult to tell who it was, especially when a swarm of microphones and cameras came waving toward them at once.

"Oh, *Shit*!" Officer Franco blurted.

A group of reporters crossed over the line. The Smiths got rushed to the front door, as the police officers pushed and held back the reporters. They kept on fishing.

"...Did you really see..."

"...You have any..."

"...Enemies?"

"BACK UP!" Officer Franco demanded.

"NO COMMENT!" Officer Riley plastered a camera lens with his hand.

The house, their home, was as monotonous as a downpour of rain from black clouds. Even the exterior cream-colored paint appeared paler in the current overcast weather. Lucia inhaled deeply, her eyes turned lukewarm as she and Matt got pushed closer to the cement staircase.

Riiiinnnnngggg...

In one ear and then out the other. Matt grimaced and reached for his ears, but the police sandwiched him. His hands were forced to remain at his sides. Everything faded away. It was noises off from then on for him.

The ringing in his ears intensified, grew louder, and forced everything around him to echo. Question after question, numerous mouths opened wider and wider, even into grotesque shapes. "NO COMMENT! NO COMMENT!", Matt assumed the officer said to the nearby reporters on the grass. Snapshot after snapshot. He blinked at another camera flash.

Beet red, the little drummer boy pounded on the inside of Matt's head and pulsated this raw ache to his shoulders and back. His body hunched forward, but he still glanced around.

Left to right. Right to left. Up and down. Down and up.

The reporter's faces turned crimson, especially at their lips that—in Matt's eyes—opened and closed slowly as the officers nudged them to back off. Matt caught snippets of the surrounding voices that screeched through his ears and drained out the last bits of sound, except for…

"Matt—"

While his body was here, his mind turned elsewhere. Far and distant, in front of himself he saw another version of himself in the middle of railroad tracks. He just stood there.

"Matt!"

He opened his mouth to scream, but nothing came out; just his lips shaped in an 'O'.

"Matt!"

The hair on his arms spiked like metal. He slapped his hands over his ears. His hands dripped with sweat. The little drummer boy pounded harder and faster, as though dragging a pitchfork through his chest.

"MATT."

And there it was. They all came to a stop as soon as Matt did. It was there just for him…a *reminder*. Miniature signs with bold numbers trailed down the cement staircase. The steps were blackened all over—

Matt spun around; his breathing grew harsh. A flash zapped through his mind—

The stranger in black.

'Welcome home,' he thought as two officers dragged over a plastic sheet to cover the black…the dried-up blood, his blood.

His legs jostled left, and then to the right. The crutches turned into jelly, detached from his armpits, and hit the grass stained with his blood. He limped forward, until the individual behind him tugged the back of his shirt, pulling him up before he hit the concrete driveway face flat. "Come on, kid," they said and scooped him up.

"Matt!" Lucia screamed. Officer Riley urged her to move, making them hurry into the house. But it was too late.

Click. Click.

Every newspaper became infamous for the homecoming photograph of a fourteen-year-old teenage boy, cradled in the arms of a teddy bear size man in a trench coat.

10.

"ON YOUR MARK…GET SET…"

He gripped the sides—made from cotton.

"GO!" Jamie gave his back a push.

Budamp. Budamp. Budamp.

Matt slid down the staircase with the bottom half of his body wrapped in a Spiderman sleeping bag. His face plastered back in a grin. The adrenaline pushed back his brown spiky hair (the top of the spikes green). His cheeks looked redder than an American Beauty rose.

At the flight of the staircase, Derek tossed his shrimp-sized fist into the air. "Yay!"

Beside him, Lisa winced. "That's going to hurt his hiney." She ducked her eyes beneath her plaid blouse to prevent herself from watching further.

"Go, Matty!" Jamie clasped her hands and bounced up and down, as did the pink ribbon atop her head.

"Whoaaa!"

Matt soared off the staircase like a snowboarder on the last half of a slope. He slewed across the cold tile floor. The three munchkins at the flight of the staircase grew tense and their eyes went bloodshot as their friend went down, down, and down. They got a bit too close to the computer desk.

"Oh, shhh—"

Matt slapped his hands over his face in preparation for CODE RED.

But he came to a halt, just inches from the bottom desk drawer. He continued to pant, pale as a ghost. Eye to eye with the bulky wooden desk.

"Is he alive?" Lisa asked, still in hiding.

"Matty…" Jamie descended a step, her shoulders adjacent to her earlobes.

"That…was…" Matt chucked his arms into the air; his grin was back. *"AWESOME!"*

Derek jumped up and down chanting, "Victory! Victory!"

Lisa poked her head out like a turtle. Jamie sighed with relief. Matt toppled down onto his back. Every inch of his body felt lighter as if Mother Earth herself lifted from his shoulders. He laughed. It was one of his happiest moments.

* * *

It was an invasion. These unwanted guests at work. Items were picked up and set down. Some were captured in a camera snap or dusted off for further evidence. Men and women in blue stood in every room of the residence. At least, that was what *he* saw through blurry snippets.

Matt zipped in and out of a twilight zone. In the corner of his eye, Lucia hunched forward, not sick but resistant to any form of movement. Her knees appeared locked. One police officer held her left arm. Riley had her right. The area seemed to part ways. Other police officers stepped out of their way…

The teddy bear size man, still wearing a trench coat, carried Matt in his burly arms, sprawled out because life wanted Matt dead, one too many times. They all watched as he and Mr. Barry passed by. His grandmother, Riley, and the other officer's faces elongated into weird shapes and sizes, as they grew distant.

* * *

"Gonna see what time we're leaving." Matt tossed his Spiderman sleeping bag onto the floor, dashed back upstairs, and curved around the hallway. Thankfully, no sign of a cut, bruise, or limp.

Jamie, Derek, and Lisa eyed each other and then the Spiderman sleeping bag. "MY TURN," they demanded.

Matt ran by his bedroom, where on the wall he had taped a poster of Ash and Pikachu in the middle of blue lighting.

"Derek," he heard Jamie's order at a distance, "you're supposed to—"

"Yahoooooooo!"

Derek dove on top of the sleeping bag and his body traveled down the bumpy ride, until the very last step. Jamie rolled her eyes. Lisa, stuck in a trance as if whiplashed, popped a squat by the staircase railings. At the landing, Derek lay flat on his belly. His neck looked scarlet from the carpet burn. The more it burned, the brighter it got.

"Owe," he croaked.

Matt lingered in the doorway. A few moments later, his hand dropped from the doorknob. The bulge underneath the floral comforter brought him worry. "Grandma..."

He took his first step into the bedroom as the budamp budamp budamp of his friends' bottoms hitting the steps was audible, until he closed the bedroom door behind him.

He circled the chestnut bench, his Batman ankle socks pointed toward the bed, when he stopped in front of Lucia. She was sound asleep.

"Oh, honey," she said, as soon as she sensed his presence. Eyeing the alarm clock, she pushed herself up to her elbows. The comforter slipped down to her waist. "I must've dozed off."

"You always do."

Her eyes met his. His attention was leveled at the floor. "Honey..." She reached for his hands; his eyes never left the carpet.

"They've wanted to meet them for a while." Now he looked at her; his eyes looked bulgy with red veins and tears. "You promised this time."

His stare intimidated her. Lucia inhaled and exhaled profoundly, as something raw glistened her own eyes. "We'll go...I just need...Few more minutes." The comforter went up to her chin as she slid back down into the bed sheets. She rolled onto her side, her back to him.

Matt sighed and turned on his heel. He snailed his way over to the door and took one last look at her. He saw the tears streaming down her face. Without another word, he walked out and caught the last audible sniffle from her—

Lucia pulled the comforter over her head.

* * *

Matt tossed and turned in bed, his legs and arms sprawled over the navy blue and gray comforter. His eyes twitched, on the verge of opening.

* * *

"Matty?"

Jamie sat at the edge of the bed, her face the same length as the untied ribbons, tangled in her bee nest-hair. Derek and Lisa dawdled behind her, rigid as winter's ice. Matt lay face flat on his Power Ranger bed sheets. His feet dangled off the bed. Corpse paralyzed, he stared off into nothingness.

"Matty," Jamie said softly and placed her hand on his bony back. "Are you… crying?"

"No." He rolled onto his side his eyes dilated. His cheeks turned lukewarm from the two mini red circles on them. "I think it's allergies." He dabbed at his eyes with his white long sleeves.

Derek and Lisa glimpsed at each other. Jamie kept her eyes on Matt, tempted to address him, but the words just stuck to the base of her throat, speechless.

"We should…" Matt pushed himself up and his elbow jostled and pushed him to hunch to the side. Motionless, ambiguous to his own reality, he accidentally said aloud, "Is this really

happening?" Noticing their perplexed faces, it was time to recover.
"I mean...Yeah..."

"Maybe we should go another time," Jamie suggested.
"Only if you —"

"No. No. We'll go." In seconds, Matt wobbled to his feet
and brushed by his friends, going straight for the door. "Lucia's not
coming. She's not feeling well."

That last part had air quotes. But he gave them no chance to
say anything. By now, Matt already headed down the hallway, in
the opposite direction from Lucia's bedroom.

"She's never feeling good," Derek said, tunneled into his
own lost island.

"I've noticed that, too." Lisa spat out a piece of her
fingernails before she started to gnaw on them again.

"Yeah, me three." Jamie dropped back down onto the bed;
her misty eyes never left the empty doorway.

* * *

Matt staggered out of the upstairs hallway bathroom—
zombie mode—and closed the door. He was already out of
breath. The bulgy cloth on his lower leg still weighed him
down, not to mention those damn crutches wanted to move
slower than him. Nobody else was in sight, including Lucia—
he could hear a few voices and some movement downstairs.

'The stranger in black.'

"No," Matt murmured to himself. "Go away."

A sudden rush pulsated throughout his skull. He
leaned his head back against one of the lemon-colored walls.
Sunlight seeped through the small openings of the curtains
beside him. It hissed onto his lower back and his navy blue T-
shirt clung to his skin like caramel. Sweat traveled from his
cheeks down to his not-so-hairy chest and way south.

Matt balked away from the satin, forest green curtains. The curtain's touch was a bit jarring, soft against his rough skin. He turned on his heel—a bit too rapidly—and everything rocked sideways again. He took a step toward his bedroom door as every inch of his body grew heavier. Slowly, he drifted onward and backward but made it into his bedroom. *Something* broke through the haziness—an item— and made his sight crystal-clear again: Jamie's gift.

The collage stood against the wall by the bedroom's door, plastered with posters of AC/DC, The Doors, Nirvana, and The Who. Pokémon was the old days, his childhood days. "Happy Birthday!!!!!!!!!!!!!!!!!!!!!!!!!!!!" with one too many exclamation marks circled around the collaged photographs, imprinted on the frame border. It created an endless funhouse.

* * *

Derek did a high leg kick in his penguin suit. Beside him, Lisa side swept in her emerald dress. Both of their scores skyrocketed to another level on Dance Dance Revolution. "Yeah, boi!"

Derek pumped his fist in the air.

* * *

Those photographs individually aligned from the past to present.

* * *

"Salty and sweet. Never a treat, until we have to say farewell. Then, we eat!"

Underneath the cheesy slug line banner, Jamie in line at the coordinated table, piling four plastic baggies with mini chocolates and sour candies. All the boys had noticed her and did a double take on her hip-hugging dress. She did not notice.

* * *

Slouched over, Matt slapped his hand on the wall, barbed by further details of the night of the promotion dance.

* * *

At the far back table on the right, he sat with his clammy fingers locked together. He dabbed at his sweaty forehead with one of the red napkins that once sat on the black tablecloth. The bass of the latest pop, hip-hop, and rap songs vibrated throughout his ears. The dressed-to-the-nines crowd booed whenever a rock-n-roll song played. Some even left the dance floor.

* * *

Matt grabbed his shaky hand, until it was the other's turn to do the same. Pressure escalated from the pit of his stomach.

* * *

His heart skipped a few beats as she scooted into the folding chair next to him at the white folding table. She handed him one of the plastic candy baggies. "Something sweet for someone sweet," she said sardonically.

His eyes boggled out. His tongue swelled up. Now, he squeezed his shaky hand, tucked underneath the table to prevent himself from passing out. A tight, band sensation tingled around his head. It just felt like one bad, ongoing migraine.

"Hey." She reached out for his hand. "You ok?"

'Yes,' he wanted to say. But instead, he sat up straighter and what soared out of his mouth was, "You wanna dance?"

* * *

It helped with his raspy breathing; he kept his eyes closed and slowly inhaled and exhaled: *'One—Two—Three. One—Two—Three.'*

* * *

He gulped, as her baby doll amber eyes glazed back at him. "Uh," he said. "We don't have—"

"Shut up." She backed up her chair and ascended to her feet. "You are my date, aren't you?" She held out her hand.

'Oh, that was a statement.' Matt smiled and so, did she. They locked fingers.

* * *

Matt exhaled deeply, as something lukewarm fizzled at the back of his throat. Higher and higher it climbed. It tightened his chest and any instant now—"Shit!"

Clump.

His head flung back. Whatever was inside of his chest stopped. Right in the heart. It felt heavy like his bones would cave into his insides at any given moment.

Thud.

Motionless. He listened in as the little drummer boy pounded faster and faster into his chest. "Grandma?"

Budamp. Budamp. Budamp.

He took a step forward, but his legs were too heavy and weary, as though invisible strap-on ankle chains were the reason for his delay in pace. He stumbled along the soft beige carpet; his toes scraped against the spotless fibers. The afternoon sunlight blazed down upon the amber leaves of trees that reflected onto the hallway walls. It made Matt's silhouette visible. The riiiinnnnngggg crackled to life in his ears.

The shiver sent chills throughout his body, as if venom pumped out of a snake bite. He felt exposed—naked in the open—even though a soul was *still* not in sight. Just a few voices—police officers. Every now and then, their radios echoed off the walls. He shambled on by with his crutches, the venom shooting down to his knees, ankles, and feet, turning everything numb, weakened by the seductive poison. The tingling sensation then shot straight to his head, everything tilted sideways. The walls elongated, like the sturdy barbed wire gates of a governmental base. He kept going; his shoulder brushed against one of the many lemon-colored walls for support. It kept him on his feet, not those stupid crutches that just dragged at his side.

Three doors down, no more than fifty feet, stood her bedroom, the door left ajar. He reached for the cold doorknob and applied a soft push to the silent door.

* * *

"No, no!" She turned around on the bench; The middle grays in her hair were now in sight. "What did I say about closed doors?" Lucia asked.

"That you can't hear me if there's an emergency." He removed his hand from the cold doorknob. His Hot Wheels Velcro shoes lit up whenever he moved—red and blue. "I gotta go! Cookie Monster's on TV!"

"Okay," she chuckled and turned back to the dresser mirror, her reflection in proximity with her real self. "I'll be there in a few."

Matt stumbled backward until his neck perked up. It forced him to a halt in the bedroom doorway.

* * *

His hand slipped off the doorframe, flimsy as Taffy. '*What the…*'

It was all in motion. Everything had a whisper of its own suddenly—Drip. Drip. Drip from the hallway bathroom sink.

Scratch. Scratch. Scratch—from tree branches against the glass of the windows.

"I'm going to get you! I'm going to get you! I'm going to get you," said the children outdoors in a game of hide and seek and freeze tag.

Statured at the chest bench, like shadows of a midnight nightmare, Matt skimmed his hand across his lukewarm forehead, soaked with puddles of sweat. Lucia lay on the right-side of her body, curled up in a housecat ball in the middle of her lavender comforter. She purred in her sleep. Matt eyed the right end table, where drops of red liquid sat at the bottom of a wine glass. He looked to the left, where novels and magazines were aligned vertically in alphabetical order in the four-row bookshelf. The stillness of her bedroom constricted something thick in his throat, as he sat the crutches down on the bench. Then, he progressed forward.

About a foot or so from the bed, lay a small wooden box, tipped over onto its side. There were 5x7 index cards spilled onto the floor from the mouth of the box, pointed in his direction.

That little drummer boy jabbed those drumsticks against his chest. Sucked in a hazy tunnel, Matt sashayed over to the object on the floor. He breathed ever so slightly, as he dipped down to his knees. He tensed from the shoulders up.

A burning sensation pulsed from his lower right ankle and consumed his leg. Lucia's eyes remained shut and off each snore, the side of her body peaked a few centimeters up.

Matt reached for the small wooden box and glimpsed around—no sign of the closet door or drawers being open. A stranger to the box, he glided his fingertips over its glossy exterior, a coating of protection fine as silk. The rectangular shaped object was no bigger than an eight-and-a-half woman's shoe box. It resembled a miniature treasure chest since the bracket was gold. He scanned around some more.

More stacks of 5x7 index cards lay underneath Lucia's legs, her feet diagonal from each other.

The cards were not blank.

There was color, backgrounds, clothing, faces, and people.

The index cards were, in fact, photographs.

That rigid feeling returned to his chest and forced him to suck in his belly as the air refused to depart his nasal passages. He turned over one index card next to his leg.

It was a photograph of his eleven-year-old self, his face scarlet from the grin that stretched his cheeks back like a Stepford Wife. He held a sheet of paper tightly, a congratulations award in recognition for being on the sixth-grade honor roll list, the reason for his goofy grin.

"I did it! I did it!" his premature voice chanted in his head.

* * *

"Just remember," Lucia said, a slight hoarse in her tone, "there are no big or small achievements in life. Everything is larger than life."

* * *

It was a trip down memory lane,

Faces and bodies danced as he flipped through the bundles of photographs—his elementary and early middle school days. Penned on the back right-hand corner of one of the photos were the date, location and two—*somewhat*—recognizable faces. *'Who da fuck is Sav and Abdul?'*

The photographs made him smirk, as his fingers skimmed over three recognizable faces.

Jamie had rosy cheeks and pigtails. Derek stood on his hind legs, *still* the shortest out of the group. Lisa had her hair down—as usual—her yellow locks longer than a horse's mane. And there he was, Matt, happier than any camper. He always had his arms around his friends' shoulders and flashed his pearly white teeth at the camera. Sometimes, they were captured in a candid moment and cracked up over something funny that was said or done prior to the camera snapshot.

Something lukewarm thickened a lump in his throat and made his eyes water. He remained on his bottom, cross-legged, as he shuffled through more photographs. He arrived at a new category of photos where he was absent, not included at all. The hairdos and clothes on the subjects were so *tacky*. It forced Matt to his knees, as he flipped through the new mini booklet. On the back of the photographs were *their* names…his family.

The photograph was a shrunken down portrait of two twenty-something-year-olds, both incredibly striking to look at. The bride stood on a pedestal—*literally*; the top of her hair tied up into a bow—*literally*. Her dress puffed out like a vanilla cream cupcake. The tall and slender groom stood beside her. Their arms placed atop each other's emphasized their wedding bands. *'Grandparents' wedding day.'*

As for the next photo, a 5x7 of his grandparents were in their early to mid-thirties, apparent by their "happy life" weight gain. Also, his grandpa sported a mustache and his grandmother cradled a newborn in his arms. The newborn was wrapped in a white blanket: '*Dad...*'

An endless timeline of the original three Smiths flowed, as Matt flipped through the photographs and watched their lives flash before his very eyes: diaper duty, baby over the shoulder to burp, baby smiles, baby in tears, possibly the father, and his grandpa, too. More of the baby, his father. Baby grows up. Toddler on its feet or belly. A close shot of the naked toddler's butt in the air was nothing but the pure innocence of a child laughing and cooing in life.

There was another 5x7 photo of the family. The man, his grandpa, Frank, had a pot belly. Lucia was heavier because of the slight curve in her hips (now she was just skin and bones). The boy, his father, wore a goofy grin, which outshined his thick light brown locks. Pampered in matching red and green sweaters, they stood awkwardly in front of a Christmas tree surrounded by presents: '*The Smiths...*'

An 8x11 photograph included around fifteen to twenty students, who either stood or sat on bleachers. A middle-aged adult stood off to the side: '*Dad's childhood...*'

Only, he could not spot his dad in the class photo.

More class portraits, holiday gatherings, and just...life. The lives of Frank, Lucia, and Jimmy were captured in candid moments. And then, his hands came to a shrunken downsize of a senior portrait. The fair-skinned gorgeous woman had on a white lace top and Farrah Fawcett, feathered, shoulder-length hair. She smiled at the camera; her eyes as vivid as her Hershey Kiss brunette hair: '*Holy shit. It's Mom.*'

11.

THERE WAS NO MOVEMENT or even an increase in his breathing. It was minutes before Matt snapped out of it and set aside the captured photograph (memory) of his teenage mother. He carried on with the remaining bundle of photographs. His fingers seemed to grip on tighter and tighter to the photos as he shuffled through them faster and saw: *Grandpa. Grandma. Dad…*

Soon, he was included in the captured moments—an infant in the smiley faces' arms: *'Grandpa. Grandma. Dad. Me…'*

A crease formed in the middle of his eyebrows; his breathing became shallow: *'Grandma. Grandpa. Dad. Me…'*

He did a double take on the penned labels on the back of another photograph and only saw: *'Grandma. Grandpa. Dad. Me…'*

Another photo—*'Grandma. Grandpa. Dad. Me…'*

And *another*—*'Grandma. Grandpa. Dad. Me…Grandma. Grandpa. Dad. Me…'*

GRANDMA. GRANDPA. DAD. MATT…LUCIA. FRANK. JIMMY. MATT.

The following picture had a newborn, cradled in someone's arms. The next photo had the same newborn— now a toddler—in midst of rolling around on the floor. Sometimes the toddler flew in midair after being tossed up. Him—a man, who was not God. There was a man present with the toddler, who suddenly became a child, as the mini booklet progressed in speed. A man as a new parent. A father with his child, but a son without his mother: *'Me.'*

The photographs slipped through his tingly fingers and rained down. Matt pressed his hand to his chest. The pounding of his heart pulsed from the IV tube ballpoint hole in his wrist to his forehead, where sweat sweltered out from the bulgy veins, underneath the bandage. His jaw locked. He gritted his teeth and his temperature skyrocketed to the moon and beyond the universe. His skin broke out into scales of goosebumps. The tightness in his chest, on the verge of closing. *'Can't...breathe...'*

He shut his eyes and inhaled deeply and carefully. The flowery sweet pea scent of the bedroom bristled through his nasal hairs. It tickled and sent a strong warm sensation to his eyes, until he exhaled. His nasal passages cleared. Again, he breathed in slowly...in and out...in and out...in and out...

When he was brave enough, he opened his eyes. The knots twisted back onto his shoulders.

Lucia.

She faced the other side, toward the wall, away from him. He leaned in for a closer sound. She was sound asleep, almost humming. Relieved, he sat back and sighed. His eyes dropped to the floor and then he saw *it.* A white tip stuck out from underneath the small wooden box. It looked like a piece of someone's clothing. Another mistaken blank index card and a piece of evidence that he somehow *missed.*

Matt stole another glance at his grandmother.

The side of her body continued to rise along with her soft kitten purrs. He scooted closer to the box and vigilantly picked it up. The faced-up photograph displayed a shrunken down portrait of two men who stood in front of a sky-blue backdrop. They beamed at the camera. The older man, with salt and pepper hair and stubble along his chin, stood beside the late teen/early twenties clean-shaven man with light brown hair. A sound asleep newborn was bundled up in a blanket in the younger man's muscular arms.

Matt flipped over the photograph. At the bottom, right-hand corner in blue ink read: *Aug. '92. Frank, Jimmy, Matt—Ohio.*

He lowered the captured memory. A slight stab pained through his chest as his eyes zeroed in on Lucia.

"No, no!" he heard her voice. "What did I say about closed doors?"

"That you can't hear me if there's an emergency," he heard his younger self answer back.

* * *

"I gotta go! Cookie Monster's on TV!"

"Okay," she chuckled and turned back to the dresser mirror; her reflection was in close proximity to her real self. "I'll be there in a few."

Matt stumbled backward until his neck perked up and it forced him to a stop in the bedroom doorway.

Out of her sight, he watched her through the dresser mirror; Lucia still had her back to him. She turned an orange bottle upside down and gave it a shake. Something rattled out onto her palm. Her eyes never rose to the mirror. She tilted her head back and tossed something into her mouth. She moved to the small glass in front of her and gulped down the rest of the clear liquid inside. The drink made her burp, and, moments later, she peered over her shoulder.

Matt coiled out into the hallway and almost slammed against the wall. Carefully, he peeked back into the bedroom and watched while she placed something underneath the bench, as she thought the coast was clear.

The orange prescription bottle sat on top of...a small wooden box.

* * *

'I remember that, but...'

Matt gazed at it all from the dresser without a mirror or a bench (no more hiding spots), to the photographs all over the floor like blood spilling out of an open wound, his eyes returned to that one shrunken down portrait of his grandpa, father, and himself as a newborn.

'...I've never seen any of these—at all...'

12.

"WHAT THE...MATT!"

Lucia chucked the item onto his camouflage-bed comforter. The red and white Marlboro box only gawked at him with Devil's eyes. The color drained from Matt's cheeks, when he spoke it was like his tongue swelled up (unless it was all in his head). "What? That's not—"

"Really? You're really going to pull that stunt right now?" She crossed her arms and chuckled. "Look, I was young once. I get it. Experimenting and stuff."

He dropped his backpack to the floor. The dribbles of sweat on his forehead brought a tingling sensation to his fingers; his heart picked up the pace. Pound. Pound.

"Well," she said.

"We were just...curious, like you said. You know. We see some of the eighth graders sneaking off and hiding behind the dumpsters. So, we, uh, chipped in a $1.25 each to, you know, ask an eighthie to get their older sibling to buy us a pack...To try at home."

"It was here?"

Sadly, he bobbed his head. Lucia rolled her eyes, although her mouth plastered back into a grin. Matt lowered to the edge of the bed his eyes bulgy like a sad puppy. After a huff, he said, "I'm sorry—"

"Save it." She approached and tapped the bottom of his chin. He met her sight. "You just need a better hiding place."

It got a chuckle and a glimpse of his red braces that resembled a pool of blood.

"So, Jamie, Derek, and Lisa were too chicken to take home the cigarettes?"

"Really? But their parents are at work all day!" She gasped and was the splitting image of the Screaming Man from Edvard Munch's painting. "Not only would their homes have better hiding

spots, but you would've been able to smoke there for hours." She lowered down next to him.

On the floor, specks of dust floated by like feathers in the wind. Matt's gaze never left the floor.

"You could've asked," she said softly. Her tone made him less anxious. He finally shifted in place, no longer rigid "I would've felt a lot safer if you'd just—"

"Trusted you?" Then, he brought his attention to her, "It's a lot cooler to do it secretly."

They smiled, humored by the thought. She gave his shoulder a squeeze. "No more secrets." Her tone sounded serious now.

"No more secrets."

* * *

Their teeth sunk into the mushy tomato sauce, melted cheese, and smoked red hot pepperoni pizza. Jamie continuously patted her mouth with her napkin—all prim and proper. Derek dug in for seconds, or thirds, he lost count as well. Lisa tossed her pizza crusts onto his plate.

"Thanks," he burped.

She failed to burp back. "You're welcome."

"Derek," his mother admonished.

"Lisa…" Her parents eyed her down.

Crumbs of greasy breadsticks sat at the bottom of the pizza box. Two jumbo size pizza slices remained untouched on Matt's paper plate. He sat there with his arms crossed.

Across from his seat, on the opposite end of the dining room table, Lucia guzzled down her glass of red wine. "Fill me up," she said with a laugh and waved around her empty glass.

'Jesus.'

Mr. Peralta glanced at his wife. Mrs. Peralta peered at Ms. Castellanos, who sat across from her. Ms. Castellanos peeked to her left, where the Santosos looked at each other. Mr. Santoso shrugged. Mrs. Santoso sighed and brought her attention back to Mr. Peralta, Lisa's dad.

"Well." Lucia shifted in her chair while the anxiety heightened in her tone. "I can't wait all day."

Jamie turned to Matt, tempted to speak, until her mouth closed. She looked to her left side and met Derek and Lisa's sight. Matt only glowered at *her*; *everything* and *everyone* tuned out, as his grandmother's lips met another round of alcohol.

"Well, I don't know about you," Lucia said and reached for the wine bottle, "but I could use a real drink!"

The adults sipped on their own glasses of red wine, except for Mrs. Santoso who pushed her full—untouched— glass toward the apple and pear centerpiece.

"Hey." It was Jamie, only her voice filled up his head because he never bothered to look at her. He felt a tap on his shoulder, but his attention never left his grandmother. "Matty, are you okay?"

"Peachy," his own voice echoed back in his head.

* * *

Matt tossed aside his Levi's. He had on a pair of gym shorts. "Stupid pants won't go over the cast. Fuck!"

Jamie lingered in the bedroom doorway; her fingers were bundled in knots. Everyone else's voice bounced off the walls from the first floor—Derek and Lisa were ordered to set up the table for dinner, while Lucia told the adults to follow her into the kitchen.

"We wanted to stop by earlier," Jamie said, a bit too cautiously, "but your grandma told us you were sleeping…"

"Yeah." He shoved the top drawer of his black dresser shut. "So?"

"Maybe we should stick with soda," they heard Mrs. Santoso suggesting.

"Just get some glasses," Mrs. Peralta responded.

Matt and Jamie held each other's gaze. His look appeared rough, tiring, intimidating, and scary.

Uncomfortable, she peered away, worried.

Down the dim staircase, the commotion of a wine bottle being corked open and the serving of glasses, made the second floor less quiet.

"Matt," she finally said and brought her attention back to him. He mimicked her, not fully aware of it, and started his way over to her too.

"Pizza's ready!" Ms. Castellanos shouted from afar.

* * *

Everything seemed to grow louder; his Spidey senses kept tingling. It was a carnival tilt-a-whirl, as the clock on the wall went tick, tick, tick.

"...Maybe you should slow down," Mrs. Santoso suggested.

A prickle sensation boiled at the pit of his stomach...

Tick. Tick. Tick.

"...It's just been a tough day..." Lucia chugged back her drink.

His intestines were tangled in knots...

Tick. Tick. Tick.

"...Lucia..."

'Those photographs,' he thought to himself, and saw flashes of them flicker on the tablecloth in front of him.

Memories. Not dreams. The universe wanted him to *remember.*

Tick. Tick. Tick.

"...Lucia..."

Remember.

'*That...fucking BOX!*'

Tick. Tick. Tick.

"...Lucia!"

Tick. Tick. Tick.

"Matty."

By her touch, he shot up on his good foot; the cast grounded his other foot already. Jamie gasped.

A flame of fire huffed and puffed out of his mouth—at least, it felt like it did, since he tasted fumes and charcoal. Everyone was startled, except for Lucia.

"Honey," she said nonchalantly, "what is it?"

"Shut up."

Clink. Clank. Bonk.

The adults nearly dropped their glasses. Mrs. Peralta's glass tipped over onto its side and stained the tablecloth with red. Jaws dropped. Scraps of food rolled off Derek's tongue. Shoulders tensed back. Eyes went watery from the alien dilation, their pupils all rigid and black. Still...They were all too motionless.

"*Excuse me.*" Lucia straightened herself up. "Just who do you think you're talking—"

"Oh, my God! For the *love of God*, SHUT UP!"

"Matt," Jamie beseeched, but he stepped away before she had reached out for his hand—skin to skin. Warmth to warmth.

"Honey..." Lucia's voice trembled, matching her shaky hands. "You should really eat. After all, the doctor said—"

"FUCK what the doctor has to say!"

The rectangular box dropped out of Lucia's grip. The cheesy garlic bread sticks flew out and landed on the table, next to the red wine stain that only lengthened across the white tablecloth. Mrs. Peralta and Mrs. Santoso seized a hold of every clean napkin and patted down the stain. Their husbands helped as best as they could. By the time Lucia looked up, *he* was already gone. Everyone listened as Matt's foot and cast clobbered up the staircase and down the hallway, followed by a—

Whack!

The slamming of his bedroom door sprung off the walls like a Sonic Boom. Everyone flinched in their seats. Derek covered his ears. Lisa gripped onto her parents' hands. Ms. Castellanos tugged Jamie into her arms. Jamie was stiff, non-reactive to the comfort of her mother.

Lucia wobbled back down into her chair, silent for a moment. "Must be the medication."

She gave a few sniffles before the tears showered down her cheeks and formed unwanted swimming pools onto the tablecloth. The adults jumped to their feet and ran to her side to comfort him. There were more crocodile tears by the seconds. Derek and Lisa remained in their seats as their eyes swept from each other and over to Jamie.

She stood at the dining room archway; Matt's outburst paralyzed her, unable to process what had just happened. Lucia tossed back the remains of wine and repeated the action after she poured herself another glass of Merlot. Practically, she choked on the wine but kept pounding it back.

13.

AN INVISIBLE FORCE FIELD extended around the boy and the unknown man. "Wait!" Matt croaked. The boy stretched out his arms; starting at the tips of his fingers and working its way down his wrists, forearms, and arms, a blaring, blue light shone.

Matt squinted as the light traveled through the white cloud storm, forcing him to look away. Yet, he dared another look and watched as the blueness took over his fingertips. Using his hands to shield his eyes from the spinning light ahead of him, he saw the 5'8 silhouette of a man walk further into the light. Matt's world.

"Wait," he bemoaned.

But the man dissolved into thin air.

Matt panted and the white air clouds that escaped his lips were the only evidence of life. He squirmed his way around, but his body was only consumed by the air he breathed in. "Come back! Please…"

Gasping and screaming for air, Matt felt the rumble of the steady earth fall apart underneath him. The white air dragged him by the feet and began to swallow him whole. Gradually, he slipped into the black abyss into the world below, ready for a hello or a welcoming arm. Panting, a sharp pain started at the bottoms of Matt's feet and worked its way up to his abdomen.

He cried for help, but deeper he went into the abyss that now reached his torso. "Help!"

Matt held onto the ledge of a cliff, dangling between the black and white worlds. With his arms shaking, he closed his eyes — a refusal to look down or up. At a sling-shot distance, a girl's voice ascended, "Matt! Matty!"

14.

THUMP.

"Matty," he heard beyond his bedroom door.

Still slowly awakening from the unknown, Matt was startled by the moving doorknob–

Twist. Bolt. Twist. Bolt.

"Come on…" Jamie removed her hand from the doorknob. She leaned her head against the white doorframe.

Matt's bedroom door remained shut and locked. "Everyone's downstairs?"

"It's just us," Lisa chimed in. She and Derek lingered beside Jamie.

The adults' voices were still audible from downstairs.

"He's just upset. The accident…" Mrs. Santoso lowered her tone. "It just probably took a toll on him."

'*Lowered my ass*,' Matt thought to himself.

"Like the rest of us," Mr. Santoso added on.

"He's going through the emotions." Mrs. Peralta sounded all fuzzy. "It's like grieving over a death."

"He doesn't hate you," Mr. Peralta said softly.

"If anything," Ms. Castellanos chimed in, speaking the loudest in the group, "he's wondering about the 'what ifs.' 'What if nobody found me that night? What if I fell another way?'"

"Hey, Jamie," Lisa whispered. "Maybe we should, you know, let you handle this one on your own."

"Yeah." Derek eyed Lisa back. "Because after all, you've known him the longest…"

They glanced at the dim hallway that guided their eyes toward the narrow staircase. Jamie stared at them a bit longer in silence. Cat got her tongue.

"You're his friends, *too*," she retorted.

"And you're his *bestest friend*."

"Really? *Bestest*? That's something Derek would say."

"Shat up!" Derek stuck out his tongue.

"Well," Lisa tugged a hold of Derek's arm. "We'll be downstairs—"

"Wait. Lisa! Derek!"

And then, they were gone.

"Shit," Jamie mumbled to herself, or at least she had hoped so.

She sighed and rubbed her forehead that was breaking out with a tidal wave of wrinkles. Long, feathered shadows were pasted on the walls in front of her. She turned around and saw through the ajar curtains, glimpses of tree branches, turning into living creatures. They wiggled around—possibly from a night's breeze.

From the yellow-brown hue and a few darkened spots around her, the walls seemed grayer by the second. Jamie took in a deep breath and the air chilled her lungs, as if from a brain freeze. Tight, it made her shiver. She turned back to the bedroom door and nearly bumped into a shirtless Angus Young, who strode his guitar in midair. Beside Angus was a poster of Jim Morrison with his arms spread out, his fingers slightly off the frame. His dark, intense eyes…

She was spellbound, and it made her weak in the knees.

"Matty!"

The door creaked open with a loud click. Matt hobbled out from the dark room and into the light. He had on a pair of gray gym shorts, which were a bit longer than his pair from earlier, and a black AC/DC T-shirt. "Hey," he mumbled and rubbed the sleepy dust out of his partially closed eyes.

"No, he *doesn't*," Mrs. Peralta said from afar.

"Sorry. I, uh…" Jamie took a took step back. "I didn't know you were asleep."

"Lucia," Mrs. Santoso admonished.

"Yeah, well…" Matt rolled his eyes at the sound of the first floor commotion. "The medicine makes me a bit—"

"Matt!" *It* garbled closer. "*Matt!*"

"…Out of it," he said and squeezed his eyes shut to surpass a fat scream.

"MATT!" *It* slurred with hiccups.

A gap remained between them. Jamie was tempted to step forward but instead, she only stared at him. His face crumbled from the pain and rage that just built and built, as his fingers curled into fists.

"Matty," she said.

Breathing shallow, his nostrils opened and closed, matching his rapid breaths.

"Matty!"

"Matt," *It* echoed closer and closer.

Tightness climbed and burned up his throat, his hands turned clammy. Then, his eyes shot wide open. "Now *WHAT*?!"

Jamie reached for his arms, but he bypassed her like whiplash from a car accident. That voice tugged him closer and closer to the staircase. He hopped his way there until, he quickened his pace.

"Matty!" Jamie trailed after him.

Paralyzed in the dining room archway, Derek and Lisa's eyes and mouths were widened in horror and fear. No more than ten feet away from them were the adults, who had skid to a halt at the bottom of the staircase, where Lucia swayed side to side and then backward…

The wine glass in her hand tipped over. The last bits of Merlot dribbled onto the wooden floor and formed tiny wet circles—a strong resemblance to crimson blood. The women bounced to Lucia's side. The men tentatively wrapped their fingers around her chicken size arms. But Lucia was oblivious and simply did not have a care in the world.

"Matt!" she hollered, ascending the steps and seizing hold of one of the pillars for support. "We need—"

"Lucia!" Mrs. Peralta choked back the tears, "Why don't you come back into the dining room—"

"We need to talk!"

"Lucia," Ms. Castellanos admonished, "you're scaring the kids."

"See this?" It was rhetorical, but Lucia wiggled her fingers. "You judge me for drinking too much tonight. Well, let me tell you, *ma'am*, three more are pointing back at *you*. Don't be a hypocrite!"

"At least they can hold their liquor!" Matt stepped out from the yellow-brown hue and into the navy blue lighting. The moonlight came through the circular window on the wall and reflected onto his cheeks; there was a spotlight for him. Jamie swerved to a stop next to him at the flight of the staircase. "You're *embarrassing* me."

"You can't just be angry with me!" Lucia spat out. "I'm the *adult* and you're—"

"LOOK AT YOURSELF! YOU'RE HAMMERED! IN FRONT OF EVERYONE! WHO'S THE IRRESPONSIBLE ONE NOW—"

"MATTY!" Jamie pulled him by his arms in time. He was unaware that his foot was about to skip over a step. She possibly saved him from another fall. In the meantime, the adults and Lucia were in shock. Their mouths dropped open. Lucia had her hand on her chest that moved up-up-up and down-down-down from her shallow breathing. Matt looked crimson, matching the Merlot drops on the floor, and nearly out of breath himself. His glossy eyes gave a twitch.

"I saw..." The words squeezed up his throat and out. "I saw them!" He wrapped his hand around Jamie's wrist. "You're a *liar*!"

"Matty." Jamie was too afraid to remove his fingers that squeezed tighter and turned her wrist blood red...

But the look on his grandma was a giveaway; she *knew* what he was talking about.

That one hurt Lucia too, especially since his glare turned darker. She burst into tears and flung off the multiple hands on her.

"Lucia!"

She was already inches from the front door.

"Lucia!" Ms. Castellanos ran after and the other parents scattered off one by one.

Matt coiled around and ran down the hallway.

"Matt!" Jamie hounded after him, back into the tunnel of sunset colors.

"Dad!" Derek chased after. "Wait—"

"Just stay here!"

Thwack!

Derek stood an inch or so from the closed front door. His shoulders stooped forward. Lisa dropped to her knees, throttled by her tears that splashed all over her clothes and onto the floor. "What…is…*happening*?"

Upstairs, Jamie stomped across the carpet while the shadows of the tree branches reflected off her skin. Some of the tree branch tips cuffed against the glass (*screech*). "Matt!"

Slump!

"What was that?" Derek looked at Lisa; her eyes were already pointed up at the ceiling, which many spiders called home.

"MATT!" Jamie picked up her pace and pursued toward the speck of light that glowed from the doorway, three doors down—no more than fifty feet from Matt's darkened bedroom.

Thud. Thump. Ping. Clash.

Object after object like a toddler using the kitchen pots and pans as drum cymbals. "Fuck!" Matt's groans echoed down the hallway.

Jamie skid to a halt in the doorway to Lucia's bedroom. She panted for air. "What are you *doing*?"

Matt proceeded with his frenzied search and destroy in Lucia's bedroom. Drawer after drawer. Item after item. Objects got snatched up and then slammed back down when the original placement unsatisfied Matt. None of them was what he was looking for. Everything else appeared untouched, except for his cast, which he rammed a few times into an object. He was losing it.

"SHIT. FUCKIN' SHIT. FUCK. FUCK. FUCK YOU!"

"MATT!" Jamie cried. "You're going to hurt yourself—STOP!"

Derek and Lisa came on running...and started a shitty Domino effect once they had reached Jamie—

"Guys!"

Derek crashed into Lisa, who rammed into Jamie. Jamie hit the side of her face against the door frame and screamed, "Motherfu—"

"Where is *it*?!" Matt walloped one of the lavender pillows back onto the bed; it rolled over onto the floor. "I know she's hiding—"

"Hiding *what*?!" Jamie chafed her scarlet cheek.

"EVERYTHING."

Then he eyed the bed and dropped down to his knee, on the good leg. He shoved his hands underneath the mattress. "Come on! I know you're hiding it here...or over on this side...Okay! Then, it has to be on *this* side—Son of a bitch!"

The three of them were no longer sidetracked by Matt's grunts and, "Shit this, fuck that, fuck, fuck, fuck, fuckadee fuck." Derek tapped on the girls' shoulders and pointed to the small wooden box that tipped over on its side in the middle of the bed. The lid was off, the box's opened mouth facing their direction. They saw the blank index cards around the mouth until Lisa tapped their shoulders and pointed out clue number two: a photograph was in the mix, but the faces were hard to identify. Before they asked—

"'I'll be seeing you…'"

Everyone jumped in place. Lisa let out a yelp…and so did Derek. It was Billie Holiday who brought a tang of the nineteen-forties into the bedroom through the clock radio. Matt growled and stomped forward, sucked back into that tunnel again, where everything but the clock radio blurred away.

"Matty—DON'T!"

Matt snatched a hold of the digital clock radio from the bed's end table. The cord yanked out of its socket and put an end to Ms. Holiday's singing. He raised his arms, the clock radio in midair,

"STOP!", Jamie jumped and clawed a hold of his wrist. "Just LOOK at *yourself*!"

She chucked his arms to the side. The alarm clock radio hit the floor…and something rattled across the wooden floor. Derek and Lisa crouched, as a small unopened bottle rolled to a stop in front of them. Half colored baby blue and white capsules were all around the floor.

"Fluoxetine," Lisa said once she got a closer look. "20 mg…"

"Fluoxetine?", Derek also had a few pills in his hands to examine. "What is—"

That discomfort ascended his throat again. Everything squeezed inward and forced Matt to gasp—

Jamie whirled around, facing his way. "Matty?"

He slumped to his knees.

"Matty!"

Everything around him elongated and distorted into grotesque shapes, like faces of witches and demons. Matt cupped his fingers over his Adam's apple as he wheezed in and out for air…

"DO SOMETHING!" Lisa wailed.

"DAD! MOM!" Derek cried out.

"MATT!" Jamie screamed, but her voice only merged with the blockage of his haze that took over his eyesight. Her face stretched out vertically as if she were straight out of a fun size carnival mirror and ready to hunt. "MATT—"

"No, no!" he heard his grandmother's voice bounce around in his head. "What did I say about closed doors?"

"That you can't hear me if there's an emergency," his younger voice echoed back in his head.

* * *

Lucia still had her back to him. She turned an orange bottle upside down and gave it a shake. Something rattled out onto her palm.

A half baby blue and white pill spilled out of the orange bottle called, Fluoxetine 20 mg—

Moments later, she peered over her shoulder. The doorway was empty. Around the corner, Matt looked as still as a puppet without its strings. His chocolate swirl eyes dilated to the size of marbles. He held his breath until the door shut.

* * *

"It...makes...sense," Matt panted, his hands pressed down to the floor to steady his balance, so he would not completely tumble to the floor.

"What does?" Jamie asked while she guided him through a breathing relaxation exercise for a few more seconds.

"The drinking. The crying..." His inhales and exhales stopped matching hers. It was ruthless—exhale, exhale, EXHALE. He felt his entire body taken over by a numbness; sweat—slewing down from his hairline to his neck and then onto his T-shirt—crawled along his spinal cord.

The clock radio remained on the floor, close to him and Jamie. Its bottom faced up, toward the ceiling. There was no longer a cover, just an opening, a perfect fit for the prescription bottle that was once hidden from him.

"Jonathan Brown," Lisa said and looked up from the Fluoxetine 20 mg bottle in her hand. "Isn't your doctor named, Dr. Brown?"

"GO GET HELP!"

Jamie grabbed a hold of his wobbly hand. His face broke out with tints of blue and purple as he choked for air. Lisa scampered out of the bedroom and screamed for help, but, eventually, her and Derek's mouths only moved up and down. There were no words. Their voices were gone.

Jamie cupped her hands beneath his chin. Matt investigated her eyes and, simultaneously, she leaned in.

BOOM. BOOM.

The lights zapped out. The Smith residence went pitch black. A colorful wheel painted the sky, like paint splattered on a canvas. Through the hallway windows, outside of Lucia's bedroom door, glowed the faintest hint of summer's moonshine. It turned the firework explosions in the sky into shadows on the walls of the hallway. Matt and Jamie held each other's gaze, inches apart, as they breathed in summertime's humid air. Jamie pulled back once the lights flickered on and off.

"Lisa!" Derek bellowed from afar.

The lights remained off. Matt tasted the gust of air that vaporized into his mouth like water steam.

"You guys!" they heard Lisa screaming in the darkness, followed by her footsteps.

The lights flicked on and off until the light vanished.

"Oh, THANK GOD!" Lisa stumbled back into the bedroom, out of breath, as if she saw a ghost.

Matt remained on his knee and ceased shaking. Just motionless. Jamie fell back onto her bottom. Those baby doll eyes of hers stayed on him as though it was just the two of them existing in the room and the *entire* universe, as his lips drifted apart to speak.

"Hey, guys." Lisa strolled over to the bed. "Is that..." Derek already stood at her side by the time she picked up the photograph that was lying face up on the bed.

It was a photo of Lucia. She looked the same as her present-day self: petite, short, still wearing cream-colored blouses with a black button-down sweater and a pair of gray slacks. She was squished in the middle of a man, who had salt and pepper hair, and a lanky eighteen-year-old boy with light brown locks. The youngster wore a baby blue cap and gown. Hundreds of individuals, most blurred out, surrounded them like moths at a light bulb. Goofy, happy smiles were on Lucia and these two men. Obviously, it was a proud moment for the Smith family trio.

"What are you two doing on the floor?" Derek asked.

Jamie jumped up first, all hot and flustered and wide eye, preparing her excuses. Matt could not keep his eyes off her. The longer they held eyesight with each other, the redder Jamie got. It took a moment before the mystery dawned on Lisa, who let out an, "Oh...I get it now..."

'Fuck it!'

Matt reached for Jamie's hand, but she already headed their way. "Let me see," she said and took a hold of the photo. She turned it over. "'1987. Us. Jimmy's high school graduation.'"

Lisa kept her eyes on Matt, who still sat on the floor. He looked dazed, preoccupied with a trillion thoughts: *'Did I do something wrong? Did I fuck up? Bullshit.'*

Then Jamie noticed a small bump at the corner of the glossy 5x7 photograph. She skimmed her finger over it. It was a crease mark next to Matt's father in the photo. It was a candid moment that was truly meant to be for them only, cherished forever. Jamie placed her fingers behind the crease mark, the back of the long time memory and brought a flap forward—

"Whoa," Derek said, as he and Lisa circled in.

It was the missing link to the photograph: Tootsie Roll curls spiraled an inch or so past her shoulders. She had a pearlier smile than the solid white cap and gown. Skin so fair like white oleanders. A teenage girl with Hershey Kiss brunette locks matched her eye color.

"Matty…" Jamie sounded all raspy, as her fingers trembled. "…It's your…"

Something thin whispered onto the back of their necks.

The three of them coiled around—Derek even yelped, "Stranger!"

It was Matt. He stooped behind them. His intense eyes were bulgy and wet as though any second now, they were about to burn a hole into the nearest object…or person in front of him.

'Blink.'

"Tell me about mommy," his younger voice rushed back to him.

* * *

"Please," he begged, his voice squeaky. "You never want to talk about her."

As his round sausage-fingers reached out, Lucia pulled away and ascended from the edge of his bed. She moved to the shudders, where streaks of moonlight brushed against her beautiful face. She closed her eyes, lost in the memories, painful ones. "Your mother," she finally said, "was a beautiful lady. I just don't…I just don't know what had happened to her. What she did to…"

She turned around and met his round chocolate drop shaped eyes. The look that came to her, the sight of him, it killed her. His bottom lip quivered, as he just sat there, all wide-eyed, so naïve and filled with innocence.

Lucia stormed off and went straight for the bedroom door. Matt remained atop the covers and pressed his footie pajama feet together. "Every year," he muttered to himself. "Every year on my—"

* * *

"Birthday…"

It certainly grasped his worried friends' attention. After a moment, Matt carried on. "Memories," he repeated. "I don't think it's just the stuff she's been hiding from me. The pictures. Family albums. I mean, I kind of recall seeing a photo or two of my mom as a kid. But both times, Grandma got all, panicky, asking where I found the pictures and took them away."

"Why did she do that?" It was a good question, at least coming from Derek. "People just don't hide stuff."

"They do if they don't want to get caught for something."

Matt squeezed Jamie's hand back. "I think…she has something to do with my mother's disappearance."

"But you said your mom left you—"

"Lisa," Jamie admonished.

"*What*?! That's what he told us year after year—no offense, Matt. I mean, you said so yourself! That your grandpa and dad's deaths were too much for your mom to handle so taking off was easier—"

"Lisa!" Jamie shot her another glowering look, like cat's eyes in the dark.

"So, what you're saying," Derek chimed in, "is your mother *didn't* leave you?"

That got everyone to shut up. Then Matt bobbed his head. "Yeah," he finally told them. "I don't think my mom left by choice. I think she was forced to leave."

Silence took over. Matt interlaced his fingers with Jamie's shaky ones. Then the sky screamed—

Boom. Boom.

The lights zapped out at once. In...every...single...room.

15.

DARKNESS.

The moonlight poured through the uncovered windows on the first floor, the small one above the front door, and the second story hallway where it bordered with Lucia's bedroom doorway. The fireworks only progressed.

Boom. Boom.

Lisa shrieked and clawed a hold of Derek's arm. Jamie remained in place, as though her feet were stuck in quicksand. Hints of moonlight glistened through the slightly parted lavender, sheer curtains on the windows and into the bedroom. A trail of light guided to the empty spot behind them.

It was just the *three* of them. No sign of—

"Matt." Lisa clasped onto Jamie and Derek's wrist.

"Matty!" The adrenaline just kicked in and Jamie dashed out into the hallway. "Matty!"

"Jamie!" Derek and Lisa bellowed a few ways down.

Every…Single…Room…was electrocuted by spurts of color from the fireworks that shot into the sky—

Boom. Boom. Boom. Boom.

She veered to a halt at the staircase. The wall next to her bounced off laser beam reflectors, until she realized it was a red colored firework that blew up in the sky. Tiny red lights kept on going. She panted heavily, as her eyes dropped to the first story, where darkness swam, like open water past dusk. Pitch black. A shark waiting for its next prey.

"Matty."

She stretched out her foot to the first step, her eyes circled in on the speck of light that streamed through the square window on the front door. Just as she reached for the following step, a breeze swept toward her. The chilled air thrusted against her skin. Every inch of her body broke out with goosebumps. Whoever wanted her to be still pressed her back against the wall forcedly. "Matt!"

"Jamie."

"*Jamie!*"

Here it came. She listened to the footsteps that trampled closer to her. Soon, it was a collision because once all the lights flickered on, Jamie turned around in time and collided into Derek and Lisa.

"RELAX! RELAX!" Derek grasped her shoulders. "IT'S JUST US!"

"Where the hell is Matt?!"

BUMP. BUMP. BUMP.

The three of them spun around—

Matt.

At the dining room archway, he looked ill, paler than a blood donor. They did not know it, but he did. It hurt. It hurt to see them. It hurt to see her. He grimaced and clutched his chest; his heart battered and battered (nails clawing a chalkboard, a nail being wedged into human flesh). He shivered, but his hefty breathing was not from the cold.

"Matty."

The blood rushed through his icy blue veins, away from his head, and his eyes dilated.

Boom. Boom.

The lights burst into explosions—one by one. It was a different firework show that ensued, as the glass turned into clouds of silver glitter, and drifted all around them. "Matt."

"Matt."

"*Matt.*"

Their voices traveled faintly through his ears. Through a silver gust of cloud, he watched, as the three of them lunged away in time from big chunks of the unbroken glass that fell straight to the floor.

Slash. Slash. Slash.

By now, Matt slumped over onto his side, until his friends grabbed him by the arms and pulled.

"*Dammit!*" Jamie screamed, as his arm slipped out of her hands.

The withdrawals of their breath grew small, smaller, to the smallest puffs of clouds.

It seized their attention and forced them to a stop. A complete deadly silent stop. The four of them glimpsed at each other, their breathing...ruthless, thickening as they breathed faster and faster. "What da fu—"

POP. POP.

Derek was cut short.

The light bulbs of the dining room chandelier burst open, one by one to their game of ring around the rosy. Screaming, the four of them huddled together. The air chilled their systems, as if something stored them in a basement freezer. A hollow sound of nightfall's eve trickled closer and closer to them. A placemat slapped onto Derek's forearm. It was stuck.

"Get it off!"

It took three tries before Lisa unpeeled the slimy placemat off him. It sailed away in the air. The other placemats and utensils scratched, scraped, and flew off the dining room table by some...force. The mightier breeze drove toward them and chafed against their skin.

"I saw your grandma close the windows," Jamie mentioned.

A utensil smacked onto the floor in the black sea, followed by a loud creak. The chandelier detached from the ceiling. The entire household got struck by a sonic boom.

"What was that!" they heard someone bellow from outside.

"KIDS!" It was a man's voice.

"Dad!" Derek shouted.

POP. POP.

The glass from the chandelier soared into the air. It was a tsunami of glass.

Jamie yanked Matt's T-shirt. Derek and Lisa already running, and the three of them dragged Matt backward. The dark gray sparkles of glass pierced the floor where they sat seconds ago. "You guys," Matt said faintly, his eyes set on the...

The doorknob jingled and jangled side to side. Derek unfastened the lock and bolt, but, as he pulled the knob, the door remained shut. "DAD!" He yanked harder, but not even the sound—*click*—of the door locks existed. Not a single movement from the door occurred, as Derek pounded his fists on it. "DAD!"

Jamie crept in for a closer look. Even from afar, it slowly came into crystal-clear sight: something bolted around the doorframe, slithered around, and concealed every crack, every possible sign of the outside world's visibility. Whatever it might have been looked silver, like chains.

Lisa high kicked a nearby window, but nothing shattered, not even a thud or thump. Instead, she was pushed away. She fell flat on her bottom, as the glass made an imprint of her size six and a half Converse shoes. The glass thinned, ready to break. Lisa and her mother, on the outside world, backed away from the window and took cover.

But the glass shifted back into its perfect aligned pieces. Unharmed. No breaks. Untouched. No more shoe imprint. The mothers pinned to the window. They were stunned and horrified on what they just witnessed. It was only seconds before Mrs. Peralta backed away. "SOMEONE CALL THE POLICE!"

"Mother!" Jamie tapped the window, but something immediately pushed her aside. She toppled over onto her side. She began to shake in response to her slapped hand. The top reddened, a red handprint from someone else.

"JAMIE!" Lisa charged toward her friend.

Derek went to Matt's side. Everyone started to notice as their eyes shot from the windows to the walls. They were imprisoned inside. Everything closed in already. The silver wrapped around the front door and the windows. It dripped down the walls like syrup, but as soon as it hit the wooden floor panels, it turned to fog that remained at ground level and slowly began to rise.

"We're trapped," Jamie panted. "WE'RE TRAPPED!"

POP. POP.

The light that dangled from the ceiling above the staircase burst. It was an eerie scene: a waterfall of the same silver glitter; glass sprinkled into smaller pieces. Then, it formed into fog. "Matt." Lisa scooted closer and her pupils grew twice its size. "You guys…"

* * *

AT LAST: Maple Oak Street—his street. He walked straighter—the booze already lost in the air.

* * *

He wheezed for air. The sweat from his forehead dribbled down onto the floor.

"MATT."

* * *

A whistle—It echoed through one ear and out the other. It had a sense of its own, chillier than the actual atmosphere. He shivered and buried himself in his pull-over, still wearing his hood. He revisited the night of his fourteenth birthday.

* * *

The screaming never stopped—or the *voices*. The porch light popped into pieces—at least, that was what the outside voices claimed, as many of them screamed—

"Jamie!"

"Matt!"

"Derek!"

"Lisa!"

"HELP!"

"THEY'RE TRAPPED!"

"GET AWAY FROM THEM YOU BASTARD!"

Jamie, Derek, and Lisa begged for their parents' rescue...something about their cell phones not working.

'Cell phone.'

Matt dug around in his pockets...there it was. It was off. No matter how many times he tapped or held down the power button, his cell phone remained off. Dead. Their parents' voices faded into the bottomless black hole, as the silver goo spread across the windows and turned them black. It shut out the last bits of light.

"You guys," Derek said, all shaky.

The fog glided an inch or so above their knees and made everything possible to see. Whiter than snow, the fog almost came off as a flashlight glow. Glimpses of Jamie revealed her top half in the shadows. The fog ascended higher, passing their thighs and abdomens.

"GUYS!" Lisa, as well as the others, choked as the fog climbed higher and higher, touching their mouths.

But it bypassed them— all together—and went straight to the ceiling, like an abandoned balloon. Only a few bursts of light wobbled around. All the windows were covered in fog, and resembled dancing cobwebs. There was a loud BEEP—

BEEP. BEEP. BEEP. BEEP. BEEP. BEEP. BEEP.

No signal. Zero bars. It became real for the four of them as soon as their cell phones decided to turn off all by themselves. The screens all remained black. It then played out for Matt—fast:

The cold air.
    The breeze.
    And the stranger.
    That night. That NIGHT. THAT night. THAT NIGHT.
    Caught in the midst of his own white wonderland, he listened to the stranger's black robe from the wind.
    FLAP. FLAP. SWOOSH. SWOOSH.
    Even the fog around him turned black.

* * *

Matt gave a loud, hollow gasp. He heaved and heaved for air, which suppressed all the screams that he wanted to lash out—

* * *

Matthew.
    Matt…
    Riiiiiiing
    MATT!
    Yellow and white lines.
    He went headfirst on the asphalt.
    He lied there, able to see but his vision weakened by the second, as life slowly drained out of him—blood. A pool of red formed around his head—pre-diaper bandage. There were tints of black. It started at the top and bottom corner of his eyes, worked its way to the middle of his vision.
    Flap…Flap…Swoosh…Swoosh.

The wind pushed up the bottom of a long black graduation robe and exposed a pair of bones. There were two skeletal feet in front of him. Before everything blacked out, he saw no skin or even any sign of human fluids…

…because it was not living, but dead.

* * *

"It's here!" Matt said, his eyes twitched and reopened, all bold and wild.

His head jerked sideways in the opposite direction of them, and he screamed with all his might. His friends each pounced away, as his eyes twitched opened and closed. For a few moments, his body convulsed around, and bubbles formed at the corner of his mouth, but his eyes remained their natural color. "Help me," was all Jamie, Derek, and Lisa heard.

The three of them covered their ears and screamed themselves. The fog above them turned into an eerie off-color white lighting, as it pulsated like a heartbeat…an extremely fast one, in its own strobing light show of WHITE-GRAY-WHITE-GRAY-WHITE-GRAY—

Three sets of white clouds repeated exhale, exhale, EXHALE, near each other. Jamie, Derek, and Lisa bundled together as they watched the fourth set of white clouds growing thinner.

"MATT!" Jamie dropped to the floor and neared him. His chest caved in more than it went out. "Don't leave us! Someone HELP!"

Screech.

Gasping for air. The fog departed from the ceiling and headed their way.

SCREECH-SCREECH-SCREECH-SCREECH-SCREECH.

They peered into the dining room. The noises assaulted them from outdoors. Through the ajar beige curtains, they saw the Charlie Brown Christmas tree bumped against the window. The short and scrawny branches clawed onto the glass faster and faster. Something powerful and sadistic swayed it from its root—right, left, left, right. Behind it, the faintest sight of objects soared through the air.

Weakened at the knees first, their entire bodies became heavier. Something churned their inside. All the way around—round,   round,   round.   An endless…merry…go…round…

Derek tossed his head to the side and dry-heaved. Lukewarm liquid sat at the bottom of his throat and burned. They saw a lone figure through the fog outdoors, just standing there. It was tall and lean, and wearing some sort of black attire.

A cough. They turned and saw Matt. He was better. His normal complexion was back. He remained on the floor and his eyes scrolled side to side before he asked, "What happened?"

"Oh, no…"

"What?" But Jamie had then noticed as she returned to her feet, pulling away from Matt once more. The individual was gone—no longer in the fog.

Lisa pointed. "Look!"

A twenty-foot maple tree hung onto its roots, no more than forty feet from the exterior of the center dining room window. All the nearby shrubs and flowers shredded up, like a piece of flesh and thrown around by the mighty wind.

WHOOSH. WHOOSH.

The veins in their eyes shot from red to purple, as if they were pulling an all-nighter. The light from the fog strobed all around, as it maneuvered up and down—over their heads and below their waists. It was difficult to see what it was; whatever was outside.

WHOOSH. WHOOSH. WHOOSH.

The dragon wing sound grew louder and quicker and sent pieces of glass around them like dust. Their shirts and hair flew up. They were rock-solid, as if they just stared Medusa in the eyes. Jamie, Derek, and Lisa coiled around as they felt a frosty big huff on the back of their necks.

Matt.

"HELP!" Screaming for dear life, Matt kept throwing his arms around, but failed to escape the arms of the figure in the black graduation-like robe. The stranger had somehow got Matt and tossed him over their shoulder, like a rag.

"MATTY!"

"Jamie…" Lisa bewailed.

A tear at its roots, down went the forty-foot maple tree in the direction near the center dining room window. The tree landed three feet away from the dining table. The wind and whistles rushed in. The fog stayed at their eye levels, and blocked their vision, but they heard his cries. They stepped directly onto the pieces of glasses; the crunch was audible. Harmed but numbed to the prickles and stabbings from the glass, they came to an abrupt halt. Somehow, they were in front of the staircase. The wave of fog spiraled its way down the staircase like its own tornado; misty yet warm. Their eyes shifted to the top of the staircase, where the fog parted and formed an aisle.

Jamie reached out for the first step, but the wind came at them with full-throttle-force. A riiiiiiiing shot into their ears. They screamed until their voices cracked, lips gashed open, a red line down the middle, like a splinter. Everything around them went mute. Their shaky knees forced them to drop to the floor; the breeze crept along their backsides. They landed on pieces of glass from the picture frames that had fallen from the wall behind the staircase. Their teeth prattled, their lips bloody. Blood covered everything.

Then, they noticed what was at the top of the staircase. Held in a hostage grip was a moving black T-shirt and gray gym shorts.

"NO!" Jamie screamed out all her strength.

But it was no regular hand. Three off-white, yellowish, skeletal fingers gripped around Matt's AC/DC T-shirt. The fog covered his feet, but his friends knew for certain that he floated a few inches off the floor. The great and powerful wind shoved the three of them further away from the staircase.

"JAMIE!"

"LET HIM GO!"

Jamie fought back first and threw herself forward as her legs gave out. It turned into a crawl, unable to get back up. Derek and Lisa followed her lead. But the more they toppled over, the more pieces of glass wedged into their skin as they pressed forward. They wailed with horror, no longer numb to the pain.

"Let me go, *please*," Matt whispered. He saw the black hoodie and silhouette, but no sign of a face. "Just put me down!" He swung around and twisted his body side to side. His cast foot went over the edge of the step behind him.

Slowly, he fell backward. The skeletal hand lost control reached back out and grabbed Matt's T-shirt; Angus Young crinkled up. The stranger's fingers went through Angus and his guitar and then clawed Matt's skin. Pain electrocuted throughout his body, as he felt bones scrape and dig deeper into his chest.

Down he went.

The blood prolonged across his forehead bandage, as if he popped a vein. His bottom slammed into a middle step. With his lips spread open, his nostrils elongated like grave holes. Matt soared backward in midair.

The stranger remained at the top of the staircase— distorted and demonic looking, as the lights strobed, revealing a black outfit in sections, as the multicolored fireworks shot into the sky and reflected off the walls—reds, greens, and blues. The stranger had no feet. They floated in midair. The friends whipped their heads around. Pieces of glass drove toward them, nipping and jabbing parts of their clothes and skin. They still hauled themselves forward, their blood painting the floor with streaks as they clawed closer to the bottom of the staircase. They kept their heads as close as possible to the wooden floor. They did not need to dodge the table and chairs, swooped up and tossed aside like garbage by the wind.

Matthew.

In the final moments in the air, a twinkle in his eyes leaked out a tear that merged with the sweat on his cheek; his body reached the floor. The last drops fell from the air and showered down onto his friends. Matt lay face up. Reeking of burned oil, crimson blobs stretched across his chest and poured over the sides of his body, into a pool of his own blood.

"MATTY!" Jamie lamented as the sirens whirled closer. She, Derek, and Lisa got smothered in their dear friend's blood.

Red and white lights spilled through the no longer blacked-out windows. It was all gone. Everything was gone, by the time the paramedics had arrived.

He was gone.

'Good…bye…'

16.

"NO! THEY'RE NOT on any medication!"

"*Mom!*" Jamie clasped her mother's hand, so she sat back down on the couch.

It was back to Night One. The brown-nosers crammed together on their tippy toes outside. Most of them dawdled on the asphalt and others pushed toward the grass. The **Police Line Do Not Cross** tape circled endlessly around the front yard of the Smith residence. Police officers moved in as soon as a few neighbors took their first step onto the grass.

"BACK UP!" A male officer puffed out his burly chest to a group of adolescents, who only mocked him back.

Inside the Smith residence was crazier than a zoo. Police officers were *everywhere*—upstairs, downstairs. The talk of the town was the dining room and staircase, where crime scene specialists moved in for a closer look.

CLICK. CLICK. CLICK.

More infamous photos would be added to the collection of the boy who took a nasty fall on the night of his birthday, and the night after.

"All done," the paramedic said to Derek, after the final bandage got wrapped on his left wrist.

The eight of them filled up the living room La-Z-Boy sofa and two red chairs across from two police officers, who questioned them for the past hour. This inspection room was supposed to be the least crowded and least busy one. *Liars.* The cameras, which loved anything that could be perceived as evidence, continuously went off and lit up the living room, as if they were all sucked into a vortex. All the employees' voices—workers reporting statuses to their bosses for the night—circled around the Castellanos, Peraltas, and Santosos, like dust. It was all an entity to them.

No sign of Lisa's footprint on the window. The glass was perfect—not cracked, never touched—even though pieces of glass were swept up, after pictures were taken of their alibis.

"No," Jamie responded and let that one sit for a moment before she peered away from the window. "We don't smoke or drink—"

"Don't touch, sweetie," the paramedic ordered, sitting in front of Lisa.

The bandage looked like a giant cream puff got slapped onto the left side of Lisa's face. Her cheek broke out into wrinkles whenever she spoke—and so did the bandage, as if it had a life of its own, more like a brain of its own. Derek and Lisa were not the only ones smothered with bandages from head to toe, so was Jamie.

Bandages on bruises. Bandages on cuts. There were signs of some desiccated skin that peeked out on their arms, legs, face, and feet. Small patches that were harder to hide away from blood and gore-phobics. White bandages were wrapped around their knees. There were red stains on Derek's legs; shorts could not protect him. Their—stained clothes were smothered with blood from head to toe. The blood was darker, fresher, and crimson the closer it got to the bottom of their T-shirts, thighs, and calves. Most of the blood was not even their own.

Jamie already stood on her feet. She paced for a bit. Too much to process. A few moments prior, she saw a line of miniature signs with bold black numbers that descended the staircase. Those signs came to a stop at a pool of blood at the bottom.

Matt.

Jamie gasped and turned away. Nobody else went to her, except for her mother. The rest sat in silence. Derek and Lisa were also in a trance of their own haunted memories, of

Night Two. "As we said," Ms. Castellanos forewarned them, "they saw what they saw. End of story."

"For the love of *God*!" Mrs. Santoso scooted to the edge of the couch, intense and all raw—tough as nails. "What kind of *shitfest* do you think you're running here—"

"*Hon*—"

"No!" Back to the two youngster officers in front of them, "You two keep *repeating* yourselves when they've all given you goddamn answers!"

"Ma'am—"

"*Ma'am*?!"

"Mom," Derek grumbled.

"Don't you dare talk to me like I'm some sort of old hag in a retirement home, *Missy*."

That got the female officer's eyes to expand, as she stared at the eight individuals on the red La-Z-Boy couch and recliners. She opened her mouth to speak, but the sight of rundown mascara and eyeliner on the mothers was just too heartbreaking.

"We know what we saw," Jamie spoke up. "I just..."

"Look," the female officer carried on as *carefully* as she could, especially with Mrs. Santoso's glare on her, "I understand how you all must be feeling, and I apologize for offending you in any way. But I'm just—"

"Just what ROOKIE?!" Mrs. Santoso leaned forward— her bottom hung off the cushion with her attention centered on the timid eyes of the woman with black hair, who sat directly in front of her. "How *old* are you anyway?"

"Hey," the handsome male officer at Ms. I Am About to Cry's side interjected, "we know it's tough, but the more you tell us, the better chances we have of finding this...person."

"*Thing*!" Jamie retorted. "We know what we SAW. Our story isn't changing."

"Yeah," Lisa agreed and crossed her arms to second on that.

"Got that." Derek leaned back on the couch. *"Capiche?"* He even squinted for his part in the imitation game, not bad for a first-timer's impression of Bobby De Niro. Well, sort of. Toward the end, it only looked like he needed to sneeze since his nostrils flared up.

Their parents glimpsed from their little darlings to the two officers, rigid as stone. Ms. Whatever-Her-Name-Was cocked her head to the side, toward Mr. Good Looking, "Hanson—"

"Officer Samuels…" someone else chimed in.

They brought their attention to the front door, where a man in a beige Dick Tracy trench coat stood. Why move when just one stare was fuckin' intimidating enough. "I'll take it from here," he said.

"Sir," she stumbled over her words, "I still have a lot to finish—"

"Please, Samuels. Take a break. You've both done enough for tonight."

On the first step leading down into the actual room, his first step into the living room—became slow motion. He meandered to the red suede couch and almond-colored coffee table. Then, everything around him went into slower motion. *Real. Slow. Motion.* At least to the parents and three adolescents. Officer Samuels (Ms. Whatever Her Name's established identity) glanced at those eight faces transfixed by every move of the teddy bear size man. Pampered in black shiny shoes, his feet stepped on the edge of the gold and moss green carpet, and she jumped to her feet.

"Whoa," Derek let slip out. He scanned the man up and down. "You're like…super tall."

"Samuels." Mr. Iron Man, who towered over his two colleagues by—*at least*—a foot, gave a nod. "Hanson."

"Mr. Barry," they said in unison.

"I'll take it from here now." He reached for the 5x8 notepad in Samuel and Hanson's hands. They were hesitant. "I'll add on."

"Thank you, sir—uh, Mr. Barry," Officer Samuels said, before she and Hanson wandered out of sight.

Mr. Barry flipped and scanned through the pages of the notepads, as he circled around the coffee table—

Derek and Lisa watched on, terrified. Derek even gulped.

"All right," Mr. Barry started, and lowered onto the coffee table vigilantly.

It was Lisa's turn to gulp. The parents and children winced, as the legs of the table gave a squeak. It even startled Mr. Big Foot himself. "Maybe I should…"

Mr. Barry moved around and the other half of his bottom—or body in his case—now hung in midair. The table no longer squealed like a dying animal, but his leg—the one out in the open—trembled a bit from holding the rest of his weight 'up'. The redness from his cheeks diminished, which brought back his caramel complexion. He gave a nervous chuckle.

"Now that's all settled." He crossed a foot over the other and the table gave an urgh. Only the eight people in front of him noticed it, unless Mr. Barry was ignoring it. "Before we proceed, do you have any questions?"

"Yeah…Who the *fuck* are you—"

"Hun—"

"Mom," Derek murmured, which broke his mouth out of an Elvis Presley lip curl.

Ms. Castellanos rolled her eyes. "Really, Carol."

"*What?*" Mrs. Santoso rolled her eyes back. "We've *only* been sitting here all night. I think it's about time that everyone stops questioning our children!"

Silence fell over the other officers and crime scene specialists; most of them retreated to work a second later.

Uncrossing his feet, Mr. Barry moved into brighter lighting. One too many gray hairs stuck out more than his receding jet-black hairline. "Look," he said, "I don't blame you for feeling the way you do. Perhaps, we should take a step back? A few, in fact. You could all bring me up to speed if you don't mind..."

"Well, *perhaps*," Mrs. Santoso responded with a grin, "you could start by giving us your damn name."

Mr. Santoso nudged her shoulder. "Hun..."

"No. No. I apologize. She's right." Mr. Barry removed his badge from his coat and whipped it open: the metallic symbol was a *stunner* in its black leather protector. "Officer Clyde Barry, but Mr. Barry will do." In one swoop, he whipped his badge closed and back it went into the interior pocket of his coat pocket.

"So..." Derek straightened himself up. "Since you're the only one wearing a scientist look-alike coat—"

"Derek," his father said with a wince.

"You're like da boss man around here?"

Mr. Barry put up his hands. "Caught me red-handed."

"*Nice.*" Derek smiled. "Far out."

"Derek, *please.*" Jamie covered her face from embarrassment. She went from pink to a dark red.

"Shouldn't you be at a desk?" Lisa chimed in. "You know, like at an office? Why aren't we there doing all this questioning stuff?"

"That's a good question." Mr. Barry chuckled; it caught them off guard a bit. "I see my colleagues and myself as equals; therefore, we pitch in the same amount of energy and time into our work. Nobody is 'higher' up or 'better' than anyone. It's just a little rule I established a while ago."

"That doesn't make any fuckin' sense—"

"Jesus, Carol." That time it came from Mr. Santoso, who ascended from the arm of the La-Z-Boy. "Anyone care for a smoke?" He eyed Mr. Peralta...

"Be back in a few." Mr. Peralta pecked his wife and daughter on their cheeks.

"Unless…"

Mr. Santoso pulled the cigarette out of his mouth and waited for an approval by Mr. Barry, who then said, "By all means."

It was eerie to witness. The two fathers approached the dining room to get to the back door. They were guided around a pile of crushed glass. The rest was swept into a pile with the other pieces and pushed into a broom pan. Sixty minutes and thirty-eight seconds went by since the beginning of Night Two. Time sure had a funny way of life.

Mr. Barry brought his eyes back to the three mothers and three adolescents. Derek in particular held most of his attention. "So…your name is spelled the same way as a blue*berry*? You know, blue*berry* muffin?"

"You must be Derek Santoso."

The most chivalrous smile appeared on Derek—like an eagle perking out its wing and landing atop the American flag. Mr. Barry went down the line, as he scanned their faces, "Mrs. Santoso. Lisa Peralta. Mrs. Peralta. Jamie Castellanos. And *Ms.* Castellanos."

"Not 'Mrs.' like that little girl had called you," Mrs. Santoso mumbled to the single mother of one.

The dry humor made Ms. Castellanos chuckle. It was phony for sure, one of those, "Oh ha-ha-ha," bullshit laughs. Mr. Barry had not noticed. Preoccupied, he scrolled through the notepad pages where perfectly aligned penmanship turned into chicken scratch toward the middle. So, he grabbed the second notepad.

"Anyway," he progressed, "do any of you have further questions or concerns?"

His expression screamed concern. Silent. One page had the word, 'someone,' circled. Another page had the sentences: 'in the dining room when the power went off' and 'then heard noises.' Behind the next page, he saw an arm wave around in the air.

"Yes, Derek."

"Do you like blueberry muffins with coffee—"

"Derek!" Lisa snapped. "You're *really* asking him that? Everyone knows that food goes best with—"

"*Orange soda,*" they hymned together.

"Lisa…"

"Derek…"

The horror on their mothers' faces. Mrs. Peralta caressed her forehead, as if an ongoing headache was triggered again. Mrs. Santoso shook her head. Ms. Castellanos glanced at Jamie, already beet red. She breathed a bit faster— something *heavy* was around her heart; the explosion happened from the outside in.

"What the hell is wrong with you two?!" she said to her friends.

"Jamie."

"Our best friend almost died tonight—"

"Jamie," her mother raised her voice.

"Do you two even *care*?!"

"Hey!" Mrs. Santoso shot up to Jamie's level, on the edge of the cushion. "My son may cope with situations differently than you, but he *cares*."

"Same with Lisa," Mrs. Peralta added on.

That face of hers congealed, resistant to any sign of human emotions. "You guys are *pricks*! All of YOU."

"Jamie!"

On her feet, Jamie bolted for the dining room. The tears already oozed out. "Hey, kid!" a nearby officer bellowed. "Watch out for the…"

Jamie hopped over an un-swept pile of glass, adjacent to the office desk, kicked over to its side. Ms. Castellanos daubed at her eyes with her sleeve, but one tear, too thick and juicy and impossible to miss, dropped straight from her cheek to the floor. "I should…go."

Mr. Barry only gestured a "Please".

"She didn't mean it." Ms. Castellanos ascended to her feet and eyed a solemn Derek and Lisa. "She's hurting like the rest of us, but, sometimes, we just need to grieve, alone."

Off she went, out of the light and down the grayer, blacker area.

A sudden darkness took over them. Lisa and Derek had difficulty acknowledging each other, but not what stood behind them, the staircase. Behind it, the deserted wall no longer held the dozens of framed photographs of the Smith family. A family with dirty little, "Secrets," Lisa uttered.

"What was that honey?" her mother asked.

"Lisa." Derek's eyes already popped out of his head.

Mr. Barry studied them for a closer look. Lisa turned back around in their direction, primarily Mr. Barry's, and said, "It's nothing. Just…It's just sad. That's all. First the car accident…and now this Night Two."

"The car accident," Mrs. Santoso said and for the first time locked in herself in haunted memories of it.

"I can't imagine." Mrs. Peralta sniffled. "The loss of a husband, son—"

"Matt *didn't* die, mom!"

"Oh, I know, Lisa! It's just when we left earlier and went walking around the neighborhood, Lucia just kept saying how she'd just die if she lost Matt."

"Nothing serious, of course," Mrs. Santoso pitched in, as soon as Mr. Barry's eyebrow furrowed in concern. "She'd never act upon…well, you know."

"Do you think this is the best time to discuss?" Mrs. Peralta gripped a tighter hold of Lisa, who buried her nose into Mother Hen's shoulder.

"Look, we've all seen it before. Their arguments on *specific* family matters."

"Yes." Mr. Barry cleared his throat. "I'm aware of the Smith family tragedies."

"When do we get to see them?" Mrs. Santoso asked. "There must be *so much* coming back to her mind...Poor Lucia." She choked on that last word and grabbed a tissue from her purse.

Mr. Barry glanced up from the black notepad. The open page had a circle around 'Matthew Jimmy Smith;' and underneath that read, 'Abused?'

"Mr. Barry?"

"What?"

"No one's in trouble, right?" Derek asked, now in full volume for Mr. Barry. "You know, our parents were all drinking wine—"

"Derek."

"Lucia did have a bit too much, though." Mrs. Peralta gave her friend a shrug like, "Had to be said."

Matthew Jimmy Smith/Matty/Abused?

"No, Derek," Mr. Barry reassured him, his eyes still lingered on that notepad page. "Nobody's in trouble. Promise."

"Good." Derek sighed and plunged back into one of the many pillows on the couch. "I hear that a lot of people are arrested for that."

"Occasionally. But when there are complaints from the public, then it becomes an issue."

The cursive writing grasped his attention once more. He resembled a puppet on its strings as his spine straightened and arms lowered to his legs. All he saw was, *Matthew Jimmy Smith/Matty/Abused?*

"Mr. Barry?" Mrs. Peralta removed her hand from his. "Sorry, it's just that you...dazed out."

He tracked her eyesight, as it lowered to the notepad, which stayed wide open and faced their direction. Mr. Barry whipped it shut. Their eyes remained on his. Something that ate away at her conflicted Lisa, slowly from the inside out. A hint of irritation scratched at the back of Mrs. Santoso's throat as she asked in a raspy voice, "Is Lucia with Matt?"

"Yes," he responded, too quickly and flipped to the next page of the notepad.

More circled words: 'fingertips' and 'of a skeleton'.

"I, uh," he started again, "spoke with her before coming here. Matt's been asleep." He closed the notepad, amazed that their sets of eyes never left him. They were dedicated fans of the dirty details. "There is something that I do want to ask, but you're not obligated to answer..."

Before Derek asked, his mother beat him to the punch, "It means forced, Derek."

They went motionless, at the edge of their seats, as if atop a roller-coaster's big dipper and awaited the unanticipated arrival of all the blood that would rush away from their head. The hesitation only prolonged. Mr. Barry, who appeared more rattled up as he eyeballed them back and forth; his fingers tapped onto the edge of the coffee table.

"Did any of you actually *see* the cuts being imprinted onto Matt's chest?"

It was a deeper wound that zero staples, stitches, and bandages could ever heal. Derek and Lisa pressed their eyes shut, and the veins on their eyelids bulged out. "We didn't..." Lisa shook her head.

"At least not their face," Jamie finished. She and her mother emerged back into the dimmed yellow-brown hued living room.

Jamie's complexion and eyes turned scarlet, and her voice sounded stuffy. "We thought we were next," she whispered, "but they—whoever it was—just took off. It didn't want us. Matt...It only wanted Matt. He must've had something that we didn't."

"You *sure* there's absolutely no one and, I mean, *no one* who'd want to hurt Matt or any of you?"

Jamie, Derek, and Lisa shook their heads.

"I mean," Lisa was the first to go, "we are isolated in our own clique, but who'd want to hurt any one of us? We're nice to everyone."

"Because sometimes others will hurt the ones that we love the most," Jamie muttered, almost too robotic.

"Maybe it was one of the 'Cool Kids.'" Lisa used air quotes for the last two words.

"'Cool Kids?'" Mr. Barry added the words themselves to the page, just centimeters below, 'Matty' and 'Abused?'

"Yeah, well, you know…" Lisa inserted her finger into the opposite hand shaped in an 'O'.

"Oh…I see." Mr. Barry turned red velvet himself. "You could've just said…Never mind."

"I know—slutty."

Lisa scooted closer to the edge of the couch. Mrs. Peralta pulled Lisa back into her arms and kissed the top of her head. Lisa's entire face still looked a glory Pepto Bismol-pink, unable to look Mr. Barry in the eyes.

"We've never got invited to parties," Jamie progressed further into details. "We don't drink or smoke. We don't have like hundreds of friends, whether in real life or on stupid Myspace!"

Derek perked up, all wide-eyed and flustered. "Did you know that some people actually have five hundred Myspace friends. *Five hundred.* I'm lucky if someone accepts my friend request, like Sandra."

"Sandra?"

"Yeah, Matt's …"

Jamie and Lisa's look of, 'Don't you dare,' was already too late. Mr. Barry clicked the top of his pen open. "Matt's…?"

The three friends refused to move until Jamie sighed and gave in, "Sandra Lee. Matt's ex-girlfriend." Mr. Barry's pen hit the page, forcing her to stumble over her words. "But they like broke up in the seventh grade!" Redder than ever, she fanned herself off. "She, uh, dumped him via email."

Mr. Barry scribbled it all down in bigger cursive writing than Samuels' tidy print: 'Sandra Lee—ex-girlfriend.'

"It's hot, right?" Jamie waved her hands underneath her armpits. "We should ask someone to turn on the AC." As she glimpsed around, possibly to find an officer, Ms. Castellanos took her daughter's hands. And kissed her wrist. It worked, Jamie settled down, and her hands dropped away from her damp pits. After a deep breath, "She's not in trouble, is she?"

"Of course, not—"

"Because he was, uh, really into her."

"Into her?" Lisa made a face. "More like in *love*."

"Or lust." All eyes turned to Derek, who even blushed, "What? I see it in the movies a lot."

"Only, this isn't a movie—you *moron*!"

"Hey!" Ms. Castellanos tapped Jamie's arm.

"Well, with technology advancement," Mr. Barry took over now, "so many youngsters—kids, teens—and, sometimes, even adults get bored. Tonight, could've been a prank, or one of many pranks..."

Jamie slipped over to the coffee table and planted herself inches from Mr. Barry. "So, you think whoever was here tonight is the same person from the other night?"

"Possibly."

"So, let me get this straight, Mr. Barry." Mrs. Santoso shifted to her right-side, her tone stern, "Basically, tonight and the other night are the media's fault."

"No, ma'am, that's not what I—"

"Maybe," Derek surmised, "it was someone from the basketball team!"

"And *why* would any of them do that?" Jamie quarreled. "They know what had *happened* to Matt the other night. Lucia called his coach, who informed the team—"

"And *how* do you know that?!" he mocked her bitchy pierce tone.

"Because my mom told me you, SHITHEAD!"

"*Really?!*" Mrs. Santoso looked Ms. Castellanos straight in the eyes. Jamie's mother tugged at her own shirt, guilt-ridden.

"Look," Mr. Barry cut them and *anyone else* short. He ascended from the coffee table, which gave a squeak. When his portion of the table dropped, Jamie titled an inch to her side from the heavyweight being gone. Nobody even cared. All eyes were on Mr. Barry. "You've all been through enough. I think that it's best—"

"You do believe us, right?" Agony crept back on Jamie. "I mean, we know this all sounds…bizarre but you *have to trust us*. Maybe it was not skeletal fingers that we saw. Maybe, they were white gloves or gloves with a skeletal design…"

"Baby." Ms. Castellanos rushed to her side. Jamie gripped her mother and buried her nose in the sleeve of her mother's blouse.

"Just promise that you'll catch her or him or them," Lisa implored.

Possibilities. All assumptions were suddenly forced into sudden facts.

Blanched faces, their bodies hardened and curved and twisted in inhuman ways. Their eyes were drained from exhaustion and teary, filled with fright, as they watched Mr. Barry. Nobody blinked—red veins mixed with blue and purple. "We'll do everything we can," Mr. Barry said as a deep wound of sorrow haunted him behind his eyes.

17.

GASPING AND SCREAMING FOR AIR, *Matt felt the rumble of the steady earth fall apart underneath him. The white air dragged him by the feet and began to swallow him whole. Gradually, he slipped into the black abyss below, ready for a hello or a welcoming arm. Panting, a sharp pain started at the bottoms of Matt's feet and worked its way up to his abdomen.*

He cried for help, but deeper he went into the abyss that now reached his torso. "Help!"

Matt held onto the ledge of a cliff, dangling between the black and white worlds. With his arms shaking, he closed his eyes, a refusal to look down or up. In a sling-shot distance, the girl's voice ascended, "Matt! Matty!"

He looked up, but only saw the white abyss of clouds and someone gasping for air.

"Matty!" she called out as her voice grew distant.

"No-no-no! Hey! Come back!"

"Let me go," the Abyss Girl screamed at whatever stopped her, forcing a distance between her and Matt. "He needs to know. He needs to know."

The blaring light spun at the end of the abyss, somehow, and with all his might, Matt pushed his weight down onto his arms. He wormed his way upward and the tears and screams began. He screamed in exasperation but kept going, soon only his legs were swinging off the ledge.

"He's doing it!" The Abyss Girl's cheers shot around like a pinball. "He's almost there! Matt! Matt!"

With his nostrils flared, the snot sputtered out and ran its way down onto his neck. Although the air grew chillier, Matt's forehead broke out into a hot sticky, sweat. He reentered the white wonderland, escaping the black abyss that screeched for his goodbye. Over his shoulder, he caught a glimpse of the skeletal face.

'And then…I woke up…'

18.

IT WAS ALL MR. BARRY SAID. "We got to go! NOW."

He slammed his foot down on the gas pedal. The police cruiser vroomed off at seventy-five miles an hour. It was a maze of its own: nothing but sharp twists, turns, and zigzagged to get out of the Smith neighborhood. The four passengers looked very green. Derek fiddled to click in his seatbelt for safety. Jamie glanced over her shoulder: a second police cruiser tailgated them with Derek and Lisa's parents as the passengers. Car honks blared off all around, mainly from the angrier drivers.

"Watch it!"

Mr. Barry flipped on the red and blue lights. Sirens.

"My bad!" angry driver four shouted out his window.

"I think I'm going to be sick," Lisa groaned and tilted her head toward the backseat window.

Matt—he saw it. A speckle of white emerged into the darkness and prolonged. He saw the foot first. It was all snippets from there on. He could…hear *them*—

"We're alive!" It was *Derek*.

Light. It came from above. The warmth tickled Matt's feet and then his abdomen, and soon, it moved up-up-up.

His lips twitched, his breathing too harsh, but nobody noticed or, perhaps, even cared. "ROOM 402," Mr. Barry panted.

Ping!

The elevator doors veered open. At least that was what Matt imagined, until his assumptions turned into reality. His own mini movie played out before his eyes.

Jamie, Derek, Lisa, and their parents skidded, stopped, and skidded some more across the tile floor, in pursuit of Mr. Barry's track. Derek slipped, as soon as he made a turn like he wanted to purposely trip the cute nurse who rounded the hallway's corner. "Sorry!" Luckily, his father pulled him up, before he made a bigger ass of himself.

Matt: The air puffed out of his nostrils. His lips parted; a thin red line seeped down the middle of his parched lips.

Them: their hair swept back, as they brushed by the doctors, nurses, and very few visitors. Their feet squeaked across the slippery white tile, like their own custom-built skating rink. The beep of multiple monitors echoed off the walls like the…

The heart monitor was no more than a foot away from Matt. Lightning bolts squiggled up and down on the screen. Next to the other robotic machine, clear liquid drip-dropped into a small plastic baggie. Beep. Beep. Beep. As his nostrils flared opened and closed, the higher his chest rose and rose.

His friends reached the door. A police officer stood guard outside of Room 402.

A comatose Matt came to life. He gasped for air and his two swollen eyes shot wide open. The sight of bandages that coated his fragile vampire skin came into clear focus. The light…

It was coming from the fluorescent lights on the white ceiling.

"*Matty!*"

Matt watched, as Jamie, Derek, and Lisa burst into the room. The tears cascaded down their red, puffy faces. He noticed the police officer at the window table; They were no more than four feet away from him. They pounced up from their seats. A cold hand touched his skin and spooked chills up his spinal cord. It was Lucia. She stood beside him, her hand atop of his. He looked at her, and his cheeks rushed to red hot.

The parents piled in and each broke down into sobs, as if it were planned on the count of three. Hugs and kisses. Kisses and hugs. Tears and laughter. Laughter and tears. It was one of those a too good to be true reunions for his mistaken death. It could have been a magical moment…if he could hear it.

Riiiiiiiing…

His ears clogged; The bags underneath his raccoon eyes grew heavier as he watched their mouths open and close, readable until they faded out of his sight.

"Maaaaatttttyyyyy," all Jamie's lips mouthed as he saw her attempting to push through his blurry eyesight.

At the doorway was a wide black blob. The room spun around, and the blob formed into a silhouette of *someone*. As the black and white spots conquered the corner of his eyes, it formed a clear pathway and directly pointed his attention to the teddy bear size man, who took his first step into Room 402. The face of a familiar stranger. Everyone else blackened out already.

"You," Matt felt his lips shape out, collapsing over to the right-side. He could not see or hear himself, but it was one hell of a guess. "You're the one who carried me that night."

And then, he drifted back to sleep. It was pitch black for a few more minutes.

19.

THAT PRECIOUS FACE grew puffier by the instant, a ghostly milk complexion in the making. The multicolored bruises and scars made him unrecognizable.

Mrs. Peralta swept pieces of fallen hair behind Matt's ear. She planted a kiss on his cheek that had the fewest pinwheel colors from his bruises. "We'll be back tomorrow, sweetheart," she consoled.

Mr. Peralta gave Matt's hand a light squeeze—the one without an IV tube. "You take it easy."

Matt bobbed his head, propped up with two pillows. Mr. and Mrs. Peralta headed out and met up with the Santosos, who waited for them at the door. They were all struck with grief; heaviness slumped down their shoulders and heads. Mrs. Santosos stepped out of the room first. She pulled out a baggie of tissues from her beige purse. The rest of them followed, one by one.

"You should tell people you won." Derek chuckled, and so did Lisa until she broke down into tears, and his voice grew hoarse, "You know," he pushed on, although the tears swirled around in his eyes, "you look like you were jumped by six big guys." He choked back a sob that time.

Exhausted, his breathing felt slow and his eyes drooped. Matt smiled, appreciative of Derek's sick fucked-up humor. "Thanks, buddy."

"Guess, it's a treat, too. Huh?" Derek wiped away the first drip drop of tears, which mostly splashed onto the bed sheet. He hiccupped the last words, "Not…getting…up…for a…few days… Other people… cleaning up… your… urine… and… shit—"

"Derek."

Lisa nudged his elbow. But Matt laughed that time. The corners of his lips gave a spasm and curled up, ever so slightly. Derek and Lisa squeezed their dear friend's bony fingers. And then, they were gone. They strolled out, sucked up into the white hallway that resembled a spaceship tunnel. For a moment, they were astronauts, ridged and anxious of what had lied ahead and beyond that. Most likely, they met up with their parents, who probably urged them that it was okay...everything was going to be just fine and dandy.

Everything was so *bright*.

Matt rubbed his eyes. Yet, the fluorescent lights were not going anywhere. They still pointed at him—purposely. It put him in the hot seat. The clear liquid from the IV tube pumped into his veins. His stomach knotted at the thought of medicine rushing throughout his insides to track down the "bad stuff," calling out a CODE BLUE.

All the bodily fluids just whished and whirled around him, until it all drained out of his system.

Drip drop. The small white plastic baggie on the IV metal rack was almost full.

"I'm right here," Ms. Castellanos whispered to her daughter, leaning in from behind her.

Jamie stared off into the opposite direction from Matt, her eyes heavy and defeated, solemn. Lucia sat in the same chair, adjacent to the bed and across from the Castellanos. The rest of the group—the four of them, including Matt—were silent. The short olive-skinned nurse, with the body of a premature adolescent boy, stood nearby to switch out the plastic baggie on the IV rack. Just minutes ago, she had injected a needle into the tube that connected Matt to the machine. The nurse left in a hurry. Jamie's nonstop, husky sniffles seemed to be her exit cue. As for her, as soon as the nurse was out of sight, Jamie gradually reached out for Matt's hand.

Matt's eyes opened and closed, opened as he gazed into her baby doll eyes that turned blue "Jamie," he murmured, "I'm okay. Don't cry."

Jamie gave another loud sniffle. She never broke focus on him. Eye to eye. Only, her eyes turned scarlet, as the tears poured down the warmth of her skin. Five perfectly shaped teardrops plopped down onto the bed comforter. The water fell atop Derek's long-ago tears; now mixed into one giant blob of water. She gave his hand a light squeeze. He weaved their fingers together.

"Thanks for being here," he slurred, using the only available strength he had left.

"I'm so sorry for barging in like this," the nurse from seconds ago interjected, now in the doorway. She had that guilt-ridden look in her eyes as though she volunteered for the pain. Their pain. Matt's pain. "But Matt really needs his rest."

"Okay," Jamie said and daubed at her eyes.

Ms. Castellanos crossed over to the opposite side of the bed. She and Lucia embraced in a firm hug. They both cried for a moment and uttered all of the, "I love you/So sorry/This is bullshit/Fuckin' hospitals/They'll find that asshole who did this"

Before they drifted apart, they took one last look at each other. Lucia gave her arm two squeezes, as if it served as some confirmation of her support. Ms. Castellanos then turned to Jamie. "Come on, sweetie."

"Okay."

As soon as her mother touched her shoulder, Jamie got up. Lucia wrapped her arms around her. "It'll all be okay," she whispered. "Promise."

Jamie pulled back from their tight hug first. She gave Lucia a forceful smile and followed her mother's high heel footsteps that clicked around the corner of the room. She glanced over her shoulder for one last look.

Matt already fell asleep.

Two police officers stood guard outside of Room 402, with cups of coffee. Ms. Castellanos waited nearby, until Jamie and the nurse strode out. The nurse and officers exchanged nods of acknowledgment. Jamie reached for her mother, who wrapped an arm around her shoulders, as the nurse walked them down the white, spaceship tunnel hallway. They dispersed out of sight in seconds.

"It's your watch," the female officer advised and pulled up a chair beside the door to Room 402. She vigilantly dipped into her seat; her lips shaped in an 'O' to blow away the steam from her hot drink.

"Roger that." the male officer entered Room 402.

Lucia still sat in her seat, slouched to her side, sound asleep; the wall served as her headrest.

The male officer paced over to the right-side of the room and quietly took his seat at the window table meant for two—empty on the other side of him. The last bits of stars in the royal blue sky shimmered down onto his complexion through the two medium size windows next to him and the table.

Matt remained asleep, like an infant after being sung a sweet lullaby.

20.

GRANDMA. GRANDMA. GRANDMA.

He emerged into the white, shutting out his childhood voice.

The itty bitty holes on the ceiling stretched on, like an endless sea of time. Matt kept his gaze on it. It took a moment before he—slowly and almost creaking—scanned around. To his left, a steamy cup of coffee, napkins, and a thin peppermint color straw sat on the table for two in front of the pushed out chair. Across from him, the wall went tick, tick, tick; the big hand on the clock struck twelve. The small hand struck five. The early moonlight gave away the time, 12:20 AM. But the object to his right-side stole his attention. The closest burgundy chair held a black pursue—a fake Dolce and Gabbana (fake name: Dolce and Gabena).

'*Fuck.*'

A bolt unlocked, immediately followed by, "Sweetie."

'*FAUCK!*'

Lucia stepped out of the bathroom; the milk-colored door gently closed behind her. Her bottom lip quivered as she repeated, "Sweetie". She rushed his way.

"Shit," Matt muttered to himself.

Lucia sat at the edge of the bed. She held onto his good hand, and for whatever reason, her eyes kept shut, as though in the midst of a prayer. Or, perhaps, she was praying—that whole bullshit "calling Jesus", when she only *needed* a favor. '*Hypocrite,*' Matt thought to himself.

The tears gushed down her face, thicker than blood. "I didn't mean to wake you," she whispered and gave his hand a peck.

"You didn't." He pulled back his hand. The most atrocious look filled his grandmother's eyes.

Betrayal.

Confusion.

Loss.

Matt's eyes broadened like an eight ball. Only, he yearned for an answer now. He needed it.

Lucia glimpsed away from him. Her eyebrows furrowed with crease marks. Dark circles, almost lavender, deepened underneath her eyes from the little to zero amount of sleep. Burned out. "Are you mad?" she finally asked.

'*Am I FUCKIN' MAD…*' Matt chewed the inside of his cheek to prevent himself from laughing.

"Obviously," it slipped through his teeth with a hint of sarcasm meant for the inside his head. That was becoming too much of an accidental habit.

A deer in headlights, all she uttered was, "Oh."

He swallowed the lump that escalated to his throat and swelled up his eyes. "I just can't remember what happened…The blood…The scars…But I do remember you."

Silence. It was a staring contest. Red to red, until she suddenly turned blue. "I'm sorry, sweetheart," she whispered. "I know that I had too much to drink—"

"Don't. You're a liar—"

"Where's this coming from?"

* * *

The pictures. Unseen family albums. His mother. Flashes of that night. The wind. The fog. The pitch black. His friends' cries and screams. The prescription. The fall—blood, blood, blood. Cracked bones.

* * *

"Matt."

In the process of catching his breath, his chest went up and down and down and up. "I...Just...Want...To...Sleep." But his body did the opposite.

Prey in the attack, he flipped over onto his side, and wheezed for air. His lungs sounded heavy and full of mucus and exhaustion. Through the window, he saw the smallest twinkle in the half-royal and seafoam blue-colored sky. The star gave another wink—a message for him. His raspy, hefty breathing began to slow down.

* * *

"Why you are singing the 'boo-boo' song?" she asked and lowered to his level, matching his height.

"So, I can take your boo-boo's away."

* * *

Lucia rubbed his shoulder blades, sticky with sweat. A soft humming sailed throughout her body. It was a familiar harmony; then, it turned into words.

It watered up his eyes, as he took one deep breath. He pressed his eyes shut, and a tear dribbled down onto the bed sheet. Lucia murmured the opening verse to, "The Wheels on the Bus."

It trapped him. '*Fucking bitch,*' he thought.

21.

IT DAZZLED IN THE CRYSTAL BLUE SKY, surrounded by cotton candy shaped clouds.

Sunlight poured into most of the rooms and bounced off the white head to toe walls. Doctors and nurses pressed a button on the vending machine and out came a brown-patterned cup with steamy brewed coffee. All for *free*. Visitors of all sizes—circular, oval, and pear-shaped—waited in line for a hot meal or a cold treat. Most of them took up the countless matching sturdy gray chairs and tables. Their bodies had compacted among each other like Mother Duck and her ducklings. As for the boys and girls, they clasped onto the hand of—whoever the taller person was—standing beside them.

At the back corner of the cafeteria, Lucia watched one of the clusters of Mother Duck and her ducklings.

A pear-shaped woman with strawberry blonde hair sat a few rows up from her. She motioned to the boy to sit next to her and eat his meal. He sported a Batman T-shirt. He made a face but picked up his sandwich and gnawed off a chunk.

It brought the slightest smile to Lucia, trapped in reminiscences. Beside her, Derek twirled his spoon into the half-empty Tampico pudding cup that sat in front of him. Lisa nibbled a piece of her chicken strip. She balked, as the footsteps screeched to a halt at their table.

"Those *douchebags*!" Hot and cold, Jamie slammed the morning newspaper onto the hideous gray and beige patterned tabletop. Lucia's "hush" and "shhs", got blocked out, as Derek and Lisa both dropped their food. His pudding tilted onto its side and its oozing chunks spilled out. Her chicken strip went onto the tile floor.

"Jeez, *woman*!" Derek snapped fully out of his reverie, "Don't *ever* do that again."

Jamie slid into the chair that was still preoccupied by Derek. He scooted over and nearly collapsed over Lisa.

"Derek."

"It's this nut right here!" He spun a finger at his ear, indicating. "She's cuckoo."

Jamie fumbled to open the newspaper. Lucia noticed how the poor girl's fingers shook with her body, as she turned page after page.

"Jamie, you really should eat." But Jamie only licked two of her fingertips and flipped to the next page.

"Since when do you read the newspaper," Lisa asked, as she rubbed her red elbow—an after effect from Jamie's erratic move into Derek's chair.

"I don't."

A split second later, her lips dropped into a frown. Her eyes scanned the page up and down.

Lucia leaned in. "Jamie…Please, honey, just put it down. No need to see it."

"Someone came up to me and asked for an autograph." Then, Jamie looked at them and flipped over the newspaper, and it was all crystal-clear for Lucia.

At the bottom, right-hand corner, on page eight, the article title for three short paragraphs read: **STRIKE TWO**

"We're all mentioned," Jamie said.

Derek and Lisa sat at the edges of their seats, literally, since he nearly slipped underneath the table and knocked his chin onto the plastic tabletop. The two of them scanned through the print. Lucia caught the attention of the boy in the Batman shirt. He stared her way. His eyes looked dark and intense—never missing a beat. His mother was gone. Some electronic waveform distorted the bleak atmosphere.

"*Lucia…*", It echoed. "*Lucia…*"

"Lucia."

Just as the boy's mother dropped back down into her chair, Lucia flinched, weight added to her hand.

Jamie's hand lay atop hers. "Lucia?"

"You shouldn't have bought it," she snapped. "You shouldn't be reading that garbage."

"Whoa…" Derek drifted back into his chair and looked bug-eyed.

"'*Names are to be anonymous for the sake of privacy,*'" Lisa read aloud, as her fingers followed along the sentences, "'*while investigation carries on…*'"

Lucia stared back at the empty void: the boy and his mother were gone, but her breathing grew steep as she saw an elderly man across the room, no more than sixty feet from her. He had turned his head toward one of the many medium-sized windows. He twirled the golden band on his left ring finger while his chest descended, ever so slightly.

"Lucia." Jamie sat up.

The elderly man's silver hair flashed to a salt and pepper color, a strobe light show for Lucia's own entertainment, and he glanced her way. His face distorted into a flicker of bones.

"*Lucia!*" Jamie gripped Lucia's hands. "You don't look so—"

"I just need to…."

By now, Lucia rose to her feet.

The elderly man's face returned to normal: skin, living facial features.

Lucia bolted away, which forced a gasp out of the three adolescents: they blanched. By dozens of unfamiliar faces, Lucia veered off and brushed shoulder against shoulder. She traveled down her tunnel of blurs, it started at the edges and worked its way into her eyesight; head to toe scrubs, knee-length white coats, and non-hospital attire flashed from white, a blur, and then tie-dyed as she ran.

"Mrs. Smith?" she heard a female's voice bounce around her head.

Lucia veered into the nearest women's bathroom— Vacant.

She zigzagged into the corner stall and slammed the door shut, locking it. She smacked down onto her knees and tossed up the toilet seat just in time to puke her guts out. When she finally managed to whiff fresh air, she bawled her weary heart out.

"Mrs. Smith," it was that *same* voice from moments ago, but it was closer now. *A lot closer…*

The short, olive skin nurse stepped into the bathroom and gently let the door shut behind her. "Mrs. Smith," she called out one last time, but she already knew which stall to approach first.

22.

IT PINGED BACK AND FORTH like a silver ball. Through the center window, the hummingbird flapped its wings to show off its spinning color wheel of feathers.

Matt watched on; his lips chapped. He had positioned himself in the most relaxed manner: his body straight, but properly aligned to the warm mattress and cold pillow. Not the slightest chance of tingles electrocuting throughout his body.

'Suck it anxiety!'

Mr. Barry sat at the edge of his chair, adjacent to the left side of the bed. The male officer stood at his side and scribbled away on a blank sheet of paper in a 5x7 black notepad. Miles of footsteps trampled by the room, although Matt had zero temptation to even bother looking. He only imagined the individuals who passed by Room 402. Some of them wore street clothes, while others had on uniforms. Room 402, his new home. At some point, a set of footsteps skid to a halt and do a double take.

"No way!" Matt heard them. "The boy from the news!"

"I got this." The female officer, now her shift to guard out in the hallway, grabbed the doorknob.

The door gently shut, but Matt still flinched; his heart sped up, only momentarily. Mr. Barry scanned the untouched tray of food pushed off to the side. It was gross. A plate with lumpy grilled chicken, soggy mashed potatoes topped off with chunky gravy, a cup of pudding, and a cranberry juice box. "You really should eat," he said anyhow, "because your face certainly agrees."

For the first time in minutes, Matt made eye contact with him and said, "I'm not hungry."

Mr. Barry glimpsed from the heart monitor machine to Matt's pale face, clammed up at the corners. "If it's too much, you don't—"

"You've said that about *forty times* already." Now, he looked up; his fingers locked into fists. "I agreed to talk, didn't I?" Then his eyes shot back down to the fresh, cotton bedsheets.

Mr. Barry tugged at his colleague's hand. He stopped writing. The men watched the rainfall of tears stream down onto the blankets and into their own swimming pools.

Matt.

He quivered and ran his arm across his eyes and rosy cheeks. The tears never stopped. If anything, it was showtime, as he buried his head in his hands. "Why is this *happening*? I can't remember a thing from that night! Just…"

Beep.

The officers watched on somberly. "Just what, Matt?"

Matt peered up at them. "Just everything leading up to coming home that morning after my first hospital stay. Nothing after that except for the big fat BAM—I see my grandmother leaving! BAM! BAM! My friend's parents are leaving. BAM! BAM! BAM! I wake up in HERE!"

Beep…Beep…

The male officer looked paler than Casper. "Mr. Barry—why…Are…We…In…Danger?" Matt clawed onto his elbow and locked himself in a forced hug. "Who…Would…Do…This…To…Us? We can't even go home! Being followed by the cops like the FUCKIN' mob is after us!"

Beep. Beep. Beep…

The officers soared up from their seats. "Get someone—"

But the heart monitor immediately cut Mr. Barry short. It just screamed and screamed.

"FIND this son of a bitch!" Matt wailed. "Whoever…I…can't…breathe…" The lump in his throat coagulated and he started to choke for air.

"Go get help NOW!" Mr. Barry ordered his colleague.

Matt's chest elevated up and down; fast and faster, on repeat.

"What's wrong?" the female officer asked as soon as the door flung opened.

Everything spun around and around for him, breathing too harshly.

"Officer Franco—find Dr. Brown NOW!"

On the ground floor, two different sets of polished black boots stormed across the tile floor. Those who sat in the waiting room chairs glanced their way. Individuals in front of them barged off to the side, as though they made some sort of a train wreck of a red carpet for Officer Samuels and Officer Hanson. They aimed their fast pace for the middle elevator that began to shut.

"Wait!" Hanson picked up speed.

"Stop that elevator!" Samuels tucked a manila folder underneath his armpit.

"MATT!"

Matt wormed his way up and he went overboard. The tray of food slammed onto the floor. Mr. Barry lunged forward but a different pair of hands snatched hold of Matt and pulled him up in time, a desperate attempt for a *hero saving the helpless* photograph for the hungry devious cameramen. Bastards. It was Dr. Brown who had saved the fish out of water boy from a face to face meeting with his destiny of DOOM. Matt lay on his back again, and his eyes dilated to the size of coal. His lips turned a parched blue…

Mr. Barry picked up on Dr. Brown's distance because he had stopped moving. The nurses pushed their way into the hazardous zone. "Matt!"

"Sweetie, can you hear—"

Blurry.
Television static.
Black.
Pitch. Black.

23.

IT WAS ALL A BLUR...that high pitch ring echoed in and out of his ears. He stared at the window in the center of the wall, where a beige-brown building stood miles away from him.

"Matt."

Dr. Brown lingered at the foot of the bed. The sun circled in and blared its brightness into the room and reflected off the shades of purple and black underneath Matt's eyes. The short, olive skin nurse eyed the plastic baggie on the IV rack, as she jotted something down on papers in her hands. Those dark macadamia eyes of hers never missed a beat, as she lifted the bottom of the page and flipped it over, scribbling away some more. "Vitals are good," she announced.

That got Matt to move. He stared at the tile floor and focused on the black patterned dots. He caught a glance of the empty chairs in the room, and the closed door to Room 402. "What you were experiencing," Dr Brown said, and his voice suddenly grew louder, "that tightness in your chest...almost like you were..."

"Drowning," he mumbled.

A short, round, orange bird bounced on the window ledge and chirped away. It was more of a squeak—a bird in premature stages, like an adolescent boy in the midst of vocal puberty changes. Everyone watched on, Matt smiled, as Mother Nature's creature jumped off the ledge and soared away into the sky, toward the golden rotation of the gliding sun.

"I'm going to..."

Dr. Brown bobbed his head, and it was Nurse Olive's cue to exit—not before she handed him a stapled stack of papers that read: **Matthew Jimmy Smith**.

It was his personal records and documentation from his hospital stay and current bullshit circumstances. Dr. Brown took in a deep breath and tucked the packet of paperwork underneath his arm. He bent his wrist—one of the bones cracked out of its tension.

Matt kept his focus on the pieces of summertime that flashed by and glistened through the window—a rainbow reflector here and there, probably caused by someone pointing a mirror at the rising sun. A bird. Another bird shaped into the letter 'M,' as it flapped its wings across the sea storm sky.

"I'm not ready to leave," he said. "Aren't I?"

"No. Not yet."

"I'll have to take something, for the…"

Matt noticed that Mr. Barry's hand spasmed. The doc. realized that his patient had watched Mr. Barry for too long. Clearly, it was something that the teenager was not supposed to see.

It slowed down Matt's breathing.

Dr. Brown inhaled through his nostrils, which pushed out his chest, and when he exhaled, the air hissed through the thin gap between his lips. "Tomorrow's Fourth of July," he said; his attempt at changing the subject, as if his panic attack got shoved under the carpet years ago.

"And you have the best room in the house."

"Yeah…" Matt sniffled and swiped his moist eyes with the back of his hand. "But for me, it's just another day to get by…"

Now, through the center window, the outside world turned grayer by the instant, at least, in his eyes.

24.

A TODDLER WITH BLOND CURLS waved around a long sparkler in his hand. "Mommy, look!"

Pop. Pop.

Beside him another boy, gawked in awe, as the colorful sparkler-dots shot up into the sky. "Yeeha!"

Evening's sky consisted of swirls—oranges, yellows, and violets that shined behind the banner with bubbly red, white, and blue letters that spelled out, "Riverfest". *It was La Crosse's annual tradition. Police officers on duty strolled along the pavement and patches of grassland. Some stood with their arms crossed, wearing dark shades, like they were part of the Secret Service. Most of them had a set of metal bracelets attached to their belt loops. These men and women either wore black or navy blue uniforms. Summer's breeze traveled down the rows of booths and whipped through everybody's hair or against bald heads. The air was still moist. Everyone daubed at their sweaty, sticky skin. Families cooled themselves off by pointing a handheld fan at their faces or drinking gallons of water did just the trick.*

"Well," *Jamie said, her hair yanked back into Pippi Longstocking pigtails,* "we can just wait till' we get back to your house."

Derek and Lisa sat on their bottoms while sketching out swirls into the dirt. A few feet away from them were booths for alcoholic and non-alcoholic drinks. Most of the booths had a stand-up sign in front of them listing the individual prices for each drink. A bottle of water cost three bucks. A Snapple or a Nesquik cost four dollars. The last drops of water slid down the bottles from the after effect of melting ice cubes,

"Refill!"

Matt fanned the bottom of his Rocket Power T-shirt back and forth, and a tinge of cool air rubbed against his lukewarm skin.

His hair looked ready to melt off. The green hair gel, meant to stay on the tips of his spikes, streamed down the corner of his forehead. He was officially the Wicked Witch of the West.

'I'm melting. I'm melting!'

"Circle, circle, dot, dot." Derek licked his finger. "Now you got the—"

"Hey!" Lisa frowned.

"—cootie shot!"

"DEREK!" Jamie balked and forcibly removed Derek's wet finger out of her ear. He grinned until he noticed the yellow crusts— earwax—caked on his fingertip.

"EW!" He shook his hands around, as though earwax was the first symptoms of the plague.

* * *

"Hey." Jamie leaned forward, pushing through the blurriness, and focusing on the clearer vision of her smile. "You're finally awake. Mom and I've been waiting."

"What time is it?" Matt groaned.

"11:30."

Matt pressed his eyes shut and reopened them. The clock on the wall, across from him, had the big hand ticking a line after the six. Nobody else was in the room…

"Your grandma's getting coffee with mom," she clarified and popped a seat at the edge of the bed.

"Oh." He rubbed his eyes and wormed his way up. She held out her arm for additional support. At first, he just stared at her arm, as if about to bite and swallow him whole. But the real attention-grabber was when Jamie giggled.

"What?" He turned hot pink. "Why are you laughing?"

"Your hair…" She chuckled again. "Here, let me."

A piece of hair on the back of his head stood up like Alfalfa's antenna. But he only paid attention to the harsh scent that tingled up his nostrils, as she leaned in to fix his hair— warm vanilla. Unaware, he held his breath.

* * *

A spiky hair boy—and green tips—and a girl with Pippi Longstocking Pigtails, zigzagged through the crowd. They aimed their eyes at the sky, where multicolors splattered into layers of wheels. Some of the fireworks spun around, counterclockwise.

* * *

Jamie went into mom mode, licked the tips of her fingers, and patted down the strand of his Alfalfa hair.

* * *

They watched in awe. Until he looked to his side.

Matt rested his hand on hers. She became still, unable to look at him.

She met his sight, as the vibrant shadows from the explosions in the night sky lit up her smile; her teeth were pearly white.

* * *

It played out all over for him again and again.

* * *

Those rosy lips of hers pressed against his mouth. Her breathing grew harsh. He held his breath. A rush of numbness overcame his body—on the verge of passing out. Seeing black and white in Lucia's bedroom that one time...on that second night. Night Two. Kissing her. Kissing him back.

She was the first to pull back. Looking at her...it stopped his panic attack. She stopped his panic attack.

* * *

Matt tugged her hand...then her arm. Jamie moved into his arms and pressed her face into his shoulder. His arms formed an X on her back, locking her into a tight hug. "You remember," she whispered, and they pulled an inch or so back to see each other.

It took a moment before he bobbed his head, '*Yes.*'

"I just remembered it now."

She let out a small gasp, but the sound effects that echoed into the room from the beep of the heart monitor, and footsteps, and doctors and nurses' pagers going off—brought her back onto her feet. The door to Room 402 was never closed. It remained open for the outsiders to peer in every so often.

Jamie paced around and swiped her fingers over her eyes, redder than ever. Matt peered away. His eyes glossy and tense, he attempted to hold back the tears. "Jamie," he croaked, "you have to tell me how it happened. How it *exactly* happened that night."

Even though she stood with her back to him, her sighs were noticeable. She tensed her posture, but then her shoulders lowered from her earlobes and everything about her relaxed. "Which night," she said.

"You know which one." As he squirmed up some more, he tilted too far to one side and grimaced. He let out a gasp.

Jamie flung around and dashed to the bed. Matt flagged an, 'I'm okay,' sign. She twined their fingers and knelt at the edge of the bed. Those baby doll eyes of hers held his attention. A twinkle of pang burst into both of their eyes. He smudged away a fallen tear of hers. Her eyes remained open, as he caressed the warmth of her cheek. She smiled a bit. "I haven't looked at myself," he began. "The nurse says that most patients ask for a mirror to see their injuries, mainly out of curiosity. But other things have been on my mind, you know?"

Jamie choked back a sob and gave a nod. She closed her eyes and turned away from him.

"Jamie...Please. Everyone's been sugarcoating what happened that night. All I know is about that nasty spill on my birthday...But I can't remember...Any of it. If I do, it's only pieces...A puzzle that I *can't* figure out and solve on my *own*."

"Matty...I can't—"

"Yes, you can." He gripped a hold of her hands.

A few tears got muffled back, as her bottom lip quivered when she simply said, "No."

"Jamie."

"Well, what do you expect *me* to say?!" She pulled back, free from his touch. "I feel bad enough already that you're lying here all hours of the day, wondering what the hell is going on."

"Then, tell me! I just want the one closest to me to tell me everything that's happened, because no one else will!" Less than an inch apart, they tasted each other's heavy breath-withdrawals.

Jamie turned bluer by the second. "I. Can't. Matty. I *can't* do that—"

"*Why?*" The desperation shot him up physically.

"BECAUSE IT *HURTS!*"

Everything rocked sideways—a whiplash of reality, the truth. Jamie broke down into sobs. Officer Grey appeared in the doorway. Matt flagged her off. "We're fine. *Really.*"

"Just try and keep it down." Officer Grey stepped out and pulled the door behind her, leaving it ajar.

Jamie was out of breath. "You were supposed to be *dead,*" she whispered, very childlike. "I won't relive that night, Matty. I'm sorry."

A few blocks away, red-white-and-blue colors decorated everything from lanterns to poster boards. Groups of children ran around in their bathing suits, even though there was no sign of water. Most of the adolescents passed around a brown paper bag and they each took multiple sips from it. Families got an early start with their lawn chairs and ice chests and walked their younglings to one of the local neighborhood parks.

Mr. Barry fished out a lighter from the interior of his coat pocket. His sausage-sized fingers trembled, as he lit the cigarette that dangled from the corner of his mouth.

Boom. Boom.

The firework explosion startled him, and he accidentally burned himself. "*Dammit!*" He cradled his left hand, where a red circle formed and burned.

In luck, an offer was made to him: a lighter pointed his way. Mr. Barry gave a nod and leaned in to inhale a long…long…long drag. "Thanks," he said a few moments later.

"You're welcome." Officer Hanson slipped the lighter back into his own breast pocket. He stood a few inches from Mr. Barry, atop a patch of grass. Beside him stood Officer Samuels, whose fingers squeezed onto the top of the manila folder in her hands. Mr. Barry exhaled, as he sat down on the closest park bench. It was not much comfort because the plastic material was flimsy and hard against his back, like nails. Still tense, he smoked like a chimney, shaken up.

"You sure?" he finally asked.

His colleagues glanced at each other before their worried eyes settled back upon Mr. Barry. "Yes." Officer Samuels eyed Hanson, who bobbed his head in encouragement for her to keep going—leaking further information. "We went over the notes. Everything's the same."

"Some of the neighbors were kind enough to let us question them again."

"*Some*?!" Mr. Barry looked at them and put out his cigarette, twisting and twisting it into the empty seat next to him. The black ashes carried off into the breeze that swept by. "Well, go back there and question them *all*. Every single house on that block."

"Sleeping, eating dinner, or watching TV. It's the same answer. Sir—I mean Mr. Barry." Officer Samuels sighed, exhausted by the second.

"It wouldn't make a difference, Mr. Barry," Hanson said with a cold, firm look of confirmation.

A clan of children skipped by; one of them smiled at Officer Samuels, who smirked back. Mr. Barry stared down at the sidewalk, his hands ran up and down his thighs. Officer Hanson crouched beside him, silent before he opened his mouth or made any sound. "Matthew Smith's friends stated that the lights went off on the night of July 2nd between the hours of 9-10PM, claiming there was fog and object movement from a socalled wind."

Mr. Barry flung to his feet. He took a few steps away, his back to them.

"If you look again at the photographs," Officer Samuels took over, "you'll see that there's no sign of any of this. The fog, the wind…"

"The lights were on that *entire* night, Mr. Barry. Nobody walked by or came *close* to the Smith residence that night. We were right all along..."

"Their stories never matched with the evidence." Officer Samuels' tone dropped at every word.

Across the forest cut lawn, a group of early bird citizens set up fireworks on the pavement. Children gathered around and their eyes boggled out in awe. "It's starting! It's starting!" A boy in Power Rangers swim trunks bounced up and down and grabbed his mother's hand.

Mr. Barry removed his hand from his forehead and lowered it, he could see raindrops of sweat on his skin. He curled his fingers into loose fists. "Okay..." He turned around to his colleagues, prepared for his undivided attention. Now was that time. "I'll have a chat with Dr. Brown then."

It was their worse fear. Silence merged between the three of them. The air was crisp and, suddenly, it dropped a few degrees cooler. Officer Samuels choked back a sigh and gazed off into nothingness—hope for a positive future. Officer Hanson gave up buttoning up his jacket; he left the top three buttons unfinished.

Boom. Boom.

"Happy! Fourth! Of! July!" the crowd behind them cheered.

25.

SILENCE SLAMMED A WALL between him and Jamie, until Ms. Castellanos waltzed in with Officer Franco at her side. "I'll see you later," Jamie said and even attempted to smile, but it was…sad. Her eyes watered up again. "Haven't been sleeping as well."

The lavender circles under her bloodshot eyes was noticeable to him. "See you then," he whispered back.

"I'll walk you guys out." And with that, Officer Franco spun around and guided the ladies out—Jamie gave Matt one last stare, as she lingered by the door. She smiled at him—that same sad, small smile.

Matt had to figure out *why* Officer Grey already seated himself at the window table for two. Officer Franco was a typical *'Slut'*. Officer Franco was awfully close to Jamie's mother.

It all sped by from then on.

Office Grey's face showed a sincere and empathetic smile, as she sat and opened a copy of the newspaper. The rotations of the small and big hand on the clock went tick, tick, tick and grew soft, like a baby angel's sweet harmony—and then very loud a few seconds later, the empty chair across from Officer Grey got pushed out from the table. It held Matt's attention, until his eyes crept over to the ajar door of Room 402. For some reason, the blood rushed to his head. He pinched the bridge of his nose, but the wooziness made the room tilt—a canted angle, as if a camera tipped over to its side. One part of the room leaned lopsided but the other was not.

The mattress was sturdy, like rocks. He wiggled around and the rock-like mattress dug deep, into his spinal cord, the edges were sharp enough to cut deep for lines of blood.

Tick. Tick. Tick.

The big hand on the clock struck two lines after the five. The small hand pointed at one. Something bubbled in the pit of his stomach. An instant later, it growled and rumbled. '*Fauck!*'

Matt eyed the pile of lumpy grilled chicken and soggy mashed potatoes with chunky gravy that leaked all over the cardboard tray, which sat atop the pull-out table attached to the bed. It was more of a tray. The worse food group skewed off to the side: a cup of pudding and a plastic cup of cranberry juice. It was not a proper meal.

He pushed himself up, and his hair touched the top of the pillow. That same piece of hair in the back shot up like Alfalfa's antenna. Only, he focused on the shitty ass food. He pulled the tray forward, away from its hiding spot on the side of the bed and dug in.

"Famished?" Nurse Olive asked.

Matt patted his stomach. Officer Grey chuckled and took a bite of the half-eaten pepperoni pizza in her hand, her newspaper in the other.

"Good." Nurse Olive smiled and grabbed his tray; it was sturdy once more. "I assume you're looking forward to dinner. Heard your…" Cat got her tongue and she stopped in place. "I heard your friends are stopping by."

The bed sheet atop his lower body felt thick and white, the light it formed nearly blinded him. His eyes looked hollow as his shoulders stood an inch from his earlobes. For a moment, he gazed out the middle window in the room. The cotton candy clouds swarmed in the ocean blue sky. The air hissed through his teeth. He closed his eyes and remembered.

* * *

Short, plumped legs bounced up and down like pogo sticks. Puffy
strawberry lips held back into grins until they opened to cheer and
shout. The actual voices, their words, went silent. A pair of light
brown, green, amber, and dark brown eyes googled out, as shots of
shadows exploded above them.

Fireworks.

"Wow," Matt mouthed to himself.

* * *

"You should be happy." It was Nurse Olive, and she had yet
to move. "Hospitals rarely make an exception for visitation
after hours."

"Guess that makes me *special* then."

Matt saw lavenders and pinks mixing into the
multicolored sky, all visible through the left side window.

"No," she said. "Grateful. You have a lot of people
who care about you."

He inhaled, and his chest puffed out. His eyes boiled
hot, a look of fury crept in.

* * *

A pair of yellow footie pajama feet ascended to their tippy toes. Eyes
dilated to the size of coal, Matt pressed his back against the wall and
peeked through the ajar door of the lavender and sweet pea scented
bedroom.

Her scrawny body was wrapped in a thick cotton, lavender
robe; her hair was held back in a burgundy towel. She sat at the
dresser, her back to the doorway to him. Through the dresser mirror,
he saw her swollen eyes that held contact with her reflection, as
though she desperately needed an answer. A second later, she tossed
her head back and pressed her hand to her lips—a quick flash of a

yellow pill. As her head leveled back down, her mouth remained closed, she reached for the glass with a yellow-greenish liquid. She chugged every bit of it.

Matt coiled around and compacted every inch of his body against the wall in the hallway; his eyebrows creased together, like a unibrow. Slowly, he sunk to the floor. He was indeed a blue Power Ranger—the color of his pajamas—holding back any sign of weeping.

* * *

"Matt?"

"No!" Officer Grey jumped to her feet and her newspaper hit the floor.

Nurse Olive pushed aside the flimsy tray and rushed to Matt's side. Officer Grey appeared frazzled, unsure how to help him. Every inch of him seemed wounded, and infected. Matt had the covers tossed back, exposing his pale skin, and the three red blotches of different sizes discolored his chest. The cold air seemed to refresh him, as he took a moment to breathe. "Let me see," he stuttered. "Give me a mirror." He set his hands flat on the mattress. "I need to see what they've done to me. I have to *remember…*"

"Matt."

He bent his elbows and gave himself an extra push.

Riiiinnnnngggg…

That monster in the mirror demonstrated his movements as he lowered his hand from the bulgy white bandage on his forehead. He glided his fingertips around his complexion and then yanked them away as the sensation of bee stings electrocuted his forehead and hit all corners of his heart-shaped face.

"Matt…Matt…" it echoed from afar.

His eyes burned as he stared longer at his discolored skin. Shades of greens, blues, purples and black mixed on him like a toddler's paint set. Desiccated pink and scarlet lines darkened around him.

He grimaced and peered away as the unknown's (*his mirrored reflection*) bottom lip quivered…

"MATT."

That got him to look up; his eyes looked bloodshot—a gory red. He shivered, even though the air was lukewarm. The monster in the mirror was still unavoidable. Nurse Olive lowered the circular handheld mirror in front him, her feet planted inches from the bed. Dr. Brown stood beside her, holding the metallic clipboard. Officer Grey, who sat on the opposite side of the two, leaned back in her chair. She already had her little black book in hand, opened to a blank sheet of paper.

Dr. Brown glimpsed at everyone…

Their trances trapped them in memories and thoughts, too difficult to address. Then, he removed the handheld mirror from his colleague's grip and swapped it for the metallic clipboard. He moved in, and the mirror came with him. "You're sure?" he asked his patient.

Matt gave a nod but made no attempt to look his way. Instead, his focus transfixed, on the sunlight that oozed in from the ocean blue sky. For a moment, it mirrored a sea of red. His body convulsed a bit unless he shivered from the warm air. His skin felt thick, like a glob of glue.

"You can go," Dr. Brown said to Nurse Olive.

Nurse Olive turned on her heel without hesitation, the mirror lowered at her side. Officer Grey closed her little black book. While Dr. Brown gaped his way, Matt sunk lower into the mattress and became isolated in his own memories and thoughts, his own cloud of dust. His lips dropped into a frown.

"Listen, Matt," Dr. Brown began. "Just—"

"I need to be alone."

Through the windows, the sunlight poured its orange hue all over the floor; most of it reflected off the nearby walls, like shadows soon to be awakened in the night. Dr. Brown traced his patient's gaze and saw a clan of crows flapping by through the corner window. It was hopeless. A sign that made him lower the clipboard and head over to the door. He caught up with Nurse Olive, who took one last look over her shoulder…

Matt switched positions, so the sunshine kissed the right-side of his face—his own spotlight, highlighting the multicolored dots, blobs, circular bruises, cuts, and scratches all over him. The monster took over his exterior. Those desiccated lips of his remained in a grim line, mirroring the flat line of the unused heart monitor screen.

Officer Franco ascended to his feet, as Nurse Olive stepped into the hallway. Dr. Brown rushed right behind her, his attention on the floor to process it all. The crowd moved by, some did a double take on the three, because of their proximity, intensity, and worried expression. The three of them made no attempt to get out of their silent stances, because that same look remained on them, as they glanced at each other. Nurse Olive broke the diversion first as soon as she stormed off. The men watched, until she turned the corner and disappeared.

Dr. Brown's hands rocked side to side. His complexion turned a seaweed color, and so did the walls, and then, the floor. Only his cheeks were a shade of red. He caressed one of his cheeks that turned redder and redder. His long piano fingers, wobbly like his appetite, suddenly dropped.

"Poor kid," Officer Franco said, his tone distorted. "Can't imagine what he's going through. First his birthday…"

The crowd was on fast forward—colleague, colleague, stranger, stranger. It was *nonstop*.

"…and now *this*…"

The sweat rolled down his skin, hotter than fire.

"Dr…Brown—" Now, the tone sounded to be in alert mode.

"I got to…"

Dr. Brown took off, further and further away, sucking into the crowd of people. They eyed him. After all, it was his hefty breathing that captured a few curious and scared looks.

"Out of my way," Dr. Brown asserted, as calm as possible to them.

The wide-eyed, almost blanched faces turned their attention from the frantic running-for-his-life doctor, to the perplexed police officer, who remained in front of the door of Room 402. "Dr. Brown," Officer Franco called out. "Hey!"

No answer: just the back of his boss, until Dr. Brown rounded the same corner of Nurse Olive's exit seconds ago.

26.

IT MIRRORED THE RADIANCE of a magician's wheel, spinning round and round in the crystal blue sky.

The sun glimmered down onto the backs and faces of doctors, nurses, and visitors who either nibbled or chomped down on their meals at the circular tables. "I don't know…" Mr. Barry gazed at the sunlight that streaked through the bulky windows on the wall. A trainwreck of thoughts trampled him. "It's a sign."

"Enough with your signs already." Dr. Brown gritted his teeth. "I'm fine *now*—"

"And if it happens again?"

Next in line, Dr. Brown set down his tray on the baby blue and brown polka dot countertop for checkout. "One swiss sub sandwich."

The cashier woman punched the amount into the register. "That'll be…"

That voice, she recognized it. A part of her past. Slowly, she looked up, her brunette locks of love poured behind her shoulders, and her pupils dilated. Dr. Brown and Mr. Barry shifted on their feet. But only Dr. Brown went wide-eyed. He recognized her.

"Shit."

"I can take you here, ma'am." A new cashier, who stood beside Locks of Love, waved over the customer behind Dr. Brown and Mr. Barry. An exhausted mother slugged her way over to the register with her two bouncy children.

"Cash or credit," Locks of Love coaxed.

"Uh, credit." Dr. Brown slid his credit card across the cold counter—a blue Visa.

The beautiful brunette shook her head and a small chuckle escaped her lips, as she reached for the debit card.

"Didn't think you'd ever see me again. Did ya'?" It was not a question. After a few more numbers were punched in, the machine gave a beep, and a receipt printed out. She tore off the paper and placed it on his tray.

"Don't think about calling me later," she said with a grin.

Her eyes glowed like a cat's, but bluer. Mr. Barry did a triple take, their breathing raspy and bodies tense. She turned her attention away first and faced the next customer. "Hi sir," she started up her phony, smiling act. "Is this going to be all for today?"

Dr. Brown snatched his tray. Mr. Barry called after, tailgating him.

"Hey!"

They squeezed through the crowd. Mr. Barry nearly lost sight of his target, until he came to stop at an empty table in the back corner. Dr. Brown plopped down into a chair and slammed his tray onto the table. It was accidental, but a few nearby customers glanced over their shoulders. Mr. Barry joined him, across the table.

"Look," he said and lowered his voice, "I don't know what the hell that was back there, but I need you to promise—"

"Relax. It was a one-time thing. Besides, how the hell was I supposed to know that I worked with her?"

"You could try *talking* next time. You know, getting to know someone before you plow them."

Dr. Brown flashed a loose grin (sarcasm at its best). He plucked the wrapper off the sandwich, one corner at a time. The plastic stuck to his fingers, like crazy glue. Soon a worried look prolonged on the man's face across from Dr. Brown.

"You're not going to talk, are you? You know, it's not right. Any of this—"

"Give it a rest, Clyde."

"We really need to…Will you listen—"

Dr. Brown pressed his hand down onto Clyde Barry's. Blobs of mustard and mayonnaise smothered over his sausage link fingers. Mr. Barry winced and jolted a bit in his seat; his pupils broadened and shot all around the room. There were two different types of groups: unrecognizable faces that brought back their normal skin tone by drinking water or eating their meals, and gloomy or bland faces that focused elsewhere, trapped in their own abyss, as they drooped lower into their seats.

"I can have you—"

"What? Arrested?" It humored the doc., but his eyes remained sharp, almost on fire. "Don't flatter yourself with that crock of shit." He removed his hand.

Mr. Barry pulled his hand back, still blobbed with mustard and mayonnaise.

"I heard you *loud* and *clear*." Dr. Brown sat taller at each syllable.

Even Mr. Barry's caramel skin grew redder. He stared at Dr. Brown, catching his breath. The men allowed the storm of silence to pass over them, longer than it really needed to be. The clangs, clinks, tinks of silverware against plates, and conversations sped by like a fast lane; every beat grew louder and louder.

Mr. Barry cringed and looked over his shoulder.

Nothing. Zero eyes centered on them.

Dr. Brown leaned back in his chair and reached for his unfinished swiss sub, until, it caught his eye—Mr. Barry's yellow, white stained hands. "Clean yourself up. I hate losing my appetite."

A rolled-up napkin hit him in the face. Wiping off the piles of lukewarm goo from his knuckles physically preoccupied Mr. Barry, and it limited his temptations.

"You know," Dr. Brown mumbled through piles of cheese, lettuce, and tomatoes that swished around in his mouth, "I've always thought you were going to become a scientist or an astronaut. You were always so *smart*." After one big bite, crumbs flaked at the corners of his mouth, "Finishing your homework right after school. Studying. Even pulling all-nighters to ace that History or Biology exam."

Chomp. Chomp. Chomp.

Lettuce juice dribbled from the corner of his mouth now.

"And you were always so smooth," Mr. Barry added in for the game; his gaze drifted into reminisces, not nice ones either, "Mr. *Casanova*. Taking every one of them, away from me." Then it was impossible to not break out into a smile, his turn for the upper hand. "I'm just curious: How did my testicles taste? You've always been a fan of sloppy seconds, even thirds sometimes."

"You just love giving yourself credit." Dr. Brown chuckled and ate more food, "But we both know that they were purer than gold. You were far from fucking any of them. They felt bad for you. You—the overweight, desperate virgin—"

"At least I treated them with *respect*!"

That got a few glimpses.

Mr. Barry cleared his throat, mortified, and even shrunk away as he dipped lower into his seat. "You're such a—"

"Whoa. Whoa. *Relax*. You're the one who brought up memory lane. Besides, it's not my fault that you and these girls you liked didn't have…'chemistry.'"

Mr. Barry dug around in his pocket and pulled out a box of Marlboros. His hands trembled, as he brought the cigarette to his mouth.

"Clyde, you can't smoke in here." Dr. Brown rolled his eyes and leaned in. "Look, if you don't relax…You're overthinking. It was just a panic attack earlier."

"*Just*?!"

The cigarette dropped to the table. Thankfully, it was not lit. Mr. Barry slammed the Marlboro box on top of it—the loose tobacco puffed out of its white wrapper. Dr. Brown coughed and peered around.

A head or two whirled their way but turned back around to their own chatty, or silent business.

Mr. Barry dabbed at his forehead with the back of his hand, his complexion already turned Bloody Mary red, like he suddenly had a high fever. He grabbed one of the napkins from Dr. Brown's tray and blobbed off his sweat. His sausage link fingers shook again, as he rambled on a million miles per hour.

"You must feel like a big shot, huh? Taking out your flaws—excuse me, *mental illness,* since anxiety attacks count as one—on me." Between more deep breaths, "You're no man. You don't have the balls to accept the facts."

By now, Dr. Brown finished eating, but not by choice. He only held onto the sandwich, squeezing it, his fingers turning white.

Mr. Barry leaned over the table some more. "You don't just have the panics. You have them too—dreams, nightmares every few weeks or maybe every night—"

Plop.

The sandwich dropped onto the table.

"Shut. Up."

"We're only as sick as our secrets."

Slump.

And there it was—the manila folder: **Case File: Smith**.

"What the *hell* is the matter with you?" Dr. Brown lurched for the closed folder, like a lion with its prey. He peered around—not a pair of eyes locked on them—and rammed the folder inside of his coat. "Now you listen to—"

"I...can't...do...this." Mr. Barry's eyes strained from torture. He started to breathe rapidly. Zero wheezing.

"Oh, sweet Jesus, Mother Mary of Christ." Dr. Brown circled around and sat beside him. "You just got to…breathe…See…" He demonstrated the breathing relaxation: inhale, exhale, inhale, exhale, inhale, exhale. "Better?"

"Not really…" Mr. Barry kept his eyes shut, as he inhaled through his nostrils and exhaled through his mouth. Eventually, his hefty and raspy breathing slowed down, "…but it's working."

"It should. It's what I show my patients." He scanned around some more, still no onlookers.

"Guess we do have something in common after all." It made Mr. Barry chuckle, although it sounded thick because his breathing was not fully manageable yet. It frightened the doc, since he looked down at the table. "If my sleep's been fucked since that night, I can't imagine what yours must be like."

"You're really killing me here." A big smile was plastered on him, like red lips of a clown. "I don't mind writing something up to make you fuckin' relax because, at this rate, you'll only burn yourself—"

"I won't."

"Yes. You. Will."

"It was 'A Tragedy in a Family…'"

Dr. Brown glowered into those dark chocolate eyes that watered up and blazed with red and purple veins. He moved in closer. "I want you to listen clear, Clyde, like a *goddamn* fortune teller's crystal ball. We were informed— pardon my French, *paid* to keep our lips shut."

"I wasn't the one who blackmailed—"

"And who'll believe you? There were no traces of evidence that someone entered the premises that night. Well, I guess now it'll be *those nights*." His tone lowered, "Remember, we all have our parts: successful doctor, caring for a failed suicidal teenager, four grief-stricken best friends, claiming they were only watching a bit of TV that night."

Mr. Barry peered off to the side, his chest rose every few seconds as his nostrils flared open.

"You said so yourself that they all looked '*on edge*' when you asked them what they were up to before the trespassing of this socalled 'stranger.'"

Dr. Brown became shinier, as his forehead clammed up. He grabbed Mr. Barry's chin and forced him to look his way. His dark chocolate, swollen eyes grew to the size of walnuts. "Now tell me," Dr. Brown coaxed, "why was everything upstairs somewhat 'decent,' except for Lucia's bedroom? Hmph? Tell me, as your colleagues find *nothing*, and you *isolate* yourself to just dwell on the past."

"Guess you just found my part in all of this," Mr. Barry chimed in. "Just say it. Get it over with it."

It made him smile. "What? A *failure*, Clyde. Is that what scares you? That you'll only be another failed cop. Well, if you don't want to be, then back the fuck off this case."

Their eyes remained locked. Mr. Barry's burly chest went in an up and down rhythm. Crease marks formed around Dr. Brown's eyes and nose while his nostrils opened and closed in a heavy matter. Drip, Drip, Drip. Even the sweat from his hairline went straight for the tabletop.

Dr. Brown cocked his head and coughed. It was not just any an ordinary cough, but the thick mucus type that burned his throat, and his eyes watered up. By the time he looked back up, Mr. Barry appeared neither rattled nor livid but upset. "Jonathan?" And he even reached out for the man's arm.

Dr. (Jonathan) Brown jumped to his feet. He coughed repeatedly and, somehow, with a tight constriction in his chest, he admonished, "Perhaps, this is all too much for you..." All the blood pumped to his cheeks, pinching them pink.

"What are you talking—"

"We have security that'll keep the press away from Mr. Smith." His cheeks turned red.

"You're *firing* me?" Mr. Barry rose to his feet. "I'm my *own* boss. Not *you* or your *socalled* perfect co-workers, who fuck, drink, and pop pills on the JOB!"

It made a few bystanders and passersby uncomfortable, and they meandered off, never looking back to see what would happen between the two men in the corner of the room. Everyone else stopped whatever it was they were doing. Somewhere in the middle, a slender blonde emerged from the small crowd. She had on a pair of light blue scrubs. "Is everything alright, Dr. Brown?"

"Sir," said one of the two beefy security guards, whose veins popped out of their forearms, as they entered the cafeteria, "some people mentioned a bit of a commotion going on here."

"You don't look so well, sir," added another pretty-faced woman, who was also in scrubs.

The cop and doc. never broke focus, until Mr. Barry cracked first, when his gaze dropped to the floor. "Everything's fine, everyone," Dr. Brown announced and turned toward the multiple strained and perspired expressions that stared back at him and Mr. Barry. "We're just a bit stressed and tired here. Isn't that right, Mr. Barry?"

That sly smirk of his, how it mocked Mr. Barry, who suddenly wiped his hands on his jeans. "Right," he spat out. "We're all just stressed and tired here."

"We'll be on our way now."

One by one, onlookers carried back to their own business. The security guards parted off into opposite directions. The two gorgeous, fresh-faced nurses gave each other a quick glance, before their attention turned back to the men. Dr. Brown squeezed an arm around Mr. Barry's shoulders and guided them away from the crowd. They headed for the door in the corner of the room, no more than ten feet away from their table, where one of the security guards waited.

Mr. Barry's breathing was steep again. "We're liars."

"Oh, Clyde…" As Dr. Brown tugged him in closer for a, 'Hey bro' hug, he flashed a smile whenever a passerby or bystander looked their way. "You're willing to jeopardize *your* career and life over some *silly* white lie." After his nod, the security guard opened the back-exit door.

All outdoor items became illuminated in a crystal-clear sight, like a tropical body of water, as the sun sparkled down upon the cement sidewalk and asphalt. "We've been protecting him since he was a baby," Dr. Brown carried on as he dragged—'hugged'—Mr. Barry across the street.

Mr. Barry stumbled a few inches behind him, far passed a tunnel of doom. Every inch they strode across the parking lot, they recognized the countless parked vehicles. There was not a soul in sight.

"You don't seem to care." Dr. Brown whirled around.

Mr. Barry jerked to a stop. The vengeance in Dr. Brown's eyes tensed up the cop's neck and shoulders, leaving him paralyzed. The doc. still held his wrist.

"If you *ever*," Dr. Brown said deadpan, "pull another stunt like that and cause stress for my co-workers, patients, and myself, I'll be sure that you'll never step foot here or anywhere in this town again."

Mr. Barry saw from the corner of his eye people and potential rescuers. But his lips remained shut. Dr. Brown chucked his arm away. Mr. Barry caressed his wrist—a bloodshot handprint stood atop of it, a battle wound. Silence fell among them, as the small crowd, probably visitors, squeezed by them.

Mr. Barry glared at the ground; his hands became wobbly.

"Why so upset, Clyde?"

"Shut up!"

"You'd never harm *me* in any way. We both already know that. After all, who would look like the bad guy if this were to all…leak out? I wonder what the family would have to say if they knew that you are *disrespecting* your *own blood*. Coming from a failed cop…Alcoholic…Emotionally and mentally damaged because you still live in 1992. The past is the past, *cousin*. Get. The. Fuck. *Over. It.*"

And just like that, he turned on his heel and stormed off and headed back to the hospital. Mr. Barry gasped for air and waved his collar up and down to fan himself off, but most of all to breathe. "Shit. *Fuck.*"

"Sir," said the security guard at the back-exit door, "you don't look so well—"

"Make sure that he doesn't come back in," Dr. Brown asserted, as he stepped back into the cafeteria.

Then he staggered and clutched his chest, which tilted his body backward.

The security guard seized his arm. "Sir!"

"I'm fine, I'm fine." He flagged him off. "Must've been something I…"

Something stole his attention: brunette locks of love spilled over her shoulders, as she picked up the half-finished swiss sub and crumpled up napkins from the table—his table. Her eyes broadened to solid hard black. She only locked eyes with him for an instant, and then, she straightened herself up.

"I wanted more," Dr. Brown spurted out and moved closer still across the table from her. He had her undivided attention. "I wanted to call, but never found the…I never…Look…" Suddenly, he turned bloody red, the kind that sets a person off. "You fucked me that night."

After her look and a sigh of disgust. "*Asshole.*"

"That's not what you said as you begged for more that night!"

Mr. Barry sat on the sidewalk; his legs rattled around, finally catching ahold of his breath. He watched the birds shaped into big and the small letter 'M's'. He closed his eyes and the downpour of sunlight warmed his face. It was like orange-yellow kisses against his caramel skin, and, for once, it seemed to relax him, as his shoulders and neck unfolded.

Dr. Brown trudged out of the cafeteria and down the hallway. He coughed and then choked for air.

"Dr. Brown?" it echoed from a galaxy far, far away. Everything around him sped to his own tilt-a-whirl, merry-go-round ride.

"Dr. Brown!" a woman in scrubs screamed, as his body dropped to the floor.

27.

"LUCIA."

Her chicken bone fingers rolled off the gray steering wheel. Lucia blinked and looked to her right-side. Jamie slouched over and looked through the passenger window, outside of the gray Toyota Corolla. Derek and Lisa lingered on opposite sides of their dear friend, close to the driver's window. "I'll be there in a second," Lucia said and turned her head back to the windshield. "Just need a moment."

Her pouty pink lips parted ways but when Lucia gripped back onto the steering wheel, Jamie closed her mouth. "Oh. Okay then…". She straightened herself up and closed the passenger door. She coiled around and tugged the grocery bags that dangled from her wrists.

"Guess we should get going," Lisa said and twined her fingers through the handles of more grocery bags in her hands.

"Yeah." Jamie started off with them. "I guess so."

The three of them strolled over to the main entrance of the McArthur building, where doctors, nurses, and visitors came and went like passengers on a subway. Lucia turned her head away from the windshield—no longer able to see them. She gasped for air and broke down into sobs. Imprisoned between a Ford and a Mercedes in the parking lot, her hands wobbled as she covered her eyes.

Her lavender shaded eyelids gave a twitch.

"*SHH!*"

And slowly peeled open.

"Don't 'SHH' me, *woman*." The tone sounded lower than the voice that spoke before, "*Wah-yah.*"

Derek emerged through the haze. He was in a Bruce Lee stance: his leg kicked out in midair and his arm elongated out toward Jamie, who stood a foot away from him. "You're such a dumbass," she whispered, her back facing Matt.

"He's ALIVE!" Lisa was the first to notice.

Officer Franco stepped out of Room 402 and left the door ajar. In the hallway, Officer Hanson ascended to his feet. "I'll go find us another chair," he said.

Lisa lit up like a sparkler and dashed over to the bed. So, did Jamie and Derek, as they released the grocery bags that plopped down onto the floor.

Gatorade and water bottles pushed individual junk food baggies across the floor like a hockey puck.

"Matty!"

The three of them circled around and imprisoned him in a closed and claustrophobic hug.

Matt gripped the bed sheet that slowly bled with sweat coming off his hands. Jamie slapped Lisa's hand away and yanked Derek back by his shirt. Matt exhaled and released the air that he held onto. "The hugs and kisses can wait," Jamie said. "After all, *someone*,"—She eyed Derek— "just had to wake him up."

Derek glared at her, only his eyes twitched in the process of playing an intimidation-game—stupidity. Silently, he elevated his leg a few inches from the floor and tossed his fist straight forward, as he mouthed, "Wah-yah," at Jamie. She just rolled her eyes.

Lisa chuckled. "Easy young grasshopper." She took a bow.

Gradually, Matt loosened his fists from the bed sheet. He looked back into those baby doll eyes of hers: they turned bluer by the instant. He sat up and rubbed the sleep from his eyes. Jamie peered away and swiped her finger across the fallen teardrops on her cheeks. "Sorry," she whispered, "for waking you."

She lowered to the floor and snapped her fingers to cue Derek and Lisa's assistance. The three of them scooped up the brown paper grocery bags and fallen items from the floor. "*Reunited and it feels so good!*" Derek swayed his hips on the way down.

Jamie's cold rigid demeanor kept her motionless, until Lisa tapped her shoulder, and she got a move on the cleanup.

"That's okay," Matt's delayed reaction came out groggier than intended. "It was supposed to be an hour nap anyway." He locked eyes with Jamie as she ascended to her feet. "Where's…"

She walked away, toward the window table. Matt leaned forward; his hand stretched out for her—

"Hey, Matt!" Derek pinged to his side. Those googly green eyes of his shimmered like an emerald, as he flashed a jumbo size bag of Doritos: Salsa Verde. "Pure…Genius…Am I, *right*?!"

"Relax, Derek." Lisa picked up a red Gatorade bottle in front of the window on the left side of the room. "Cheese flavor is still da best—fair and square."

Jamie settled the food and drinks atop the window table, her back facing the others. Lowering to the floor, she kept herself there for a moment, as though her body would give out any second. Breathing a bit heavy, he focused his eyes on her, as she sniffled and ran her sleeve across her eyes. Matt watched, as Jamie struggled back up to her feet and used the legs of a nearby chair for support. Derek or Lisa had not noticed. They kept chatting.

Jamie stepped away from the table and Matt's breathing thickened.

"But you do *know* what cheese does to you though," Derek avowed.

"What?" Lisa dropped off more food items onto the table.

Derek pointed out his finger and lifted his leg.

"Ew!" Lisa turned away and gagged.

Jamie rolled her eyes and pinched her nose. "*Really!*'

"A *warning* would've been nice!"

"Ah, *come on*! It wasn't—" Derek took in a few whiffs himself, and immediately he turned around. "Yeah, that's pretty bad. My bad, dudes!"

"Ya' think?" Matt fanned himself off. "Peanut butter waffles with honey, chocolate syrup, and sprinkles are *not* breakfast."

"And neither is PB&J with strawberry syrup and three double chocolate chip cookies, with a tall glass of mixed chocolate and strawberry milk on the side," Jamie and Lisa had both interjected.

Matt shrugged. "You're probably lactose intolerant, dude."

"Sweet." Derek went straight for the goodies in the grocery bags.

Everyone else just stared at him. Jamie rolled her eyes and turned on her heel, and then pushed her hippie color striped purse onto the table. She faced the window on the right-side of the room, as tints of oranges and yellows highlighted her hands. The golden sun sat above the orange swirls and below the tints of lavender in the sky.

Outside, beyond those olive shaped pupils, a bold pink glimmered. She pushed back the visor above the driver's seat and ran her fingers across her eyes. She grabbed her fake, black Dolce and Gabbana purse by the strap. Her hands were jolty.

"*Fuck!*"

Lucia dropped her purse onto the passenger seat. Her hands released the purse's strap. She was horrified, as if it were a dying animal. Her bottom lip trembled. She broke down and squeezed onto the cold pleather strap. Those long bony fingers of hers reddened by the second as though venom from a snake shot into her icy blue veins. Lucia finally looked up at the windshield.

Mr. Barry stood straight across from her; his eyes locked with hers. He lingered in between, a red Toyota and a blue Honda. Lucia bobbed her head and she reached for the driver's door handle. He started toward her.

In Room 402, Matt gazed off to his side; his body lay straight, like a mummy in its tomb—dead and undead. Derek dragged up a chair beside the bed, giving the floor a few squeaks. He waved around a red and a blue Gatorade bottle. "Hot or cold?"

Jamie looked away from Matt—the first to break focus—and put her attention to the right side window. Through the crystal-clear bulletproof glass, something flickered at her from an adjacent angle. She leaned forward, her cheek an inch or so from the nippy glass.

Straight across from the center window of Room 402, stood a beige-brown building. Jamie waited for a sign, but no shiny light that called for her attention, until she caught the slightest glimpse of movement through one of the apartment building's windows. She counted from the ground up; the fourth floor had a weird vibe to it.

"What are you doing?" Lisa asked and dragged up two chairs next to Derek, adjacent to Matt.

"Nothing," Jamie answered and faced their way. "Just thinking. Happy to be here with you three."

Derek raised his Gatorade bottle. "I'll drink to that."

Lisa beamed and patted her hands onto the empty seat cushion next to her chair. Jamie grabbed the Doritos: Salsa Verde bag. As soon as it soared across the air, Derek caught the bag. "*Nice!*"

"You're *welcome.*" Jamie dipped into the chair.

His bloodshot eyes gawked back into hers. Jamie gave him a small smile as her rosy lips parted. Lisa interjected, as she backed up her chair, "Almost forgot! We got—"

"CHOCOLATE!!!" Then Derek lowered his voice, as Lisa skipped over to the table. "She's on her period."

It was hard not to watch Derek popping off the cap of his Gatorade bottle and chugging it all the way back like a fraternity brother at a party. The blue liquid emptied out of the plastic bottle and dripped from the corners of Derek's mouth. The frosty blue drink looked so refreshing that even Matt gulped.

Derek puckered his lips, "*Ah,*" and licked them.

Matt jolted, as something neurotic twitched at the core of his stomach like he sat at the top of a roller-coaster ride; his eyes dropped down to the blackest pit for what seemed to go on for eternity.

"Well." Derek handed over the red Gatorade bottle. "I shall do the honors." He unfastened the cap. "Cheers." They clinked on it, Derek tossed his head back to finish the last drops of his drink, until he realized it was all gone. "*Damn!*"

Matt stared down at the pool of red liquid in his plastic Gatorade bottle. Then he leaned his head back and brought his lips to the opening of the bottle. For some reason, he grimaced, as the red liquid streamed down his throat, the drink chillier than winter's icicles. Derek burped, which got another, "*Gross,*" from Jamie.

When Matt saw something from the corner of his eye, he released the bottle from his lips, stained red; his head never moved away from his pillow, as he exhaled. There it was again—something flickered at him through the center window, directly across from him—in flawless sight. It came from the beige-brown building at eye level from the fourth floor on the opposite side. It flickered on and off, a shot pointed directly at his eye.

"Ah!" Matt peered away. "I'm fine," he reassured his friends, as soon as they bolted to him. "Probably some kid with a magnifying glass."

Jamie already gazed his way, one of their many unspoken moments. Lisa retreated to the table and returned with a plate of unwrapped chocolate candies. *"Bon Appétit!"* It was her best charm school act.

Derek pumped his fist in the air, while the other hand doves for a miniature Baby Ruth bar. "Sweet!"

28.

LUMINOUS STREAKS OF THE SUN daggered through the second story windows like acrylic fingernails clawing for its next victim.

Two hands shuffled through the stack of 8x10 black and white photographs. At the bottom, right-hand corner of each photo read, *July 2nd, 2006*. The Smith residence, a two-story household, stood alone in the faintest glistening of summer's moon. He leaned his head back against the seafoam-colored stall door. His sparkling eyes remained down at the manila folder in his hands: **Case File: Smith**.

His sugar honey tan went ashen, as his hands started to shake from side to side. He fished one of his hands into the interior of his coat. Something rattled. He pulled out a small bottle; there is was, a medication of his own: Jonathan Brown. Done in a simple take, he popped open the cap and tossed a pill into his mouth.

Dr. Brown grimaced, as he swallowed it dry. He exhaled and pressed his eyes shut. His long ghostly fingers slanted to the left side of his chest, as though he needed to reach into the center of his heart.

Room 402. Tick. Tick. Tick.

The small hand struck on the three, the big hand followed two numbers behind. *'Fauck!'*

Matt dropped his head back down onto the pillow. He removed his arm from his eyes. It was another face off with the itty bitty dots on the eerie ceiling. The ceiling had holes, like swiss cheese or tiny eyes that seemed to watch him from miles above. He got sucked into a tunnel of a white flash.

* * *

Derek tore off the candy wrapper and gnawed off half of the Baby Ruth. He vacuumed down the other half. Lisa gawked out the window. Jamie put her free hand up and pointed at the sky; her lips settled into a flat line when a few Reese's pieces trickled out of her uncurled fingers. Matt focused his blood red eyes on the window in the middle of the room. He sniffled back the mucus and tears, mentally transfixed onto something else, rather than the firework show. At some point, he felt something touching him.

Jamie gave his ankle a light squeeze. It sent a shudder down his spinal cord. He wiped his arms over his eyes, but a teardrop still bypassed and skimmed down his cheek.

* * *

The ceiling elongated like a rubber band. His limbs felt turned to jelly, as he forcefully compressed lower and lower into the mattress by some benevolent force.

* * *

Lisa grabbed a handful of Reese's pieces from the plate. Derek nibbled onto the candy wrapper of a miniature Twix.

"It's him!" a passerby said. "Oh, and his—"

But whoever belonged to the eager voice, Derek did not see, nor did Matt.

Lucia stepped into the room with Nurse Olive. Lucia closed the door, her back against it before anyone else poked in their heads, like dogs at a drug bust.

"Thought these would come in handy," she said for the icebreaker and waved a set of binoculars.

Jamie's eyes diverted to Matt, pink in the face. His grandmother's sight never left his. It was a stare down—an awkward one. Her eyes already addressed the elephant in the room. Real life. Reality, no words needed to be said.

Matt broke focus and turned away; his eyes centered on the biggest and brightest light, adjacent to the left side window, revealing the moon. The polished, outer layer of the moon blended seamlessly with the blue sky. The circular object seemed to twirl, as its glow seeped through the windows, and down upon the empty table.

"And three," Nurse Olive's voice came into focus. She held onto his hands and gave his body a light but encouraging pull. Matt ascended slowly and painfully to his feet. Every part of him shot raw with agony. He groaned, his face itching and burning to scarlet. For a moment, everything flashed to a grainy look, and then to black and white.

"Matty!"

Jamie and everyone else had lunged forward.

The black dots scattered away, and his ears were no longer stuffy. He stuck his ears out, like Dumbo, and used the other hand to massage the thin skin above his nose. "I'm fine," he repeated and repeated, "just a bit...tired." Yet, he was halfway to the floor, sort of slipping backward. By the time he looked up, Lucia was already right there with him—another stare down—as her chest elevated ever so slightly, so she could catch her breath.

* * *

The ceiling spotted black and white. Matt pressed his eyes shut and his jaw clenched.

* * *

The marvelous mixture of colors.

The exquisite textures.

The visualization after a couple's first kiss.

It was a rainbow of explosions in the midnight blue sky. Lisa watched in awe; her hands clasped together like the young girl she once was. Derek tossed his head back and shook out the crumbs from the Doritos: Salsa Verde. Jamie managed a small smile at them, but as she looked off to her left side, her lips collapsed back into a grim line.

Those Hershey Kiss eyes of his watered up. Lucia dawdled two to three feet away from Matt, behind him. It was odd. It kicked his gut. He was attached to the strings of his puppeteers. They wanted him to be a very good boy and sit up straight and just put on a smile: 'Play nice. Be a good boy.'

"Oh, neato!" Lucia zoomed in through the binoculars, her attention faced the left side window. "Look at this honey—"

Before she touched his shoulder, he already flinched, and his instant attack reaction seized ahold of the arms to the chair.

"Honey..."

* * *

Matt was grinding his teeth. He smacked his hand onto his chest...gasping...choking.

* * *

"I'm fine...I'm fine," he lied through gritted teeth and wormed his way back up to his feet. Everything around him rocked sideways. Even his friends' faces expanded and suddenly shrunk to the size of an ant—all bundled and squished up like intestines. Matt rubbed his forehead and his eyes that began to shut on their very own.

Jamie tightened her grip on his arm. "Matty..."

"He needs to lie down." It was an order from Lucia.

Jamie, Derek, and Lisa slowly loosened their grip on Matt. Lucia set the binoculars down onto the window table and then reached over for Matt's hand. Her fingers rolled out for his choice if he wanted the additional help or not. She waited, an acknowledgment for his space, but she was still not going anywhere.

He was unsure, until he gradually reached for her bony white fingers.

Chills ingested his entire body from head to toe. Her hands were freezing, unnatural, not human, but he tightened his hold on her anyway. Lucia winced a bit and gave him a long-lasting look.

* * *

The fingers on his right-hand spread out wide on the left side of his chest, breathing heavily.

The small hand settled on nine, the big hand pointed at twelve.

* * *

Back in bed, Matt lay on his side—the opposite direction from the trio of windows. He skimmed his hand over his eyes to wash off the wetness, but his pupils went from pink to a Scorsese-Tarantino red: a crossover, how daring! Jamie, Derek, and Lisa grabbed their belongings, as they headed out of Room 402. "Bye," Lisa said first.

Derek hunched on his way out. "Later, dude."

Jamie moped in the doorway for another minute, her somber gaze never disengaged from Matt's. Lucia sat next to the bed, behind Matt, his back still to her. "We'll visit tomorrow," Lucia said and reached for the back of his head. He felt his body stiffen, his eyes widened, as she stroked his long locks. "Someone needs a haircut soon. I'll see if the nurse can cut it, or maybe me."

But that last part came out as a whisper, "Me. Me. Me."

'ME. ME. ME.'

Paralyzed from her long piano fingers that combed through his stringy unwashed hair, his attention remained on the ajar bathroom door, where there was nothing but darkness—vampire pitch black. Lucia lowered and planted a kiss on the left side of his face. He clenched his eyes shut to push back the tears; it worked.

* * *

The air huffed out of his nostrils. A strong sensation burned through his system, it started at the bottom of his feet. His lips released a small gasp. He covered his mouth, but the pressure just built and built and pushed through.

Another gasp.

Another gasp.

And another one.

His throat constricted, holding back the screams. He could not stop trembling.

"Please...*Please*," he begged.

But the flashes, memories from earlier, just replayed *over* and *over* again.

"Sttt...ooop."

'*Stop*?'

His heart raced, as if galloping around a track. The worries stirred his insides, and he slouched over, heaving, until no vomit arrived—just the illusion that he spewed up every bodily fluid. The pain melted deeper and found its way to the left side of his chest, where it buried.

"ARGH!" He flung right up.

* * *

At the doorway, Lucia peered over her shoulder, where Matt curled up in a ball, hypnotized by the pitch black that seeped out of the bathroom, and came to a stop on his side of the room, the direction he faced.

Lucia sighed and clutched her loose purse strap. She turned away and meandered out of Room 402 when he burst into tears; the rivers traveled along his complexion and stung like venom.

* * *

"Matt! MATT!"

It was too late. Matter chucked off the comforter, and the bed sheets tangled up. He tumbled out of bed.

The lights turned up a notch, as Nurse Olive and her team hustled into the room and went straight to their spots. They became aware of their assigned positions and the tasks that came with it. Two of them prevented Matt's complete pitfall from the bed and caught him before he headbutted the floor. "Where's Dr. Brown?!" one of them asked.

"Matt, look at me," Nurse Olive ordered quietly as she cupped his chin with her hands. "I need to know that you can hear me."

He jolted his head up and down: '*YES!*'

But where were the words? Just tears—buckets of them.

"Breathe…"

He followed her demonstration and inhaled through his nostrils and exhaled out of his mouth, but the more he wormed around, the faster his pulse sped up.

"Matt," she said and never released his hand, "stay with me."

Matt squeezed her fingers and pulled a bit too tight.

His arms fell flat.

He grimaced. Then *screamed*, gravity yanked the IV tubes out of his hand.

The IV rack tipped forward, as a waterfall of red seeped from the small markings on Matt's hand and trickled down onto the white bed sheet.

29.

RIIIINNNNNGGGG...

Slowly, the surroundings of his bed dissolved in and out. Dr. Brown stood by the left side window. "Panic attacks."

It was barely audible, and time lapsed.

"Scheduling...Psychoanalysis," he carried on, calmly but informative.

Nurse Olive wrapped the beige bandage around Matt's right arm, identical to the one on his left. Matt kept his focus elsewhere, straight ahead, anywhere but on the hospital staff.

"...Later...Tomorrow..."

The clock on the wall elongated in height and width...smaller...bigger...shorter...taller. The thin arrow—the third hand—ticked by the big and small hands of the clock.

Tick...Tick...TICK.

A part of his heart, unless it was his soul, dragged him further and further into his own abyss.

"Matt!"

He rolled on over to his left side.

Nurse Olive emerged through the blackened spots—his night goggle vision—and rounded the bed, catching him just in time. "You poor thing," she said, with a soft stroke on his cheek, helping him back up while another nurse locked the last railing of the bed.

All along, Dr. Brown got trapped in his own bottomless pit of a black hole. He stared down at his hand, rocking on its own...side to side...side to side...side to side. He grabbed his hand with the other and gave it a tighter clench. He put a stop to the trembles, until he shivered from a chill that rattled him to the bones. With his eyes shut, he inhaled through his nostrils and exhaled out of his mouth.

But his own coaching was useless. He had to leave the room.

"But I'm not crazy."

"Nobody's saying that," the man in a brown Mr. Roger's sweater said, writing on bundles of lined yellow paper on his lap—the psychologist, who was socalled recommended by Dr. Brown. "Unless someone's personally—"

"No one's ever called me *that*." Matt shook his head, tempted to laugh; instead, his eyes grew somber. "I would never hurt myself or anybody."

The afternoon oranges and yellows hit, like lighting against Autumn's leaves and gave them a darker hue. It was beautiful.

"Another nice day today."

Matt sighed; his eyes stung to red. *'Oh sweet baby Jesus! Small talk.'*

"Perhaps, this is the best place to stop." The therapist sat at the foot of the bed and turned back to a page of his notes. Matt caught the slightest glimpse of a bald spot atop the man's head—thinning hair.

Matt sniffled and pressed his arm over his eyes. He took his time, unable to look the man in the striped sweater's eyes. It hurt, the small but thick white bandages on his inner wrist, next to the new IV injected into his skin hours ago. Blood was around the clear tubes. The man ascended to his feet and towered to his six-foot stature. It cued Officer Grey's rise from the window table.

The man…psychologist, gave one last look at the frail boy in front of him. Even his complexion matched the bed sheets. "Until next time," was all he said.

Off his client's head bob, the psychologist started off. It was then, he came to a stop about a foot or so from the closed door. "Perhaps, some sightseeing." He looked over his shoulder, and Matt's body turned right around, too. "Some fresh air will do you good."

Matt was already there. Through the window, he saw black dots soar across the limitless skyline—crows, multiples of them. "But I can't leave…"

By the time he made eye contact, he only saw the man's stretched up hand which indicated a, 'Goodbye'. Then, he disappeared, followed by a click.

Alone. Nothing but the echoes of body movements beyond the door carried into Room 402.

Officer Grey slipped back in and left the door wide open. Unaware of her action, she made her way back to the window table. Matt watched the dozens of passersby, none of them snuck a peek; none of them seemed interested enough to bother.

Alone.

All Alone.

"Perhaps," that man's voice bounced around in his head, "some sightseeing. Some fresh air will do you good."

'A therapist…A motherfuckin' THERAPIST?!'

He laughed and laughed at that one. It startled Officer Grey.

30.

THE LAST DROPS trickled into a cup with steam. Dr. Brown lowered and removed the Styrofoam cup from the opening of the coffee vending machine.

"Heard you fainted."

Dr. Brown's entire body jolted from surprise and sent a few drops of freshly brewed coffee over the edge of his cup. The splish-splashes that landed on his hand made him wince. Immediately, as he sucked off the coffee dots, he marched away without a look behind him. The casually dressed male in line behind him stepped up to the vending machine.

"Well," Mr. Barry said, already at his side.

"It's none of your goddamn business, Clyde." He turned a corner and Mr. Barry followed. "I'm fine. In case, you're wondering. It's what you do best—*snoop*." He took a sip of his black coffee.

Another corner. Mr. Barry trampled a step or so behind him and picked up his pace. "That's bad for you," he said, with a tap on the Styrofoam cup.

"Damn it, Clyde!" Dr. Brown flinched and pulled his drink away. "I can let it go the first time." Another corner but now, Dr. Brown pinned his cousin against the wall. "But the third time will send this drink flying right at your goddamn face!"

Mr. Barry broke free with one simple arm jolt. He caressed his upper arm that scorched red. "I was just checking up on you. That's…"

The cup shook in place; the black coffee swished around. Mr. Barry glimpsed up at Dr. Brown, who kept his eyes down at his hand that continued to tremble. It forced Mr. Barry to lower his voice.

"Jonathan—"

"*Goddammit!*" Dr. Brown slam-dunked the coffee into a nearby trash bin. It caught the interest of a few passersby, who peered over their shoulders, as the cousins distanced further away from the chaos.

Mr. Barry stole a few looks at the curious and wide-eyed faces that remained nearby. Most of them were in a clear shot of eavesdropping. He cleared his throat, prepared for a speech, and then, a rattle sound snapped his attention back around.

Dr. Brown wiggled a white bottle side to side to pour something out onto his hand. And there it was again on the front side—the label with his name: Jonathan Brown. Before Mr. Barry could tell what it was; his cousin tossed his head back and covered his mouth. While he took some sort of medicine, Dr. Brown wormed the small bottle back into the front pocket of his coat. He winced in disgust, as he swallowed the pills dry. He took a moment for himself, his eyes closed, breathing steeply. It was baby steps onward for Mr. Barry, who watched his cousin's skinny hands fall into a slow rocky tempo. Then it all came to a stop—no more body shakes.

His eyes peeled open. Dr. Brown chafed the front pocket of his coat, which sat directly on the left side of his chest and clinched his heart. He turned a rosy color, both of his cheeks and eyes darkened.

"Jonathan," Mr. Barry almost whispered, tempted to move but he did not dare to do so.

Darker and darker, his eyes went bloodshot and deepened the red and purple veins beyond the pupils. "Don't," he gritted his teeth and tightened his jaw. "Just...Fuck off, Clyde." And he turned on his heel, toward the silver elevator doors that stood at the end of the hallway.

"He'd never hurt himself," it finally tussled out of Mr. Barry's mouth like a thick loogie. It got his cousin to stop in place again. "Nor would she—"

"Shut. Up." Dr. Brown whirled around and sprinted back to him. He snatched a hold of Barry's collar and dragged him pass a trash bin, where two double doors stood behind...

They burst through them and entered a storage room, where utensils and dishes were neatly packed and compressed into tiny boxes. Mr. Barry was thrust back against one of the compiled shelves. Dr. Brown towered over him...*oddly*...even if he was a lot shorter. For the first time, he never released his cop relative; if anything, he held on just a bit tighter. "What the *fuck* is with you?" His tone was low, but firm, to prevent any echoes or giveaways for anyone to check in the room. "You're such a fuckin'—"

"A psychoanalysis, Jonathan—really?"

"For fuck's sake, stop calling me that!" He released him and stepped aside, his back to him.

"Why? That is your name: Jonathan Brown. You're ashamed of who you are."

Dr. Brown's silence was enough, even when he turned back around, eye to eye with Mr. Barry.

"But most of all, you're so ashamed of who you'll become."

It was enough. The doc. trampled by and burst through the double doors that flew open. He elbowed his cousin in the shoulder. Mr. Barry flinched as soon as the doors slammed shut.

Dr. Brown ran down the hallway, as though his life depended on it. As he neared the elevators, he caught the slightest glimpse of his reflection on the silver door. For a moment, he only stared back at his reflection, intriguing but also terrifying, his hands wobbled again. He heaved for air.

On the right-side of the wall, the light panel with the floor numbers pinged to an orange-yellow color as it gave a ping. The doors opened wide. He barged into the elevator and his knees gave a jolt, sending him straight to the floor. Down he went, straight onto his knees, which blared to a dark red.

Gasping for air, his eyes watered up. Unable to rise, he tapped his long fingers against the cold tile floor of the elevator. Off another ping, the elevator doors started to close.

Through a vertical line from the smaller door opening, Mr. Barry moseyed out into the hallway. At a distance, they still found each other and locked eyes, as the elevator doors were closing. They realized that they were all alone, not a single soul in sight. The elevator doors closed.

31.

THE SUN TWIRLED; its radiance rained down on the fresh cut grass that turned greener by the instant. The crystal blue sky stretched on like an ocean of timeless thoughts and choices.

Matt gazed out the middle window of the room; his chair was nearly pressed against the wall. Officer Grey sat across from him at the table. She glanced every so often at the shaggy-haired boy. He had knots and waves that needed to be flattened out with a horse brush, or a water hose.

"I got it from here." Officer Franco entered the room with two cups of steamy coffee.

Officer Grey picked up her magazines—*Vogue* and *People*—and headed out. "Thank you," she said and took the coffee cup that he held out. He slipped into the chair across from Matt.

The sad faced, shaggy-haired boy's eyes never left the window. Focused, across his way were five windows atop each other, high above the ground.

"Hope you don't mind," Officer Franco disrupted his train collision of thoughts.

"Be my guest," Matt said without a look.

The five windows, high above the ground, belonged to the beige-brown apartment building.

Officer Franco blew at his coffee, and it swirled into small puddles, like windmills in the springtime. He slurped his coffee—a loud *slurrrrrrrrpppppppppp*.

Matt's Hershey colored eyes crawled over to his right-side. '*Son of a—*'

"Used to hate hospitals," Officer Franco said nonchalantly and *uninvitedly*. "Yeah. Used to have it really bad, actually. 'Nosocomephobia'. It's what my doc once told me, 'Fear of hospitals.'" He looked over his shoulder like the boogeyman was out to bite him. To settle his nerves, he brought his cup up.

Slurrrrrrrrppppppppp.

Officer Franco kept his attention on the right-side window. Matt, who winced at Franco's many *annoying* sound effects, flexed out his fingers that clammed up. "I'm sorry to hear," was all he said. His sincere tone even threw himself off, as he leaned back into his chair and crossed his arms. It was room temperature.

"It happens. Life is nothing but an assault. It messes with you and won't ever take the blame for it." Franco shrugged and took another sip of his coffee.

And there it was. That thing.

Matt moved in closer to the window, plastered with tiny air clouds from his breathing. He watched. On the far-left side of the apartment building, a white, milky, luminous glow of the sun blocked off window one.

Window two—to the right of window one—had a curtain halfway pulled down, exposing bits of color—reds, oranges, yellows, pinks, purples.

"Fucker." Matt bumped his nose against the window, and his air clouds formed into a big blob of white onto the glass for a moment before it cleared up.

"Whoa." Officer Franco coughed and nearly choked on his coffee. Before Matt gripped onto the arm of the chair, "Whoa, little man."

Matt squiggled to his feet, his face shot to red velvet, as he seized ahold of the edge of the table.

"Hey," Officer Franco pestered, "you don't look too well…"

He saw it! It spun like a spider's web in front of him, around and around. At a distance, quick flashes of light flickered right to left. Left to right. Matt staggered to the window.

"Grey!" Officer Franco stood up and rammed his knees underneath the table, directly on a piece of metal. It sent his coffee straight to the floor. *"Damn it!"*

Through the center window, he noticed the frilly pink walls across…

"Matt!"

Slowly, someone emerged from the white—window one—as the rotating light reflected into his eyes.

"AH!" Then, he saw for the first time—a short silhouette.

Riiiinnnnngggg…

It was back; his ears clogged up. Unable to hear his own cries, he covered his ears and watched the silhouette come to window one—*That night.*

He saw the flashes in his head—Jamie, Derek, Lisa, and that thing from *that night.* He watched his own reality unfold in front of him, just a few feet away—long curly hair and skin of a porcelain doll—a girl. It was a child, who looked no more than five or six years old. She just stood with her short, petite hands resting onto the glass of window one.

His legs jolted, and the window pulled away from him; forced by a greater and greater distance among them. Everything spun around, including the girl, who slanted left and right. Matt's eyes gave a few twitches, and his body tilted backward. Those black dots spotted out his vision—before the back of his head slammed onto the floor.

He felt body warmth instead of the cold tiles. Before he met with the chilled pitch black, he realized whose arms he was lying in.

32.

THE WHITE LINES elongated for miles and miles as the tires sped across the asphalt.

Derek and Lisa sat in the backseat, their bodies slouched toward their own windows, where miles of green zoomed by. Jamie had her eyes level to the floor as the car vibrated at fifty miles an hour. Those baby doll eyes of hers turned bluer than frostbite. Lucia peered away from the passenger seat, where Jamie sunk and then gazed out the window.

The elderly woman gripped onto the steering wheel, as her foot inched down onto the gas pedal. The speedometer arrow wiggled toward sixty in the forty-mile neighborhood zone.

"What do you mean we can't see him?!"

"Jamie." Lucia tugged her arm until she wiggled free.

"No! It took us thirty minutes—not to mention the traffic—to get here."

"Yeah." Derek and Lisa crossed their arms, along with Jamie.

Dr. Brown stared back at the three red, angry, small faces. He dabbed the corners of his face with his sleeve. Lucia swallowed whatever it was that seemed to constrict her throat—her fingers kept tightening, although they were already locked into balls of fury. Before she said anything, someone screamed, "Lucia!"

She spun around, and her eyes broadened with horror.

Mr. Barry rushed over, out of breath by the time he came to a halt. Those bug eyes of his also grew wider—black like an alert raccoon—when he saw Dr. Brown.

"Mr. Barry," the doc. said, and his eyes dilated, slowly.

"Dr. Brown…"

"*Well?*" Jamie tossed her arms down in exasperation.

"Honey," Lucia chimed in, her attempt to console worked somewhat. Jamie sighed and kept quiet—for now.

Mr. Barry glanced at the three shorter bodies. Everyone was still so tense, their shoulders touching their own earlobes. Passersby squeezed by in the lobby of the McArthur building, which prevented any sort of dead cricket silence among the angry visitors and a distressed doctor. A footstep here and there; a sneaker—tennis shoes. Even a few high heels clicked and clucked against the tile. Someone—a runner—collided into Jamie's left side.

"Owwe!"

"Sorry!" The voices echoed, lost in the crowd.

"You know," Dr. Brown began, rapidly, facing the three and Lucia, "why don't I go check and see if Matthew is taking any visitors right now." He looked at Mr. Barry, the Joker smile was plastered on his face. "Mr. Barry, I just remembered that your colleagues wanted me to get you—"

"For what?"

That invisible pinball smacked right back at him. Dr. Brown became flushed, as the rosiness in his cheeks dropped to white. "Why don't you four go check in," he said to them fast, a bit too fast, because he was already out of breath. "Mr. Barry and I have something to discuss." He reached for his arm at a vigilant pace. He pinched his fingernails—each one of them—into his cousin's flesh.

Mr. Barry flinched, but it was already too late to say anything or react, as Dr. Brown guided them further and further away.

He left the four perplexed faces, shrinking to the size of ants.

"So…" Derek looked afraid to ask. "We can see him? I'm confused!"

"So am I," Jamie agreed.

Around the corner, as soon as the closet door whacked shut and closed off any sign of light, and outside voices, Dr. Brown released his cousin. "Clyde, what the *fuck*!" He shoved him long and hard.

Mr. Barry grimaced as he slammed against the wall like a rag, inches from an overloaded, three-row shelf. He pressed two fingers onto the back of his head. There was a small bump, but no sign of blood.

"Just what in God's name are you thinking?!" Dr. Brown continued.

"Relax! I was just outside and—"

"Saw an opportunity." He stepped closer.

Face to face.

"You're not going to let them see him." Off his cousin's cold, rigid look, Mr. Barry broke focus and gazed off; his eyes dropped to the floor. The floor was dark, like a black hole. "Thank God Meemaw isn't—"

Dr. Brown whipped around—his lab coat made a sound—his fingers swerved through his salt and pepper hair. His hair became tussled, as he gripped a few pieces at its roots.

"…the monster you've become," Mr. Barry spat out.

"And may *God* rest her soul!" The tears engorged his eyes, and he pushed his fingers against them; his eyes remained puffy pink, by the time he had looked his cousin back in the eye. "*Fuck. You.*"

The doc. flung open the supply closet door and barged out. The door remained ajar, and the fluorescent lighting from the hallway trickled against Mr. Barry's face.

Still. Very still.

Mr. Barry was only able to move an inch. He kept his back against one of the many shelves piled with the opened and unopened supplies: tissues, wipes, and bedpans. Darkness held the rest of his body captive. For some reason, he panted heavily and jerked further back into the shadows. He fumbled through the interior of his coat. Then he brought a portion of the plastic cover—almost like a sandwich baggie—into the light.

It was a copy of an article. Due to its rich ice-white paper, every word appeared readable.

Mr. Barry brought the top portion into the light. An evidence bag…

The New York Times

A tragedy in a family…

For the Smith family, it was a day that would infamously be remembered until the end of time. On the night of August 4th, 1992, sixty-two-year-old, LUCIA SMITH, had received the worse news of her life, involving the whereabouts of her husband of forty-three years, FRANK, and their only child, JIMMY. The incident that had changed their lives forever.

33.

TWO BULGY EYES watched as Nurse Olive set a lunch meal atop the bedside tray. Matt wiggled up in bed, his lips around the tip of a straw. He sucked in the water from a plastic cup. The mix of water and sugar entered his blood system—his very own drug, as his eyes widened for a few moments.

Deadbeat.

His body was tender, like uncooked meat. Even his lips puckered, as he slurped in the last water drops. He reopened his eyes: those same two bulgy eyes, plus Nurse Olive's, were still on him. They stood around the bed, stiff as a rock, as if ready to recruit him into a cult of some sort. All they needed was a pair of matching robes with a cape.

Cape.

Something funny punched him in the gut. By the look that crept onto Jamie's face, he knew it was time for a plan. So, he smirked, but the center of his bottom lip cracked open with red.

"Ugh…*Gross!*" Derek peered away for a moment and gagged.

Nurse Olive dug out a tissue from the large abdomen pocket across the front side of her T-shirt scrub. It was a chain of effects, as she passed it over—slow motion—until it landed in her hands. Being Lucia, she took a moment, her eyes locked with his grandson's. Matt grimaced, as he reached over and yanked the tissue from her. It got a small gasp from her.

Immediately, she hurried over to the right-side window, adjacent from the cup of coffee on the empty table. The coffee steam evaporated into thin layers in the air.

Derek and Lisa turned their attention away from Lucia and looked to Jamie, who already narrowed her eyes to the floor. Neither of them would speak nor address it.

They were already lost in their own trance.

Nurse Olive picked up the tray with scraps of leftovers from the window table, where the morning's meal of gooey oatmeal, a cup of watered-down fruit, and a crushed-up orange juice box sat. She peered at Lucia, who only gazed out the window. Those dark chocolate, brownie eyes of hers looked grayer than her own hair, as she gave another sniffle.

Nurse Olive headed for the door, without another glimpse over her shoulder.

Matt pulled out the utensils from its plastic wrapper and then stabbed the fork into the middle of the chicken breast on his tray. A small amount of liquid gushed out of the deceased animal. Its juice circled around the plastic plate and mixed with the buttered toast and neighboring steamed vegetables.

Lucia wiped away the tear that squeezed out of her eye and rolled down her cheek. She set her hand on the window and toward the glass. All that was visible to her was mania. Four levels below Room 402 was a swarm of frenzy bodies. Arms aimed at cameras, and hands waved around microphones at the moving burly man.

Mr. Barry avoided any eye contact with the brown-nosers: the press. He sandwiched between Officer Grey and Officer Hanson, until they had reached his parked vehicle in the lot. The officers flagged up their hands and asserted, "No comment," at the hungry-eyed reporters and their damn camera equipment.

"We have the right to know!" a woman reporter demanded.

Grey and Hanson, somehow and thankfully, got Mr. Barry safe and sound into the police cruiser. They were the ones to slam the door shut as soon as he slipped right in.

A beep echoed through the parked police cruiser once the doors locked. Mr. Barry removed his fingers from the lock panel on the driver's door. He watched the security's hustle and bustle: their attempt to get the crowd to back up (Or, "BACK THE FUCK UP" from a few of them). Hopeful, he started the cruiser up and somehow, his two colleagues—screaming at the top of their lungs—got the crowd to back the fuck up. They must have because an aisle formed for him. He made sure to get the *hell* out of there.

Tires screeched, until he reached the street and sped off into the soon to be dark night.

"My God…" Ms. Castellanos removed her sunglasses, "…they're just everywhere."

"Come on," Mrs. Peralta said, with a squeeze on her husband's hands. Then Mrs. Santoso clasped her husband by the arm, as the five of them headed off.

"*Move!*" Mrs. Santoso snapped, as they squeezed through the crowd.

Three sets of high heels and two pairs of shined dress shoes clicked away from the asphalt and onto the curb. The chaos turned crazier as—one by one—the reporters chased down Mr. Barry—a pathetic attempt, since most of them stopped to gasp for air or get into their vehicles. They realized walking on foot was a bad, *bad* idea. As for the rest, once one of them recognized the faces of the five adults heading for the hospital entrance, they were targeted. The camera lights went back on and microphones were raised up again.

"*Hey!*" Ms. Castellanos retrieved the string of balloons from a greedy bastard, just in time, before the sliding glass doors shut. A few security guards and police officers ran outside.

"BACK UP!" one of them ordered.

34.

IT MOVED AROUND IN SWIRLS.

The crystal blue water stretched out, waving around, translucent from the sun beating down on it. A round-faced boy with rosy cheeks bounced on the diving board. "'The wheels on the bus go 'round and 'round, 'round and 'round, 'round and 'round.'" He hopped closer to the edge. "'The wheels on the bus go 'round and 'round, all through the town.'"

Young Matt took in a breath of air: his cheeks puffed out. With his nose plugged, he pressed down hard onto his feet—cannonball position.

That light brown hair of his and Power Rangers trunks flared up, as he soared into the air. Body into the water. Red into blue.

Streams of tiny bubbles escaped his nostrils and surfaced, as he sank further into the deep end of the pool.

He glided down to the bottom of the swimming pool and looked up. The sun twinkled at him from above the water.

* * *

Matt opened his eyes to the darkened room. Through the three windows, glimmered the slightest glimpse of a crescent moon. He peered to his left side—at the window table—where Officer Grey rested upon her arms. Her small kitten purrs were audible to him. Sound asleep.

Then he realized how the green fluorescent light above his bed only captured bits and pieces of himself and the bed in its color. He sniffled and wiggled back down onto the mattress and snuggled up against the solid white pillow. That was when he felt something warm against his cheek, and he flinched.

Their blotches trailed from the corner of the pillowcase to the bedspread in front of it. Matt elevated himself an inch or so for a closer examination to find large and diminutive blobs, circles. He reached out and skimmed his fingers against them—soggy. Beyond the sleep crusts, something else was itching his eyes. He sniffled again, and a lukewarm string dribbled out. He used his fingertips to smudge away the sticky goo that piled above his lip.

A mushy booger sat atop his finger. The sensation grew stronger, as the tears burned down into streams along his cheeks.

'*I was crying in my sleep*,' he thought to himself.

"Matty. Matty…"

The room shone too brightly. The sunlight hovered over that familiar face, like a halo.

"Jamie?"

"Hi." She sat on the edge of the bed and held his hands. Something strong already watered up her eyes. She was hesitant to speak.

"What is it?" he asked and reached for her cheek. "Tell me." And then it dawned on him. It took one scan around the room.

Three windows and an empty table.

He scooted himself up, his eyes engorged with whatever thickened the lump in his throat. Jamie gave his hand a squeeze, probably unaware of her natural reaction, as her complexion evolved to pink. "They're interviewing," it escaped her mouth in a mouse whisper, "all of us."

"What? I thought we were supposed to avoid…They're supposed to keep those goddamn reporters away from us—"

She closed her eyes, and the slightest air hissed through her parted lips.

"They don't believe us?"

"No," she defended, "that's not what I meant."

"Well, they must have a reason," he retorted. "Otherwise, why interrogate the goddamn survivors?!" He needed a breather, but he remained red, blood red. He fumbled for the remote attached to the bed and clicked the nurse assistance button.

"Matty?" The wariness took over Jamie.

Buzzzzzzz....

"What the fu…Why isn't anyone coming in already?!" He clicked and clicked away.

Buzz. Buzz. Buzz.

"*Matt*!"

BUZZ. BUZZ. BUZZ—

"Hey!" he shouted at the ajar door. "*Hello*! I'm trying to get your help you fu—"

Jamie snatched a hold of the remote and put a stop to that stupid buzzing.

"Could you at least, go get someone," he demanded. "I'd like to enjoy one meal, before I start getting accused AGAIN of being a socalled liar—"

"My mom's downstairs." She sounded so monotone, but still appeared grief-stricken, as if a good cry would happen *now*, but it did not. "I'll be back."

It started at the nose and spread across his cheeks, before it hit his eyes and turned them red, too.

"Matty?"

It was in her eyes.

They both felt it.

First, it was him, until she pushed right into him and compressed their lips for one slippery, sticky hot kiss. His hands tussled through her hair. She pressed in further and enclosed any heat that was to possibly escape out into the open. But as soon as they pulled away—she was the first one—he saw a look of disappointment on her. She remained close to him—no attempt to move. He kept his hand on the back of her head, so their foreheads touched. Those baby doll eyes of hers were no longer in his sight. They gazed down at the mattress, still trying to catch her breath...for once.

"You know," he panted, "I care about you. *A lot*."

It got them to inch apart to see each other. He brushed a fallen strand of hair behind her ear. That got to her, and she broke out into soft kitten sobs.

"You were there that night, Jamie—"

"I know...I know..."

"But I don't blame you." He brushed away her fallen tears, "As long as we know what had happened...the truth...it'll all fall into place."

"Matty?"

But he hauled in closer and held onto her tighter. Her arms formed an X around his bony back, as she buried her nose into his skeletal shoulder. He kissed her cheek; his bottom lip trembled from the coldness that took over his system.

"I don't know what to do," she wept. "What do I say? They're almost making us put on some act."

"I don't know," it was all he repeated. "I don't know..."

* * *

The car was parked against the curb. Her hands fumbled, as the key wiggled backward. Somehow, it made it out of the ignition. Lucia leaned toward the driver's window, as she clenched onto the dark beige steering wheel. The sun shot right at her, highlighting her eyes, her red eyes. It was obvious that she had been—was still—crying.

Almost in unison, men and women in navy blue carried pieces of the house: small to big, short to tall, circular to square, down the stone staircase. Others became gulped up whole once they stepped into the roaming darkness of the premises, the Smith residence.

Lucia winced as her trimmed manicured fingernails stabbed the top of the steering wheel. Police officers carried out plastic baggies that contained any sort of evidence: a picture frame, pieces of glass, and paperwork or articles of clothing.

Lucia reached for the door and gasped once her fingers came into contact with the silver handle. Her head drooped forward. She ran her fingers through her hair; strands of it only turned grayer, as every part of her ripped into emotions. Tears showered down her very green complexion. She covered her mouth to prevent any sort of escape. Her skin crawled with raw tenderness, as she sank lower and lower in the driver's seat, as if into a bottomless, black pit.

Out of sight.

The job never came to an end across the street. Plastic baggies were opened. Objects were being removed from their plastic protector. The yellow caution tape was yanked down from the front yard and no longer circled around the Smith residence. Officer Samuels and Hanson worked as a team and rolled-up the police tape, from opposite ends. Both were glum and blue, like a blizzard.

Mr. Barry and his colleagues ascended the stone staircase. Somewhere, during his busy day—*so far*—he peered over his shoulder.

The gray Honda Accord sat—remained—beneath the lamppost, about forty yards away from the premises. The only visibilities were the leaves that danced with the wind; their pigments of reds, oranges, yellows, and greens reflected through the crystal-clear car windows. The trees and flowers also waved in sweet harmony with the chirping birds.

No sign of Lucia.

With his hands buried in his pockets, Mr. Barry gave one last dry sigh before he turned away and led his party into the dark residence.

35.

"...THE 'LUCKY ONES' OR WHAT OTHERS have come to know as the Four Angels who were saved from above...'"

It played on the semi-flat screen: footage of the entrances and exits into and out of the Smith residence, and the curious and googly-eyed faces unable to bypass police officers, who ordered everyone to remain back. It was all on an endless loop—wish wash, wish wash. 'Round and round...and round their life was like a *damn* washing machine.

That pretty-faced woman, with a tight little bod. Centered on the television screen, boobs—tucked under a black blazer—probably would have screamed, 'Tits', if tits could talk. The microphone hovered inches from her mouth, as she addressed the camera with poise and confidence. "...This is Sharon Melendez. Channel 17. WLAX News."

The television screen faded to black.

Jamie lowered her arm and the remote plopped down onto the cushion beside her—an empty red seat. Derek looked at Lisa, curled up in a blanket. They were seated across from their dear-dear-dear-DEAR friend. Jamie gazed off into nothingness, her eyes down at her bare feet. Today, she had on a pair of black Converse high tops. She eyed the pair of low tops and flip-flops that sat seamlessly with each other on the short-haired, porcelain carpet in the dining room entryway. It looked awkward—just a small square of carpet and tile everywhere else. Every inch of that piece of carpet was spotless, and perfect—a perfect, spotless clean, little carpet. At least, that was what her furrowed brow appeared to scream.

"Jamie?"

It was too late. The remote was already midair and went directly to the flat screen television that cracked at the bottom. Jamie jumped to her feet and pierced the entire room with her screams. She shoved the couch back, lifted and chucked the matching cushions across the room. Picture frames dropped, snapped, and burst into pieces; random objects were chucked their way. And those windows, the glass was clearer than the fine sheer white curtains, guarded behind a set of cream-colored silk ones. Ugh, two curtains.

"Fuck! Fuck! FUCK!"

Jamie dropped to her knees, her hands clenched into fists, as she bawled out every bit of energy from her system. She tipped sideways and rammed into the brown leg of the tattered couch. Derek kept ahold of Lisa, who wept into the blanket that elongated down to the floor like the train of a Met Gala dress. There was a tear in the cotton blanket, up until the middle, and strings of royal red swung sideways.

Utter silence.

"It'll kill him." Jamie hiccupped and finally looked up at them. "Seeing how she truly is. She's not…"

"I know," Derek said; it jarred the girls. "I know when I'm seeing it. She has a problem."

"A big *one*," Lisa disrupted and straightened herself up, bringing her knees to the bottom of her chin. "We'll have to tell him."

"I know," Jamie whispered.

Bam!

They jumped and whirled around, toward the bookshelf.

A vase shattered onto the floor and the marbles from inside rolled across the white tile floor, their aquamarine color shaped like teardrops. The marbles stopped at Jamie's feet. She backed away, affected by their silky coldness, as though touched by the plague. Her breathing grew steep, like a daily smoker in their later life…if they ever made it. It made her cough; she ascended to her feet. Petrified, her eyes were bolder than ever. She grimaced to prevent tears.

"I'm so…tired," was all she said.

Then the sound of an engine roared close to the house. She inhaled some air but never quite exhaled to breathe. In fact, none of them could breathe. They were all too tense, unable to remain seated. Lisa dropped the blanket to the floor, adding it to the rest of the mess. It was only seconds before soft echoes of their voices carried from the outside world and into the room.

Jamie shivered, as the tears poured out and cascaded down her face. She plopped back down onto the floor. Derek dipped into the white leather chair, adjacent to the couch, his eyes broadened with horror. Lisa was motionless, on her feet, unsure where to go and what to do. She cried out; her shoulders slouched.

She stared at the only unbroken, untouched object in the family room—a medium built, porcelain elephant with its feet pressed firmly onto the table, glass table, somehow in great condition. Still in its original spot, the table stood between the leather couch and red striped chair. The door was being unlocked.

The first reaction was, "Oh my—"

"GOD!" Mrs. Peralta interjected.

"JAMIE!" Ms. Castellanos screamed at the top of her lungs.

36.

THE WATER POURED DOWN, and every muscle and particle of him relaxed.

The drip drops skimmed across his pale skin and down his stubbly thighs, legs, and feet. The warmth of the water hugged his naked body like saran wrap. He tensed as soon as the water traveled down his spinal cord, giving him goosebumps. It was strange: his reaction forced him to open his eyes. He looked up at the showerhead. The tiny holes, where the water leaked out, held his attention, until he shut his eyes again; everything around him turned white like Christmas snow.

* * *

"Um, isn't that a bit too much?" Lisa muttered. She was on the verge of barfing. Even with her hand pressed over mouth, she still gagged, and it made her body jolt.

Derek picked up his masterpiece—peanut butter, grape jelly, Hershey's' chocolate and strawberry syrup, and colorful sprinkles slammed between two pieces of Wonder Bread. "Hush down woman." The strawberry syrup gooed out into thick strings from the bottom of the sandwich.

"You're so shitting your pants later," Jamie said and backed up her chair from the kitchen table.

* * *

His eyes reopened; the red and purple veins broadened. He glimpsed around the shower. Empty. But the wary look on him said differently. He sensed something. *Someone* was in there with him. He covered himself up, his hands wrapped around his chest.

* * *

"You love me! You love me!" After his chants, Derek grabbed her by the face and planted one big ol' kiss on her cheek.

"EW!" Jamie backed away, her eyes livid and wild. "What the HELL, you MIDGET!"

Lisa spun a toy rattle in her hand, her cheeks puffed out as she wrapped her lips around the tip of another noisemaker. "All right!" she hollered in between whistles.

Matt stood across from them at the dining table, decked out with purple and pink confetti dots. He only had eyes for one of them there.

"Happy birthday, Jamie," he said and brought the disposable camera up to his eye.

Click. Click.

The flash was blinding, but it had still captured his friends' pearly whites, except Derek, who had his head tossed back, his lips parted in a frozen 'Muhaha'.

* * *

Stuck or it seemed that way, steam shot up from the white checkered floor-mat in the shower. Matt winced, as the water splattered onto his back—*pained*, as he stuffed away his own reaction to the hotter water. He turned redder and redder, on the verge of another blow-up. But his hand was on the lever, turning it up and up. Purposely making the water *hotter*.

SPLAT. SPLAT.

* * *

Fast and faster.

Matt.

His itty bitty Velcro's lit up, as they hit the floor. His small round face plastered back with a tense look. He panted for air, and his eyes were already bigger than a rat's. He veered to a stop, upon reaching the bathroom door.

Underneath the door—through a thin crack—gusts of white streaked out into the hallway and went toward him.

* * *

'What am I doing?'

An awakening. Matt balked away from the hot water until he retrieved back and fumbled to turn the lever down. Instead, he moved it up.

"ARGH!"

He cradled against the corner. His back was redder than blood. He pressed up against the tile wall and caught his breath.

"Stupid." He slapped the side of his face. "Fuckin' idiot! What the fuck were you THINKING?"

He was on the go—SLAP SLAP: right cheek, left cheek, right, left, right, left, right-right-right, and left-left-left.

By the time he stopped, he was breathing heavily. He clutched his chest and hunched forward. His entire body moved in sync with his gasps. It pushed him to slide down onto his bottom. His breathing slowed down. Black dots spotted out his vision again, until he blinked and reopened his eyes.

The thick steam from the water floated around him.

* * *

The doorknob—not locked. Young Matt barged into nothing but a storm of clouds that fluttered around the bathroom like ghosts. He trudged forward and the steam parted ways by his touch like a safari team making their way through a rainforest.

* * *

It all bundled up again.

Matt coughed, to clear whatever closed-up his throat and nearly choked him to death. Not frightened but pained, he slammed his hands over his mouth and his entire body trembled, as he was gulping and gasping for air.

Then he bit down on his hand—harder and harder—as the tears welled up his eyes. Tasting his own blood.

"Fuuuuuuuu…"

It was all flashes and present…flashes and present, from there on.

* * *

As his touch reached out, the last cloud drifted away. He screeched to a halt.

Lucia stood underneath the running hot water; steam floated around the edges of the bathtub and splattered onto her naked scrawny body. Her complexion turned hardcore red. She only stared at him momentarily, until the blade slipped out of her fingers.

It slammed onto the white tile with the first drops of blood, which matched Matt's spiky hair color. "GRANDMA!" he wailed.

"Sorry," was all she said before her eyes rolled back and her body dropped.

Matt raced over.

Everything from her waist down remained in the tub, while the other half of her slouched over the edge, because he held her. "Grandma? Grandma?!"

But her eyes remained shut. Thin lines of red swirled with the last bits of water drops that were swallowed up by the shower drain. Matt used all his mighty strength and formed an X across her back and gave a big tug,

Nothing.

His complexion shot to scarlet as he went to plan B and grabbed her arms. But before he even gave a tug, he saw the splice on her inner arm, just inches above her elbow. It gashed open.

The red sea poured out, ran down her hand and fingertips, and dribbled down onto the bathmat outside of the shower. Bits of it splashed onto him.

Matt stumbled backward, releasing her, and screamed, "GRANDMA!"

* * *

"...cccccccckkkkkkkk!" *It* burned through his chest and paralyzed him into a silent scream, as he landed on his hands and sobbed uncontrollably.

"Matt?!" *It* echoed beyond the locked door, followed by more knocks—

POUND. POUND.

"Matt!" Now that was a different voice.

Through the incisive door knocks, pounds—someone even jiggled the handle—Matt stretched his fingers out, toward the steamy water that circled the drainage. But all he saw and heard was his red spiky-haired self.

* * *

"Grandma!"

"GRAndMA!"

"GRANDMA!"

* * *

Everything tilted.

First, the shower faucet and then, the shower curtain stretched in and out. His body grew feeble, and he dropped forward. The shower drain got closer to his face.

BLACK.

37.

NURSE OLIVE'S LIPS MOVED as she took out a white bandage and placed it on the rim of his nose, he heard nothing except for the slightest riiiiiiing that spiraled down into his ears.

A man in a light gray sweater and black slacks was escorted into the room by Dr. Brown, who pulled up a chair for him beside the bed. Matt looked like a deer in headlights something looked familiar about the man, the *shrink*. Matt never gazed away from the shrink, who suddenly morphed from his normal size to big…then small like an ant…and big…and small…and big…and small.

"Better?" It echoed through the gunk that clogged up his ears. But it was only Nurse Olive, who adjusted his pillow.

Matt bobbed his head. She gave a sweet smile, but beyond her eyes, he saw early signs of tears.

Nurse Olive handed him some sort of clicker attached to another baggie with liquid on the IV rack beside him— medicine for the pain. She walked out with her silver clipboard tucked underneath her arm.

* * *

Tick. Tick. TICK.

Matt pressed the top of the clicker and it made a bubbly sound in the new IV plastic baggie beside him. The liquid shot through his IV and into his system. It relaxed him—a lot. The shrink was in the same spot as earlier, with the same straight posture; the same pointer finger rested against his *same* stubbly chin. "…Perhaps," he started, so monotone that Matt's eyes closed for an instant and flipped to the front page of the *same* 8x10 sheet of paper resting on his lap, "this is a good place to stop for today."

Matt wiggled his finger in his ears—one by one—as he brought a cup of ice water to his lips. The man slipped the yellow paperwork booklet—pages compiled with notes—into the brown briefcase that sat at his feet. Matt tilted backward and backward, as he slurped up the last drops of water from the plastic cup. Visible through the bottom of the clear plastic cup stood the man, Mr. Shrink, who removed his rectangular glasses.

They stared at each other. Neither one of them wanted to *address it*.

Mr. Shrink pinched the top of his nose and it boosted up his courageous next move, "Whatever it was earlier…" It was difficult; he cleared his throat, clearly not wanting to impose or, perhaps, offend him. "It's gone now. I just want you to know that. As I was saying earlier Matt, these flashbacks, as you called them, were just—"

"Suppressed childhood trauma." With his head leveled back down onto the pillow, the cup no longer at his lips, he crunched down onto the ice. He had a lifeless—not a care for the world—tone. "I heard you after the *fiftieth* time."

It soared across the room—his arms abandoned in a semi-basketball stance that made him wince—until the plastic cup landed in front of the empty window table, inches from the nearby trash bin.

"Shit," he grunted.

Mr. Shrink stood on his feet and kept a tight grip on the handle of his briefcase. He waited calmly, as Matt slipped back down onto the mattress. Instead, Matt gazed up at the swarms of itty bitty dots on the ceiling. The dots zoomed in and out, as he closed one eye, then the other, switching back and forth like a game. It made the fluorescent light go from a clear to a hazy focus: white to off-white and white to yellow.

At the doorway now, Mr. Shrink glanced over his shoulder. Even at a distance, Matt—*his client*—appeared gaunter and malnourished, due to his healing injuries, both new and old.

"Excuse me, Mr. Peterson." Nurse Olive and her colleague approached.

The shrink, Mr. Peterson stepped aside for the nurses' entrance into Room 402. The nurses parted ways and headed off onto the opposite sides of the bed. Nurse Olive spoke to Matt—all inaudible to Mr. Peterson, who remained in the doorway—as she switched out both clear baggies on the IV rack. In the meantime, her colleague, who was smaller and terrified, struggled to keep up. She was the new owner of the silver clipboard and scribbled away on one of the pages. Wherever Nurse Olive went, the trainee nurse remained close behind.

It was all a blur for Matt, and he could not care any less since he kept his chin and eyes facing the ceiling. It was not too long before he sat up, which caught the nurses off guard. The newbie even dropped the clipboard. There it was again—the slightest flicker reflected off the ceiling.

Unlike the other times, Matt caught glimpses of a rainbow in each flicker. It was a sign. Obviously, the reflector came from a mirror—a magnifying glass against hot cement. Someone was behind it. Someone wanted his attention, and they had it.

38.

IT WAS BEAUTIFUL, wherever he was. Something gentle, soft, like cotton, stroked against his skin, tickled his cheek. He was afloat, amid some sort of brightness and glided up and up into the cotton ball clouds. The sky shone as radiant as Christmas snowflake's reflective lights.

"Oh! Yes of course," It said.

Matt looked around. The voice echoed around him—his own Darth Vader. He came to a stop, but not by choice. Something clutched his ankles and pulled him out of the new world…away from the spinning white that grew farther and farther away from his reach.

* * *

Matt's eyes peeled open. Over his bed, over him, hovered the outline of bones.

Thump. Thump.

His palms clammed up. His toes curled inward, and nails pressed into his skin. He clenched his eyes shut and blinked hard. His breathing grew thicker, as if mucus got stuck at the bottom of his throat.

"It was a cut—"

There it was…*that voice…*

"Not as deep as they'd thought," *It* continued. "But he's bandaged up…again…"

And through the spots of blurriness, when he became brave enough to fully open his eyes, he saw her…his grandmother. "Yeah," she croaked, "I'm fine." She sniffled and dabbed at her eyes with her sleeve; the tears stuck to her chin like unwanted whiskers or as she referred to them, chin hairs. "No need to…"

He, his overachiever, her teacher's pet, watched her. She paced back and forth—back and forth—among the windows, until she made a pit stop at the center window. Lucia never faced him—just her back. He straightened out his neck to align it with his stiff spinal cord and head. Everything about him, from head to toe, grew heavier than a bird without its wings...headed for a downfall.

Plop. Plop. Plop.

DING DONG the birds are dead because they landed straight down on their head.

"...It should've been me," Lucia whispered and broke out into soft kitten sobs. "I just don't know what to do anymore..."

His hands slid across the bed. The television static—his imagination—fuzzed out all textures and living colors in the room. Almost there. He held onto the nurse assistance remote, and his finger in takeoff mode pushed the button.

Beep.

Not once but twice. And down-down-down he went...the bottomless black pit of his abyss.

Beep. Beep.

Down...down...the...dark...hole...

"You've got to eat," Mrs. Peralta said from the bedroom doorway.

The upper half of Lisa dangled off the bed, her eyes on the wooden floor. "No thanks," she mumbled. "I'm not hungry."

"Come on," Mr. Peralta whispered into his wife's ear and took her by the hand. "Let her be."

The sunshine-yellow comforter only made Lisa gloomier. She tilted onto her side once the bedroom door shut. She stared at the miniature collage—of their friendship—the four of them. At the top, right-hand corner, in purple and pink gel pen writing, read: **Merry Christmas chicken butt!!! Luv, Jamie!!!**

Down…down…the…dark…hole…

"Come on, Derek." Mr. Santoso waved around an Xbox controller at the family room doorway. The movement awakened the television set with a loud noise and all sorts of colorful 3D graphics bubbled up to the screen. "It's your favorite game."

Derek played with his food—a child beyond the grossed-out stage. His paper plate of McDonald's—chicken nuggets, French fries, and a glob of ranch and ketchup—was untouched. Even water circled the bottom of a cup of melting Oreo McFlurry on the kitchen countertop. Mrs. Santoso only watched her son. "How about a movie," she suggested from the kitchen sink.

But he already rose to his feet. Derek rounded the corner of the doorway and dispersed into the darkness of the living room. Mr. Peralta sighed and tossed the Xbox controller onto the dining room table. His wife strolled to his side, her eyes swollen from the tears, and wrapped her arms around his chest. Then he held onto her, too, wrapping his hand around her wrist.

Down…down…the…dark…hole…

"I just miss him." Jamie hugged her teddy bear, curled up in her mother's lap, as her feet dangled from the pink bedspread. "I just really…" The blood rushed to her cheeks and then to her eyes.

"Shh," her mother whispered a soft sailing and tightened her arms around her. Jamie snuggled in closer and buried her nose into her mother's abdomen. Ms. Castellanos pressed her lips to the back of her daughter's head for the longest time. "I know, baby. I know you do."

Everything collapsed within Jamie, as she trembled and failed to hiccup or suck back her new reality.

"It's okay, baby," her mother said. "Let it all out."

Jamie flung up and fell into her mother's arms. She burst into tears that thickened her breathing. The light brown teddy bear slipped out of her arms and drifted to the wooden floor.

Mr. Bear's arms were shorter and chubbier than his legs. He landed on his cotton ball tail.

Down…down…the…dark…hole.

"*Ouch,*" Matt groused. Now, he stood alone in the room. The moonlight glimmered outside. With his eyes squeezed shut, he wiggled around like an earthworm under the hot sun. The downpour of sweat ran down his face, chest, and legs, as his eyes shot wide open.

"OWW!"

It was a second-nature instinct and an expected reaction as he bit down on his tongue and a pool of lukewarm liquid fumed at the corners of his mouth, red, so red. It shot by quick—a million miles of shooting stars—that night. The second night…encounter…with the stranger.

* * *

Darkness spat him out. Matt smacked flat onto his stomach, in front of the stone staircase, in front of his house.

Home.

POP. POP.

WHOOSH. WHOOSH. WHOOSH.

Night vision mode, he saw them but by the looks of it, they could not see him. Jamie, Derek, and Lisa crammed together in the middle of the living room. Jamie reached for the first step, but the breeze came at them with full throttle force—'That night.'

It played out every detail for him. His friends' falls. Their sliced-up lips. Blood. More blood.

"NO!" Jamie screamed out with all her strength.

Now, he saw from a new perspective: from high above was a black T-shirt and gray gym shorts that were stained with a pizza color.

Held hostage. A hand grip…Yellow fingers. It was him…him…HIM.

A prowler in the shadows, and invisible to his friends. No matter how loud he called out for them, he watched his past-self failing to break free from the grip of the stranger.

"Let me go, please. Just put me down!"

Matt remained a fly on the wall, until he faced whoever accompanied him that night. He stared directly into the eyes of his past-self. As one of the many firework explosions painted the walls with its shadows, his past-self grew fierce with one foot over-the-top step of the staircase.

"Wait!"

A strong force poured into his current fly on the wall self and forced him to reenact experiences. Matt was back, present at that night. But he was not himself.

He was the stranger.

Matt reached out and grabbed his past-self's T-shirt; Angus Young crinkled up. Now.

Matt's fingers scrapped through Angus and his guitar and against past Matt's skin. "NO!"

He watched his doppelgänger travel down and down.

"MATTY!" Jamie lamented, as the sirens whirled closer from outside.

And then.

Matt felt something brush against his neck. He glanced over his shoulder and stared back into the two black circles…concaved…eaten out…that were once eyes. The stranger was a stranger staring back at him, as if he saw his reflection in the mirror. Tables turned once again when Matt became the helpless one. "ARGH!"

Reliving it…all of it. His body grew feeble and heavy; his head spasmed left to right…right to left. He was back in his AC/DC T-shirt that elongated forward…toward the stranger, who gripped tighter and tighter.

The stranger was, in fact, pulling him upward. To prevent the fall. Trying to help him—only, Matt saw it differently.

The thick fog surrounded them, like farm dust, and blocked out all surrounding objects. Matt screamed and winced away as soon as the stranger's claws dug into his chest with those skeletal finger bones. The sharp pain electrocuted throughout his entire body, as he watched the two black circles, concaved eyes, poke through the flaps of the hoodie.

The stranger's face looked ashen, like the mask of a gladiator. They gaped right at him, a moment of contact, until their olive shaped pupils—no longer charcoal or eaten away—shot wide open. Terror. They accidentally lost grip of Matt.

Everything spotted to black and white, starting with the walls and firework's shadows, as three sets of feet and hands and voices trampled closer his way…His friends. Free falling, Matt saw the stranger getting consumed by the darkness.

…and up…up…the…bright…light, he went…

* * *

Matt gasped for air and flung up. Everything crept into focus. He flipped over onto his side and two sets of cold hands gripped down onto his arms. He screamed and coiled around, toward the windows.

"Honey! Honey! It's ME!"

Lucia then focused in through his eyesight. She leaned over, her worried and tired, baggy eyes locked with his bloodshot ones. "It's just me," she reassured in a whisper.

"I remember," he panted. "I saw…I saw THEM!" Frantically, his eyes shot around the room.

"Honey…Honey!" Lucia lunged just as he tussled off the bed, "*Nurse!*"

But his eyes twitched and rolled back to a possession of white. His limbs and muscles turned into noodles, sending his body to the floor. He collapsed into his grandmother's long-sleeve covered arm, just inches above her elbow, where the splice would be on her inner arm. She slammed onto her bottom—hard—and caught him in time. On her shoulder, lay his head, unconscious.

"Someone HELP!" she wailed.

39.

THERE WERE SNIFFLES AND TEARS.

"What…What happened?" Matt's eyes twitched open, and closed, then opened again.

Brightness seeped through the three windows. It formed a glow around Lucia, as she lowered and pressed her lips to his cheek. Her tears fell onto him—his own sprinkles of rain.

"Grandma…What's going on?" he asked, groggy.

Outside was a different story: "Let us see him."

"Jamie—"

"NOW."

Ms. Castellanos grabbed Jamie by the arm and hauled her toward the curb before her daughter knocked over the cup of steamy coffee in the security guard's hand.

In Room 402, Lucia covered her mouth and broke down into heavier, husky sobs. His eyes remained opened, filled with wariness. "Grandma…"

A machine whirled off.

Nurse Olive and two other nurses rushed to the bed. One went to silence the machine. The other ran to Lucia's side. Nurse Olive set her hands atop Matt's. "It's okay, sweetie," she said.

On cue, Dr. Brown came in sight. He approached Lucia and rested a hand on her shoulder. For some reason, it forced her to close her eyes; she turned away and followed him out. He guided her away, completely out of sight.

"Grandma!"

"*Please*," Nurse Olive implored with her hands on his chest, so he would lay back down.

Matt listened to the beat of his heart. As though an ear was compressed to a stereo speaker, the vibrations thunderstruck throughout his fingers and then, his body. His breathing grew steep. He fumbled ahold of Nurse Oliver's arm, and her eyes bulged with terror.

"Dr. Brown," she said softly, an attempt to remain calm.

Thump…Thump…Thump…

The reek of his own sweat, a lukewarm sensation, burned his eyes and at the pit of his stomach. His brittle, chapped lips cracked down the middle with blood as he wailed, "GRANDMA!"

In the hallway, Lucia skid to a halt and spun around. She dashed back the other way,

"Mrs. Smith!" Dr. Brown ordered, forced to go after her.

"Ma'am!" a meaty nurse projected, unable to grab ahold of Lucia, who hurried back into Room 402, "Excuse me, MA'AM—"

Wham.

Lucia kept her back against the door, which jolted around, preventing them to enter the room. One and then two voices plead behind it. "Mrs. Smith," Dr. Brown said, as calmly as possible, until, "Open UP!"

Even with the ruckus around them, she only had her attention on Matt, who squiggled his way; unable to catch his breath. He had one arm on Nurse Olive for support and the other trembled and reached out for the IV in his arm.

"Don't!" Nurse Olive screamed and seized his hand.

"Don't TOUCH HIM!" Lucia jumped an inch or so from the door that gave one last HARD shake before it flung open and shoved her straight to the floor.

Two security guards hovered in the doorway. Multiple horrified and shocked faces had the chance to peer into the room from afar or ping over for a *closer* look.

"Everyone!" the meaty nurse asserted. "BACK UP!"

Another nurse used her arms for the gesture. 'BACK UP!'.

"They won't let me take you home!" Lucia wept, "*All of them! You.*" She glared down the staff, one by one. "*You. And YOU!*"

That last part, "YOU," made her eyes bulgy and targeted Nurse Olive, who tried to fight off Matt's resistance; her grip tightened on his arm. "Let me go!" he screamed.

"Do something!" Nurse Olive bellowed, fear shook up her voice, and her colleagues ran over to the opposite side of the bed. They grasped Matt's *other* arm.

"He's stronger than he looks," one of them said.

"They're the LIARS!" Lucia carried on. The security guard who yanked her to her feet got a bigger piece of her. "Put me DOWN!" She stomped on his foot, but a size four was only a pinch to the guard's size thirteen shoes.

"Ma'am," he said; his best attempt to also remain calm.

"BACK UP!" The guard who blocked the doorway flagged back the eager and curious crowd.

"You can't keep him from me!" Lucia was dragged further and further away.

"Grandma!" Matt attempted to tug and worm his way out of the two nurse's tighter and tighter grips. "Let GO OF ME!"

"I'm so sorry, Matt," Nurse Olive whispered.

"No! No! No!" Lucia thrust her elbow back, until another hand stopped it.

Dr. Brown yanked her by the arm, out of the security guard's grip and around the corner.

It lit a fire within Matt, as he gave one last pull. "HEY!"

"Matt!" Nurse Olive dove forward, but it was too late.

Matt was free.

He pounced on the bed and went headfirst, but he prevented further damage by smacking flat onto his hands.

The machine by his bed toppled over, part of the Domino effect. Matt yelped out in pain, as the IV tubes yanked out of his skin. The blood prolonged down from his wrists and onto the floor in streams.

Nurse Olive lunged for the IV rack, but instead, she soared across the bed and toppled over *immediately*. She landed flat on her back. By an attempt to turn around and catch ahold of the fallen mattress, her neck positioned itself in a crooked stance. Her colleague, Unknown, dashed over to her side and brought Olive's head onto her lap, as she cried for help and for some backup.

"Grandma," Matt said a bit louder, as he dragged himself across the chilly floor, using his upper strength. The room swayed left to right…right to left. "GRANDMA!"

"Let me GO!" he heard her from a distance.

Out in the hallway, Lucia continued to shout back; her voice echoed through every wall. She glared at the man beside her and spat, "You BASTARD!"

"It's alright everyone!" Matt heard a deeper voice follow up, his blood smearing and tracing his drags across the white tile. "Just a case of public intoxication…"

Closer and closer to the door, it caught his attention. Matt looked up, paralyzed in spots, as a train of sweat dripped away from his forehead. A silhouette hovered in the doorway, outside of Room 402. It elongated in size through the zoom in and out of Matt's blurry vision. *It* moved in and said, "*Gotcha!*"

The silhouette became darker—pitch black—and reached for Matt, who scooted backward and directly into his own puddle of blood. He screamed at the top of his lungs, until he was no longer able to breathe.

Like a fish out of its bowl, on the side of its body, Matt gasped for air. His lips began to tremor slightly. Dr. Brown knelt beside him, his eyes sharp, deep, and filled with dark pools of black. Lucia's voice only echoed further away.

"Matt! Matt! MATTY!" He listened to her. "Let GO OF ME—"

"I…want…to…see her."

"Well, that's a first," Dr. Brown mocked.

Matt groaned, after he attempted to get up and possibly sucker punch the doc in the face. "Fuckin…*asshole*." Even that took a lot out of him, and he coughed a few times; saliva spewed from the corners of his mouth and dripped everywhere. "You…can't…keep…me here…no…more…" It was worse because the color washed off his face.

"No one believes you and your friends' little *pathetic* story."

By the time Dr. Brown pulled away from his patient, the door closed, and an unknown, nameless nurse stood behind the doc, a needle in hand.

Matt groaned and squiggled around; it was the best he could do. Dr. Brown hushed him, as he cautiously placed his hand on his patient's arm. "It's okay, Mr. Smith," he said with a drip of southern charm. "This is just something to ease away your worries. Your panic attacks."

The nurse pressed the bottom of the needle, which released a few liquid squirts into the air. She passed it over to Dr. Brown; he more so snatched it from her loosened grip.

"You…bas…ttt…ard!" He was ghost white. "I hate you! I HATE…"

His pupils dilated. He looked directly into Dr. Brown's eyes that raged with numbness. Dr. Brown winced, as he pulled the needle out of his patient's upper arm. Matt went limp, like a noodle, as his cheek drifted to the floor—his cold cheek against the ice temperature floor. Everything stretched and swirled around, as his eyes flickered open and closed…open…and…

"He's losing a lot of it!" one of the Unknown nurses shouted, their hands bloodied up. They glimpsed over their shoulder for the next step. "Code—"

"Set-ups," *It* hissed behind his ear, "and criminal acts." Dr. Brown stroked Matt's thick wavy locks.

Matt's eyelids grew heavy. The bathroom door zoomed in…in…in…and out…out…out.

"Here!" one of the nurses said as she dashed over with a few towels. One of the towels was propped underneath Nurse Olive's head.

Words of encouragement and support kept Olive semi-conscious. "You're going to be alright," another nurse informed her.

"You'll be alright, son," Dr. Brown said a bit louder. "We understand that your friends were just…looking out for you." It became slower for Matt—a whisper in his ears. "Failed suicide attempts. Cops found nothing but *lies*."

"Where's…" Nurse Olive struggled, drowsy from the hard fall; her head still sat atop her colleague's lap. "Where's Matt?"

"You do know," Dr. Brown carried on, "that *lies* have multiple consequences."

Riiiinnnnngggg…

After one last twitch, Matt's eyes rolled back—white sclera to the white ceiling. He caught the slightest glimpse of Dr. Brown, who moved in closer; his heavy-duty kneecap was an inch or so from his patient's face.

Outside, people walked away. They whispered. They talked. They gossiped, gossiped about Matt. Derek and Lisa stood back, as if they were dogs with their tails between their legs. "What's going on?" Derek asked.

But their parents only clasped ahold of them and led the way, away from the hospital. Every inch of Lisa shriveled up as she bawled her weary heart out, breaking out into body-jostles. Derek was still perplexed. His father set his hand on his shoulder. "Come on, son."

"Matt! MATTY!" Jamie was blazing red; her cheeks puffed out like her beastly dilated eyes. She failed to worm out of her mother's arms. "Let go of ME! Mom...*please*...Let GO!"

"Exactly," her mother only said. "Just let *go* of it, Jamie! It's out of our hands now, sweetie."

Jamie stared at the fourth floor, the window to Room 402.

Matt fell asleep, and his body seemed to wither away as the white towels soaked up red. Streams of blood still seeped out of his wrists.

There was a knock.

Two men appeared in the doorway with a gurney. A security guard lingered behind them, as did Officer Hanson and Franco, who stared into the room—just as shocked and horrified. Somehow, they managed to get most of the nosy crowd to back up.

Someone signaled Hanson and Franco out of Room 402's sight. They gave one last look over their shoulders and followed out the last mob of people—brown-nosers. The crowd no longer watched on, as the door to Room 402 closed once the gurney wheeled in.

40.

"HE'S DOING IT!" THE ABYSS GIRL'S CHEERS SHOT AROUND LIKE A PINBALL. "He's almost there! Matt! Matt!"

With his nostrils flared, the snot sputtered out and ran its way down onto his neck. Although the air grew chillier, Matt's forehead broke out into a hot, sticky sweat. He reentered the white wonderland, escaping the black abyss that screeched for his goodbye. Over his shoulder, he caught a glimpse of the skeletal face.

The stranger opened its mouth, growing and stretching toward him. Matt's eyes turned wild and bug-eyed as his lips formed a scream but, his voice gave out. And so did his body.

"Matt!"

He went headfirst into the white abyss, until the benevolent voice of the girl returned a favor. A pair of arms held onto him and as Matt turned to look up…

* * *

He woke up and still found himself in the hospital bed, adjacent to the man in the Mister Rogers' sweaters, aka Mr. Peterson. "FUCK!"

But his screams were cut short by the drugs as they knocked him into a twilight. His eyes rolled back as darkness swallowed him.

41.

"THEY CAN'T DO THIS!"

The wine glass slipped out of the elderly woman's hands and soared through the air. It landed a few inches from the archway between the dining and family room. The shattering glass burst into itty-bitty pieces.

"THOSE PRICKS!" Lucia screamed again.

Jamie stared back at her reflection in the piece of glass lying on the wooden floor. Two bold pupils—baby blue and a red face, covered in tears. She ran her sleeve over her eyes, but it only increased the waterworks. They kept on coming and going…all the way down…down…down her cheeks. A waterfall in the dark. She kept silent and backed away from the destroyed wine glass in front of her.

At the dining room table, Derek looked as stiff as a board. His shoulders heightened, almost at the earlobes, his back raw from tension and agony. Lisa had her forehead pressed down onto the dining room table and she sniffled. It was only moments before she looked up—*scarlet-faced*—and burst into tears. The rest of *their* voices drowned out and dissolved away her cries.

"Lucia! STOP!" Mrs. Santoso lurched for her arm but tripped over the coffee table in the family room. "LUCIA!"

There it went—another one and another one. More objects whacked and crashed—KABOOM—against the walls and floorboards. Derek flinched a foot back and missed his step, until he clutched onto the back of the chair for support. It was comforting as he hunched over to catch his breath. Paralyzed from head to toe, Jamie pressed up against the archway pillar; red grilled her cheeks darker and darker.

Lucia seized ahold of another wine bottle instead of one of the eight glasses from the nine untouched dinners on the table. "LUCIA!" Mr. Peralta hurried over, but Lucia chugged back every drop from the green bottle.

"Lucia!" Mr. Santoso circled the table, inches from her, "LUCIA!"

"NO!" Not even Mr. Peralta had a chance, because the object flung across the room.

Her feet moved before the rest of her body followed. Jamie jumped away in time. A breeze hissed at her ear as the wine bottle crashed into the wall, where she stood seconds ago. The wine bottle shattered—KABOOM—into every shape and size. "How DARE YOU!" But Ms. Castellanos squirmed around, like a wild animal, until Mr. Santoso grabbed her. "LUCIA! LUCIA!"

Lucia stared in horror and dipped to her knees. Her mouth agape, her eyes filled with *regret*. "Oh, Jamie…"

Those baby doll eyes held onto hers for the longest time. Jamie scooted back against the wall and touched the side of her head. She felt bundles of knots that mirrored her shoulders. Then she grimaced.

"Jamie!" Lucia sobbed.

Jamie scratched her fingernails through her hair and sprung up. She ran out of there, before anyone got to her. A thin red line trailed down the wall, shaped like a fingernail mark. In the living room, Jamie collapsed onto the couch. With her head between her legs, she panted for air and hiccupped whatever was left of her.

"Lucia! Lucia!"

Jamie clenched her eyes shut and listened to the stifled sobs—not her own—and the footsteps that followed them. Up…up…up the staircase they went, until a door slammed and sent a vibration to the first floor like a Sonic Boom. *Another one.* Lisa screamed. Derek turned away, directly into his father's arms and cried. He just *cried*. "Dad…I'm…"

"I know," he said and hugged him back. "Me too."

"Honey…" Ms. Castellanos lowered on the couch armrest; her eyes were heavy. "Sweetie…"

But Jamie curled into a fetal position, pressing her knees to her mouth. The Smith residence was finished—zero evidence of police and investigation equipment. It was occupied as soon as Jamie's screams were no longer silent. Audible, Jamie was staying true to herself.

42.

IT WAS ALL A FLASH—the speed of light in stop motion for a second. Then the world resumed in fast forward, then it slowed down to real time.

Jamie and Derek slouched at the dining room table; only the pleas and tears from upstairs were audible and came from their parents. The Peraltas stood nearby, at the request of their daughter's comfort. Lisa began to sob, and her mother knelt beside her. More tedious, repetitive door knocks came from the floor above them.

"Lucia!" Mr. Santoso called out, followed by another door knock that went unanswered. "Goddammit!"

"Here," his wife asserted, "Lucia." Nothing. Ignored, like the rest of them. "*Shit!*"

"Seriously, you guys," Ms. Castellanos half implored and retorted until her tone lowered. "They'll hear us—"

"Like we can't ALREADY!" Jamie hollered back, her eyes at the ceiling.

"Bye, Lisa," Derek muttered and went in for a side hug. Afterward, Lisa buried her face back into her mother's blouse, wet from her tear blobs.

"Call if you need to," Mr. Peralta said. He was the last of his family to cross the dining room and headed for the front door. At a vigilant pace, the front door shut, until there was a CLICK.

Jamie kept her gaze on the front door at an earshot from her seat. Off one of her random hiccups, her eyes became soggy from all the endless hours of rage, angst—everything the human body could handle.

"Come on." Ms. Castellanos appeared at the table, across from her daughter and reached for her black purse that dangled off one of the wooden dining chairs. "We're leaving."

"All of us?" Derek peered up.

"No." She looked at her daughter. "Just us."

"*Why*?"

"Jamie," her mother said calmly, but also with a rise of sternness. She started to the living room and dining room archway. "*Come on.* I don't got all—"

"We can't *leave*! Lucia needs—"

"A bottle almost hit your head earlier, Jamie! A *wine bottle. Glass*, Jamie."

Lost for words, Ms. Castellanos stopped. Jamie dipped back down into her chair; her arms crossed tightly. Derek sat quietly, rigid as dried-up glue, and he scanned the room.

A few pieces of glittering *glass* on the floor *went* unnoticed from the earlier cleanup.

"You know, I could press charges," Ms. Castellanos started again, an echo in the night, "but with *obvious* circumstances, who wouldn't want to break *every* piece of furniture in this goddamn house!"

"Come on, Lucia," they heard Mrs. Santoso beseech *yet again* from the second floor; her soft tone made it seem that she was miles away; until—

"LUCIA!" Mr. Santoso roared; his repetitive door whams—not knocks—were ignored, and it made him knock, wham, knock, wham.

Now, she looked pissed. "Get up, Jamie."

"No. I'm not leaving. I'm not abandoning her."

Jamie choked back a sob. Derek reached for her hand that rested on the table and gave a squeeze. She gripped his hand back. Her eyes remained shut, as every crinkle accentuated the tears that welled up her eyes even more, visible to everyone. The longer she grimaced, the redder her complexion got—blood color. Derek was the only one who stared back at a motionless parent, who was neither shocked nor outraged.

Ms. Castellanos turned away and her high heels clicked across the floor—soft, loud, soft, loud, loud...louder. It was only seconds before she swung the front door opened and slammed it shut, securing it back into its bolts. Jamie exhaled for air but struggled to get it back. Derek faced her and grabbed ahold of her other hand. "Jamie," he said softly, already looking her in the eyes. "Hey..."

"No," she whispered back and kept her attention on the floor, as if ashamed to even acknowledge him, acknowledge it all, "it'll never be okay. I don't know what to do! What is *happening*?!"

Now, her head hit the table. A speck of lint floated in the air and drifted toward the glass cabinet behind them—the only unbroken pieces of glass. It landed atop one of the glass doors, where expensive China and a few framed pictures of the Smiths sat behind on another glass shelf. Baby Matt and Lucia; Toddler Matt and Lucia; Child Matt and Lucia; Pre-teen Matt and Lucia; Today Matt and Lucia.

Derek eyed the tabletop, where there were a few black-brownish dents. Stains. It looked like food, but it also looked like blood. He frowned at, what appeared to be, fingernail markings, and leaned in for a closer look.

"We're killers...We're..." Jamie pushed out the air from her lungs. She bawled even more, and her throat tightened from holding back a complete nervous breakdown. She sniffled nonstop and nearly collapsed into Derek's arms, as she leaned in, almost like she was about to get up; her nose pressed into his shoulder. "I'm...sorry."

"Don't."

"It's just that,"—She pulled back and loosened from his grip—"we *tried* and *tried* and *tried* and LOOK AT US! We're still failures—"

"We're NOT FAILURES. How could we? Like you said, we *tried*. That's all that matters. We gave it our all, but sometimes, it doesn't come back! And I wish I had the answer for that. But I don't. Neither of us does or will."

Those baby doll eyes, blue with grief, opened wider. Her lips were slightly parted, but the words got stuck and refused to come out.

"I know," Derek said. "How could someone like me know this stuff? I'm just a dumbass, right…A retard—"

"No, you're not—"

"Or, a shrimp boy." That got a chuckle from her. "Remember," he started up, "a long, long time ago in the land of fourth grade—"

"I do," she said, even blushing, "because you were really—"

"Short," they said in unison.

"Well, you still are." She smiled and so did he.

"That's it!" KNOCK. KNOCK from the floor above them. "I've HAD IT! We're leaving." Mrs. Santoso was far beyond angry…*livid*. "DEREK!"

Hands trembling. Feet tapping against the floor. Jamie backed up her chair.

"Jamie!" Derek stood with her, but she toppled back down into her chair. Gasping, she pushed her head between her legs. "Look—like this." Derek demonstrated an inhale, where he pushed out his belly, and to exhale, he sucked his belly back in. One-two-three…inhale—belly out. One-two-three…exhale and suck belly back in. She was surprised. "I saw Matt doing it a few times," he answered without her needing to. "He thought nobody was watching or, I guess, paying attention. But I was. I've always noticed."

"DEREK!" his mother avowed. "GET YOUR STUFF!" Their footsteps trudged closer to the first floor.

Now, Jamie took the lead in the breathing, semi-body relaxation; her exhales slowed down drastically. Derek continued to demonstrate—a lending hand, in case she needed it, which she did since her eyes never left him. He closed his eyes, absorbed in his own steady breathing and even counted out, "One-two-three. One-two-three."

Jamie gaped at him for a moment, stunned and grateful, until she followed through and closed her eyes as well.

"*What*?!" Mrs. Santoso said, her voice and now in the same room as them. Jamie never opened her eyes to confirm though. "Did you NOT hear?"

"I'm NOT going," was all Derek said, before he resumed back to counting with Jamie. "One-two-three. One-two-three."

A few more pieces of lint, or maybe it was dust, landed atop the glass cabinet doors. It was obvious. The tiresome merry-go-round pattern: Matt and Lucia, Matt, and Lucia, Matt, and Lucia. There was no sign of *her*. Matt's grandpa, father, or mother were not in any of the framed pictures on the cabinet shelves.

43.

IT WHISPERED THROUGH HIS ABYSS OF WHITE,
"MATT…MATT…This way, Matt…"

A pair of arms gripped Matt. Slowly, he let it all go and a rush of relaxation conquered his body. His rattling teeth slowed, as did his shaking body. Before he turned around and looked up, Matt already felt the warmth of a palm on his back — two sets of hands.

"Dad," he mumbled. "Grandpa."

But he only saw the white cloudy air as he turned around. Even the black abyss had disappeared. Instead, it was all solid white paint, like the opening credits to a nineties animated cartoon.

"It's okay, Matt," the Abyss Girl's voice echoed around him. "It's time. I know you're not ready yet."

"Who are you?" he asked. "What do you want from me?"

Silence: his panic surged, and he wheezed in and out for air.

"As sick as our secrets—the irony."

"Let me go! I'll do anything to go back—"

"Where exactly?" she asked, her voice echoing in his ear.

Matt balked and stumbled a few steps to the side. Again, his bugged-out eyes searched the air for a clue. And then, he saw the 4'10" silhouette of the Abyss Girl. Straight across from him, at the end of the abyss, she glided his way.

"Who are you?" he implored and backed up a few feet, still wary of the former entrance to the black abyss. "Why are you doing this?"

"You'll see."

44.

A KETTLE WHISTLED for her attention. Jamie slid into the kitchen and twisted the stove dial counterclockwise. The flames sizzled out. She huffed and puffed at the steam that evaporated out of the kettle's mouth and into the air came long, bony fingers.

That forced her to lean back. Fingers. Bones. The stranger.

The hairs on her arms stood up. She closed her eyes and took a deep breath, which made her a bit dizzy. She exhaled heavily and rapidly.

"They're out of sweet potato!" Derek shouted from the dining room, until he moved the receiver of his cell phone back to his mouth. "Hold on." Then he covered the receiver, "Jamie, my dad wants to know if a kid's meal will do."

"Yeah," she said, "that's fine with me."

"Yep that works—oh, sub out for two regular size fries!"

Jamie took a few steps back, away from the stove, to break out of her trance, her zombie state. Her eyes lingered on the red kettle—red as blood—still as a statue, not a peep or sound from it. The small steam cloud settled down, but it still seeped away from the stove, directly at her—those long, bony fingers.

"Not real," she whispered to herself; her eyes squeezed shut. "Not real. Not real."

"Okay. Later, Pops," Derek said back into his phone.

And by some miracle, it was the chipper, same old, sound of Derek's voice that calmed her nerves. Her breathing slowed down. When she reopened her eyes, the steam was gone. The illusion of long, boney fingers was gone. It was just the petite, red kettle, and a teenage girl.

A sigh, and her chest deflated like a balloon. She looked at the large window above the sink—the white curtains were ajar. The night was quiet, but so beautiful, like a scene from a movie. The sun hovered inches above the horizon, which added an orange hue to whatever the sun glimmered down upon.

"Hey, Jamie." Derek started towards the family room's archway. "I'm going to watch some TV." His cell phone vibrated, and he took one look at the screen—an incoming call from 'Mom'. He hit the red phone icon— rejected. His phone went silent, as he tossed it onto the dining room table. "And *don't* answer, if she keeps calling."

"I won't," Jamie replied, her gaze still on the sun. The redness on her cheeks flushed away, as she inhaled the warm, gentle air.

It was only moments before that she came to a screeching halt at the foot of the staircase. Everything snapped back on replay.

* * *

The screams. Buckets and buckets of lustrous blood stained the steps. Their feet. Their clothes. Their skin…covered in red, not entirely their own.

The crashes.

Destroyed items. Pieces of glass.

That gust of a rushing windstorm, coming at them one-hundred miles per hour.

* * *

"Not real," she mumbled to herself and squinted. "It's *not* real, Jamie."

Her knees jolted to the left side, which unlocked them, as did her thighs and feet. She clasped ahold of the baby blue mug in her hand and it steadied out her balance. Even though her hands clammed up, she was still able to adjust by wiping one hand and using the other to hold the mug tightly. Those baby doll eyes of hers broadened, as her breathing quickened.

* * *

At the flight of the staircase, Matt took the wrong step and headed her way—backward.

* * *

Jamie gasped and lunged against the wall, still in balance with the steamy mug, and somehow, *right as he came at her*, she reached and fumbled to turn on the light. All six of them that dangled from the ceiling shined their yellow-brown hues down onto the staircase and that one spot on the step—Matt's blood.

But Matt from *that night* was out of sight.

"Lucia." That tightness built in her chest. Jamie exhaled one last time. "Lucia."

The light underneath Matt's bedroom door shone with an ominous fluorescent quality.

Jamie patted at the corners of her face that became clammy. The heaviness settled back on the right-side of her chest—her chest—and it switched up her breathing again. Dead in her tracks, she did a double take at two different doors: the first and second one—Door One and Door Two. Door One belonged to Matt.

* * *

"Keep walking until you see his baby photo on the wall," Lucia said, as she guided her up the staircase. "His bedroom is right after that."

The short, chubby girl with braided pigtails scanned around, almost in awe. Those amber eyes of hers were a size too big for her small, round face.

* * *

Knock. Knock.

"Lucia…"

Knock…Knock…

Nothing.

"Shit…"

Jamie removed her hand from the door and glanced around. Only the faintest tree shadows reflected on and off the walls. She brought her attention back to the rusty gold— out of style—doorknob. It was *still* locked.

"Should've seen that one coming."

Louder than expected, Jamie dropped her fingers from the doorknob and turned on her heel, until there was a jolt. The doorknob turned left and right, followed by a click and a kitten-like squeal.

A beam of light poured out, as the door opened five inches. Most of it shined onto Jamie's cheek. Her reaction was strong, as though a knife came at her. A strained red eye peeked through the door crack. "What do you want?"

"I, uh," Jamie stuttered and blinked a few times, before hovering her hands above her eyes for a better view, "brought you some tea." She gestured to the mug, but it was probably invisible through the door crack, because of that goddamn light.

As more squeals, a batch of kittens being tormented, the door opened even more. The halo of light shone brighter and brighter, as if it were a hot rising sun in the sky on a summer day...unlike *that night*.

Jamie swigged whatever molten liquid ascended and tensed up her throat. She turned away for a moment as if a student awakening from the classroom lights being turned back on. "Lucia, could you please turn down."

There was a small thump. The stadium light-exposure diminished to a yellow-brown hue. By the time Jamie looked back at the door, her eyes bulged out and sparkled like crystals. Hunched at the doorway, Lucia held onto the doorframes for support. Her eyes were glossier and redder than ever, as though all the veins exploded, and the blood piled up. Her hair was tangled up like knots at the end of a rope. She tilted sideways and rested her head against her forearm. She hiccupped and out came a burp. That made her giggle.

Jamie coiled her head to the side and coughed, which transformed into a small gag, but the dog breath stench from Lucia already showered over her. "I, uh," it was the first thing to slip out of her twitchy lips, "also brought you some..."

Lucia moved an inch or so and pressed the right-side of her body against the doorframe. Then something took over her; it started on her belly, chest, and out came another disgusting burp. She chuckled, and her head dangled to its side. Tense, the last bits of thick alcohol stench, washed over her...*again*.

Jamie held her breath, until, "...food..." She fell silent, hard as nails.

Lucia gaped at her; and her eyes filled with twinkles of reds, purples, and now blues, like she was about to cry. But she gave a Miss Piggy chortle with a snort. It was awkward, as she wiped away the first and last fallen teardrops and whirled around. The elderly woman headed back into her bedroom, swallowed up whole by the dimness. Jamie finally exhaled—a small poof over her jeans. There was zero hesitation, as she stepped over that invisible divider between the hallway and the bedroom.

The smell was worse than before; it was strong and thick like cat shit in a litter box. The blinds were closed for whatever reason. The windows were, most likely, shut because of the muggy, lukewarm temperature that roamed around the bedroom.

Jamie yanked the top of her blouse over her nose. She was nasally like Squidward Quincy Tentacles from *SpongeBob SquarePants*. "I'll leave this here." She set down the mug, no longer steamy, beside a navy blue lamp, curved over. The face of it pointed down at the desk. Lucia had it pointed at the door only moments ago.

"You should've seen them." Lucia faced the windows, her back to Jamie. "They flipped when I had that light pointed at them." She snorted and toppled back onto the cobweb of bed sheets. "How does it feel now, Mr. and Mrs. Piggy Cops?! But you...I don't mind. They judge. You don't."

Jamie untucked her nose and scanned around the bedroom some more, as a small gasp escaped her tight-pressed lips. She covered her mouth and squeezed her eyes shut, motionless at the practically empty desk.

"They judge," Lucia repeated. "They just judge and judge..."

"*MATTY!*" she heard her own voice from that night.

* * *

The collision of footsteps. The cries and screams echoed. Four bodies sped by the firework explosions that shadowed the walls, like the splattered gunshots.

* * *

Jamie gawked over her shoulder. The bedroom doorway was empty. There was emptiness beyond it, except the unison of their voices chanting each other's names from *that night*.

"RELAX! RELAX!" she heard Derek's pleas echoing back and forth in her head. "IT'S JUST US!"

"They judge," Lucia started again, which brought her back to real time.

Jamie poked her finger into her mouth to touch the interior of her cheek. A mush of red coated her fingertip.

"They just…" Lucia stared blankly at the ceiling, where small shadows waved back at her.

From the corner of her eye, Jamie spied with her little eye—a tall yellow-greenish bottle beside the alarm clock, next to the bed.

"Why did you hurt him?" Lucia rolled onto her side, now toward Jamie. "You sat back and did *nothing*—"

"Stop—"

"*Nothing. Nothing. Nothing,*" she retorted and sat up straighter.

Downstairs, Derek grabbed the remote and lowered the volume, his eyes already on the ceiling. "Jamie?"

Upstairs, Lucia broke down into sobs, "He's all I have! I got NOBODY ELSE!"

Jamie now stood at the foot of the bed; her eyes shot from the bed light that emitted some light into the room to the wine bottle that edged closer and closer. Then, she saw a hand on it.

"Lucia," Jamie said warily, "Mr. Santoso will be back any minute now, and I think its best if you—"

"MATT!" Lucia tussled over onto her side. The bed slammed against the end table with the alarm clock and bottle.

"Lucia!" Jamie lunged for it, but the champagne bottle smashed onto the floor—tiny pieces flung everywhere.

Downstairs, Derek snatched ahold of the railing at the bottom of the staircase that stretched out and out, like the deep blue sea. He swallowed whatever got stuck in his throat. "Hello," he said and sounded shakier.

Upstairs, shaken up, her breathing only grew steeper. Jamie opened her mouth and said something—terror in her eyes—but it was inaudible. Lucia only had eyes for the tiny yellow-green glittery pieces and the red dots on—

"Oh, Jamie…"

A thin line of blood seeped out of Jamie's forearm from the few pieces of yellow-green glass that seemed glued to her skin. She dusted them off rapidly and furiously and backed away. The bed squeaked, as Lucia lifted one of her legs.

"*Don't*," Jamie snapped. "I said, DON'T!"

Lucia dipped back down onto the edge of the bed, motionless, as she gawked at the petrified child before her. Jamie, grimacing and cursing through gritted teeth, pressed her back against the wall, about eight to ten feet away from *her*, Lucia…a stranger…a monster.

Jamie gazed up at the timeline collage above the dresser. All of them. Those hugs. Kisses. And smiles…Beauty…Happiness that was long gone.

"We…love…him…" Jamie could hardly breathe and choked, as though her throat shriveled down two sizes. "Just as much as you do!"

Lucia grimaced and pressed her eyes shut. She lowered her head into her shaky palms, and her cries dwindled away. She could not even *dare* to apologize, even though her lips twitched to speak—but *nothing* came out.

"I love him." Jamie panted.

"I know…"

"I would do *anything* for him—"

"I KNOW!"

"I wish it was *me* that the hospital—"

"Don't say that!" Lucia stared her back in the eye—an absolute trainwreck. "At least, you still have others—"

"I'm not listening to this crap!" Jamie scurried to her feet; her complexion shot from pink to red, as she pushed herself up.

"Your mom," Lucia went on, and ascended to her feet at each word, "Lisa. Derek." She grabbed Jamie's arm, "Matt…and me—"

"Let go of me!" She yanked back. "Don't you get it, Lucia? All you do is just sit and pout, feeling so damn sorry for yourself." Slowly, she cracked. The tears arrived. "You have people to live for, *too*. You have all of *us*!" Now the tables were turned, because Lucia pulled back; and Jamie reached out for her hands.

"Lucia."

But she sunk into the bed and rejected Jamie's touch.

Jamie trudged closer. "Lucia."

"Don't argue with her." Derek stepped into the bedroom; his fingers locked in a tight, anxious twine. "My mom says to never argue with a drunk."

"Watch it," Lucia admonished.

"It's just…" His eyes shot wide in horror. "It's just…" He looked at Jamie.

Lucia caught that and by her deep sigh and straighter—almost proper—posture, she did not like it at all. "It's just *what*?"

"Come on, Derek." Jamie rushed his way to the door.

"Oh!" Lucia bellowed; although, her voice cracked bit by bit from the strain. "Just leave, like the *rest of them*!"

"Derek, COME ON!"

Jamie reached for his hand, but Derek scampered in, now a few steps closer to Lucia. "You know I don't blame him!" he said in between hiccups. He wiped his face that scorched to the temperature of a fever. "No *wonder* why Matt HATES you after—"

"Derek," Jamie pleaded.

"—he found those photographs in that BOX!"

"Derek!" Jamie went bug-eyed, and he scampered out. Then, it was her turn, she followed in pursuit. "DEREK!"

A bear trap gobbled up her foot and sent her straight to the floor—on her knees—as each body shake slowly, but viciously, detonated her. Lucia screamed out a wail.

Derek sped down the hallway—his feet pounded against the floor and down the steps to the first floor. Jamie never lost sight of him. She only chased after, a few feet behind him. "DEREK!"

Lucia peered up from her wobbly hands. Her face was a murderous red. She panted heavily. Eye to eye with the doorway, where the trees were visible through one of the ajar hallway curtain windows; they waved their branches of greens at her. "Lies," she muttered. "It's all LIES!"

Three steps away from the bottom of the staircase, "Come get me," Derek shouted into his cell phone. "I'll explain to you later!"

"Derek!" Seven steps to go for Jamie.

"Just hurry DAD!" Derek burst into tears.

"You SHOWED HIM!" Lucia's screams bounced off the walls and spiraled down the staircase and hissed against their backs. "Why were you snooping in my—"

Pop. Pop.

"Derek," Mr. Santoso repeated, but he received no verbal answer. The call dropped. He redialed and redialed but he only reached his son's voicemail. "Shit. Shit!" He punched the steering wheel, which set the horn off as well as pissed off the driver in front and behind him at the red stop light. Unaware that his foot mirrored his punch, the gas pedal sent him forward—a small crash and a brief electrocuted jolt from his car to the one in front of him.

"*Shit!*" Mr. Santoso took his foot off the gas pedal.

Darkness consumed every part of the house as the lightbulbs zapped out, one by one…

POP. POP.

The Smith residence turned black as the night sky. A few streams of light gleamed through the small window above the front door. The lighting was beautiful, like an ominous gargoyle on top of a grand cathedral way. "DEREK!" Jamie soared from the bottom of the staircase, as there was a louder and stronger—pop, pop, pop, pop.

A shower of silver glitter came from the exploding glass.

Jamie screamed and tumbled over the bottom step. Her body got slingshot through the air for a moment, until she smacked the side of her face on the floor; the impact continued to push her body across the floor. She wailed out bloody murder, as something lukewarm pulsed briskly throughout her system, as though her intestines wanted to escape. There was a striking pain. She wheezed in and out…in and out…for air.

"JAMIE!" Derek cried out somewhere in the sea of darkness.

"YOU GUYS!" Lucia hyperventilated from close by, then far away, and then… silence.

Jamie shrieked out again and again, and it sent her back to the floor *again* and *again*, as she attempted to crawl to her feet. Finally, she caved in and rolled onto her back. She cradled her left hand that felt swollen like a grapefruit. It was, infected, eaten up alive with reds, blues, purples, and black inflammations. Something hot and sticky climbed up her throat. Jamie lurched over to her side, ready for the forcible release, but nothing came out, except for gigantic painful gags.

There were a snap and a crackle.

In her faint sight, she saw it: the glimmer of moonlight brought in a dose of illumination, revealing lines of cracks embedded in the glass.

"No!" Jamie screamed; a red line split down the middle of her lips. "NNNNNNNNNOOOOOOOO—"

There was a loud POP, and all the windows shattered into a downpour of silver rain, followed by the swooshing of the wind. White clouds streaked out from every husky breath she took of the cold air. In came the white sheets of fog like the hallway flood of blood in *The Shining*.

There were a small TAP TAP and a gist of light emitted from a cell phone.

Derek pointed his cell phone around until he hit something—the front door. He maneuvered the light around, and then, he saw the molten silver layers between the door cracks. "SHIT!" He shivered; his breath pumped out and turned into air clouds. "*JAMIE!*"

Faster and faster the ride spun. The lights throbbed on and off…on…and off to the pulse of its own.

"JAMIE!" Lucia released ahold of the metal railing in the middle of the staircase.

The fog was out to play. The blizzard of white moved in and circled around Jamie, who was paralyzed in a crouching position. She stared wide-eyed at what was in front of her.

Black—the bottom touched the floor.

Black—a gown.

Black—an open sleeve.

Black—the pulled-up hoodie.

Jamie grimaced—her lips gushed out red—as whistles bounced off the walls like a silver ball. The sounds drilled into her ears, pushing up against his cranium. She opened her mouth, but the screams quieted down by the SWOOSH, SWOOSH, SWOOSH of the wind and the FLAP, FLAP of the sleeve that began to roll back.

"JAMIE!" Derek maneuvered the light to her, as he limped her way. "GET AWAY FROM HER!"

"JAMIE, NO!" Lucia stumbled down the last steps and headed to the light.

Almost in a robotic motion, the dried pieces of skin on the skeletal arm reached out for Jamie, close to being in a state of 'awe'. It smelled like raw meat; the chilly wind only pushed it up her nostrils. Those baby doll eyes of hers broadened with tears.

"It can't be," she whispered.

It hovered close to her, their hoodie drifted backward, falling off *Its* head. Red, yellow, and blue strings dangled from every inch of its face—veins, working bodily functions. Whistles came from *Its* mouth; *It* circulated warm air onto her cold face. Then *Its* veins turned white, until trickles of color engulfed Jamie. She burst into tears.

Her eyes twitched, and her knees gave out.

"NO!"

Lucia dodged Derek from the opposite direction, but instead, he tripped the way she tried preventing him from falling. His cell phone went flying through the air.

Lucia's weight pushed Derek. Then, Derek and Lucia sandwiched Jamie, who collapsed forward. Jamie dragged them down with her, into the arms of the stranger. A flash of white strobed throughout the entire household until there was a sonic BOOM…

No more cold.

No more fog.

No more wind.

Emptiness.

Glass and memories were knocked aside or shredded up like garbage—officially destroyed. The house stood strong but none of them did. Two cell phones were in the middle of the living room, about five or six feet away from the closed front door. One phone had a dark cover and the other was a light pink.

The navy blue cell phone lost its pulse, as soon as the incoming call from 'Dad' had stopped. The pink cell phone swerved across the floor once an incoming call from 'Derek's dad' arrived. From upstairs, a third cell phone soon buzzed off; everything was untouched and unbroken in the bedroom. Atop the lavender bed sheets was a silver cell phone.

In unison, all three of their cell phones gave a loud POP.

"Shit." Mr. Santoso hung up after he reached Lucia's voicemail. He looked to his side, where the angry driver he hit paced a few feet away. Still on a rant, Angry followed the police officer, who jotted something down into his little black book and examined the scratched-up bumper of Angry's car.

The three cell phones exploded into the air, but no pieces landed on the floor—or anywhere. The cell phones were gone, no trace of evidence. It mixed into the invisible air of nothingness. Just like Lucia, Jamie, and Derek, who were gone themselves. Nonexistent in the world.

Missing.

45.

"MATT, YOU NEED TO STOP THIS," the Abyss Girl begged of him in the white wonderland. She was about twenty feet away from him. *"Please, don't leave, Matty! You need to know."*

"Know what?" A wave of dizziness hit him, and he dropped to his knees. "I'm sorry," was all he said before tilting to his side and smacking the floor with his left shoulder.

Matt tried to breathe in the white air, but it evaporated into black smoke. He caught a series of glimpses of the screaming girl. She floated in and out of a wheel of light as it spun faster and faster, distorting her fair complexion…and Hershey Kiss brunette hair.

"Like Farrah Fawcett," he muttered to himself. "No…No! This can't be happening!"

As his eyes flickered shut, his body dropped deep into the black abyss.

* * *

The lights flashed on and off, no longer fluorescent. Two bare feet slapped against the tile–it was Matt.

Fully conscious in the other world, he raced down the empty hallways of the hospital. "Matt," he heard the Abyss Girl's voice emerging through the darkness, "you need me. I need you."

Still in his gown with both legs out in the open, there was no sign of a cast or any injuries evident. His eyes, sharp, never missed a beat, as he picked up speed, until his legs gave a jolt. But he caught his balance in time. Moving like jelly, he limped toward the mirages of his life that flashed across the roofless ceiling, replaced by the sky. A desire to go back to what once was, the tears already streamed down his face. His life circled within, what appeared to be, a burning black tunnel.

"Matt," the Abyss Girl's voice was a cold tremor, bouncing off the walls, closer to the edge. "There's something…I need to tell you something."

"Go away," he gritted through his teeth, oblivious to the girl gliding behind him. "I don't know you."

"Denial isn't good for the soul. Just look at your grandmother…"

Her tone lowered to a demonic pitch, and in a flash, she emerged from the black abyss in front of him. Her face was distorted and twitched into different static movements. At first, she laughed. In another flash, she screamed.

With gray lips and skin, it looked as though she were left for dead at the bottom of a swimming pool. "Well," she screeched, "isn't it!" On that final note, her mouth was left ajar and out spilled the maggots. The beetles and spiders scrambled across her face, going in one orifice and out the other.

Matt collapsed to the skating rink floor, silenced by his own inner screams. Cold pressed against his warm cheek. Matt wheezed for air as he flipped over onto his back and stared up at the massive black hole in the night sky. There was no sign of the girl, but he saw those faces: Lucia, Jamie, Derek, and Lisa.

The black hole spun, with the smoke fading into thin air, and picked up speed: LUCIA, JAMIE—

"Stop…It." Matt grinded his teeth.

DEREK—

"Stop it!"

LISA—

LUCIA—

"STOP!"

Their faces—memories—shuffled counterclockwise, faster, and faster and FASTER.

The curly hair boy turned crimson, as a wet oval prolonged across the center of his overall bottoms and ran down the inner part of his thighs, 'Me.'

FASTER—

The wavy-haired boy squirmed as he yanked out his first bloody tooth.

'ME.'

The wavy-haired boy wore a turquoise and light gray hoodie for the first day of school.

'ME. ME. ME. ME. ME. ME. ME. ME.'

First day. First times. First encounters.

A pear-shaped girl blushed every second.

'Jamie.'

A short shrimp-sized boy's hair flowed down to his neck.

'Derek.'

A tall Popsicle stick girl.

'Lisa.'

And those two, dismal teary eyes that belonged to the frizzy gray-haired woman—Lucia.

Riiiinnnnngggg...

Screaming, Matt pressed his hands to his ears. He watched, as their four faces stretched out; their eyes bulged out and mouths opened wider. They were also screaming.

"MATTY!" Jamie cried out.

Matt reached for their touch, but he stood a million miles away from them. Whatever yanked them out of his sight had only forced him down onto his back, pinned from the neck down.

He was paralyzed and wailed, "STOP!"

Darkness swallowed up his memories—his life—in a distorted shock. It formed a blur of red. Matt covered his eyes, until thunderbolts soared across the black sky. The redness came from his friends—melting away—and their bodies gushed red goo.

It splattered down into the hospital and covered Matt in whole, as he attempted to worm away, but it was impossible to move. He was stuck, forced to watch living greens grow from underneath him. The hospital, now, looked like the Amazon rainforest, growing all sorts of textures, colors, shapes, and sizes of Mother Nature's children—trees, bushes, flower beds.

SPLAT. SPLAT.

Raining red. Blood shriveled up and killed all her children. Next came the wind—

"NOOOOOOOOOOOOOOOOOOOOOOOOOOOOOOOOO OOOOOOOOOOOOOOOOOOO!"

POP. POP.

Multicolored fireworks blasted throughout the sky. Each explosion played out a clip from his life. Dark memories—that night—spiraled around him. The sky burst open, down in the middle—brighter than glory. Streams of black emerged through the orange-yellow rotating sun.

"STOP!" Matt called out, until it was night again, and a strong force wrenched him by the chest.

His body was taken over and curved into a distorted angle, as he jostled up and down. Possessed, his eyes turned white and bold. Growls escaped out of his mouth, as he bit deeper and deeper into his tongue.

It woke him up, and his normal eye color returned. Blood gushed out and slopped down the corners of his mouth, as he implored, "PLEASE!"

The phantom mask pressed through the ring of fire. Thunder and lightning roared the sky to life, oozing out the last drip drops of red, greens, purples, and pinks. Piles and piles of intestines plopped down to the hospital floor. Most of the muscles, tendons, and arteries wormed and melted away—a life of their own—until the red shower storm pushed out its raindrops for the bigger kill. Most of the intestines gave one final squeal, before they steamed away in hot water.

"Please." Matt wheezed in and out for air as he came face to face with the stranger, who tripled the size of any living monster. "JUST LEAVE ME ALONE!"

The flames around the stranger turned bigger and hotter. The flames framed around them for a perfect portrait. It made Matt sweat. The Devil just emerged from the soil of Mother Nature and brought hell with him. The black smoke began to fuse his way. Matt coughed and turned pale, blue, and purple, as his eye sockets shot to blood red. Pools of blood formed into circles, coming from what were once muscles, tendons, and arteries, on the floor. As soon as more raindrops hit them, millions of insects escaped from the water and ran for their lives.

Spiders. Beetles. Crickets. Cockroaches.

The stranger opened its mouth and pulled their next victim in, silencing Matt's screams, until his eyes rolled back to white, Matt closer and closer to the stranger's skeletal face.

Down…Down…Down…the bottomless black throat, until there was tranquility; a bright light pointed directly at him from high above and called out for his reach, "Matt."

So, he did what he was told and just…stretched out his arms.

"HOLDING!" a voice echoed from afar.

Matt only stared into the white, where a silhouette stood. A hand reached for him and pushed through the transparency—what divided their worlds—and chafed the right-side of Matt's face. Whoever it was had cold skin. Their fingers were strong and burly, like a man's, but softer than feathers, relaxing Matt.

"And, CLEAR!" the voice was, now, closer.

46.

MATT GASPED FOR AIR and his body jolted from, what felt like, an electric shock. The room rocked side to side; white walls were now visible. His eyes…

Nurses and doctors around the bed sighed with relief, as their patient's pale, blue vein skin darkened to a lighter sickly color, almost back to his normal warm complexion. "Pulse," the nurse said and loosened her grip from the two paddles that stuck to Matt's chest.

Matt saw that the door was shut from the corner of his eye. There was also the gurney from earlier, and blue curtains around the bed.

"Dropping!" another nurse stated.

"Dr. Brown…"

"You can't run forever, Matt," The Abyss Girl's angry voice was for his ears ONLY. "You can't run forever!"

There was a loud out-of-tune pitch—far worse than any scream—that came from one of the many nearby machines beside him. "Where am I?" Matt asked and started to gasp, his breathing thick and raw from his chest.

Wheezing.

Nurse Olive pinged to his side. She squeezed onto his hand; her eyes never left his. "Breathe," she said and demonstrated, as she inhaled and exhaled.

'Breathing relaxation.'

"Just look at your grandmother," the Abyss Girl growled in his head. "Do you want to become just like her?!"

A nurse interrupted her, addressing Matt directly, "Here."

But he freaked out when an unfamiliar nurse/*face* moved in closer with a breathing mask. Matt balked away, and a hot sensation scorched throughout his entire body, mainly at the wrists and feet, and he *screamed*. It settled down his panic attack, but he was robbed of words, when he saw brown straps wrapped around his wrists and the ankle without a cast. He was being attached, strapped down to the bed.

"What's…going…" he huffed and puffed again, "…on?"

"Matt," Nurse Olive said calmly; her eyes watered up. Her face screamed a pain of guilt, "I'm so—"

Up. Down. Right. Left. Down. Up. Left. Right…

Matt was not going anywhere. No matter how hard or fast he squirmed around, the bands only knocked him back down onto the bed. He became squeamish, as the leather constricted into his skin like teeth. His wrists and ankles turned crimson, making him grimace, as the pain forced a tight band around his head, as if a screw drilled into his skull.

"Matt," Nurse Olive croaked.

"Get me out!" Matt tugged and tugged at the bands. "GET ME OUT! GET ME OUT!"

"Doesn't feel nice," the Abyss Girl said, now standing at the edge of the bed. She was only visible to him, as the staff walked through her. She was a ghost. "Or does it, Matt? Do you like being ignored? That was my life for years, being ignored by everyone in my family, including that of your father and grandpa."

"You're not real! Hey!" Matt shrieked and jerked his head around, his eyes scanning the faces that appeared and disappeared in seconds. "Does anyone not see her?!"

Nobody listened. They were here but only dashed here and there. Some carried a clipboard and others shuffled through paperwork. But all of them ignored his pleas. Matt jostled around some more—wrists first; ankles next; wrists; ankles; ankles; wrists; wrists. The veins protruded out of his skin. His cheeks turned two red balloons, thicker than the white bandage that he still had on from *that night*.

"ARGH!" He slammed onto his back after the last pull.

Nurse Oliver's breathing was shallow as she watched in horror. The red liquid snuck out and trickled its way from underneath the bed straps around Matt.

"*Matt,*" the familiar voice spoke again.

"Lisa," Matt cried for joy after it dawned on him.

"Why doesn't anyone listen in this family?" Now the Abyss Girl lingered at the left side of the bed, next to Matt. "How come no one wants to address the elephant in the room? If more people would only address the obvious, there wouldn't be so many problems. Don't you think so, Matty? Would you ever believe me? Are you ready to know the truth?"

Matt felt the burning ring of fire at the pit of his stomach. The Abyss Girl gave him a sad smile and took a step backward as two nurses slid to their patient's side.

"Miss!" It was a man's voice. "*SECURITY!*"

"MATT!" There *she* was again. "I NEED TO—"

Lisa bustled into sight, but she only got so far—nowhere close to Matt—since her arms gripped behind her back by the oompa loompa nurse, who tailgated her into the room. A security guard followed in, seconds later. The loud and deep voice belonged to him. "Miss," he said again.

"Lisa..." Matt leaned forward, until the bands no longer allowed him to do so. "LISA!"

"ALL OF ARE YOU!" she screamed, nearly drowned out by her own tears. "*LIARS.*"

The short, stout nurse placed her hand over Lisa's mouth. It did not prevent Lisa's mutters. A few of them were *somewhat* audible such as, "Let me go/Fatass/You bitch/You cunt—"

"Goddammit, LISA!" Mr. Peralta rushed into the room with his wife; their mood did a one-eighty when they saw their daughter's physical circumstances.

"HEY, THAT'S OUR DAUGHTER!" Mrs. Peralta dropped her husband's hand and charged for the nurse.

"Whoa-whoa-WHOA." The security guard lunged in front of the oompa loompa nurse and Lisa. "I wouldn't do that if I were you."

It was Lisa's worried tone that made everyone look, "Matt."

Help was already at his side. A nurse removed the wrist straps, as two more towels were pressed down onto the bedsheets and his bleeding wrists. His shaky fingers formed a crooked, small red sea along his hands, fingers, and the white bedsheets.

"MATT!" Lisa screamed. The nurse, with help from the security guard, had no choice but to escort her and her parents out. "LET GO OF—MATT!"

A crowd already formed. Heads, bodies, and feet bunched up at the doorway; most of them attempted to push into the room with zero windows and a lot of lights dangling above the bed. The heat sweltered up Matt and increased the red on his face. A dozen security guards asserted, or flat out, shoved back the onlookers, brown-nosers, most of whom had a notepad and pen in hand, and flash photography.

"GIVE ME THAT CAMERA!"

It was all still visible to Matt, until he locked eyes with him and only *him*: Dr. Brown was inches from the doorway to the surgical room, near the chaos, but hidden behind the door. His eyes turned googly, a sense of perplexity and fear in them as he grew ashen. He took a step forward, his mouth ajar.

"Say it," he mumbled; his voice was scratchy, strained from the trauma. The nurses now added the final bandage wrap around his wrists. "You…You…"

"FUCK!" The oompa loompa nurse nearly collapsed from the pain—teeth marks in her hand. Security guards were already on it.

"LISA—"

"DON'T!" Her mother turned around in a panic, until one of the guards yanked her back, further from the surgical room.

Lisa went straight to the bed. "THEY'RE GONE, MATT."

"LEDGER," Dr. Brown ordered, "escort them out NOW."

"MISSING!" Lisa continued and tackled her way over to the foot of the bed. "THEY'RE MISSING!"

A taller and heftier, meathead security guard grabbed her arm and towed her to the exit. Another hand slapped over her mouth.

"YOU *BITCH*!" were Lisa's last words, as she was forced out of the room; her hands squeaked across the tile as she wormed her way around, but there were zero chances of breaking free. The security guards got a hold of her ankles and continued to pull and pull her.

That was all it took. Everything around Matt...objects...people...more photography flashes...slowly tilted around and around...

In between it all, he saw the Abyss Girl. She remained at his bedside; her head was hanging low in disappointment. With her eyes shut, she sniffled. The tears rolled down her cheeks.

"No one will ever believe me," she wept.

Mr. and Mrs. Peralta glanced over their shoulders, unable to lock eyes with Matt. The three security guards behind them kept moving forward. They were being pushed out of the room like their daughter was seconds ago.

It baffled Matt; how the two male nurses were not the ones who cleaned up and bandaged his wrists. The original nurses were already gone. "Wait," he begged, "don't—"

But the two men pinned down his arms, as other two new nurses prepared the straps.

"STOP!"

His wrists were reattached to the bed railings, but it was the last drop of medicine injected into his upper arm that stole his attention. "You just need to rest." The needle was in Nurse Olive's hand. She could not bear to look him in the eye, "Forgive me."

She ran out and even flinched away from Dr. Brown's touch. As soon as she rounded the corner in the hallway, her legs jostled and gave out. A crowd rushed up to her, as she broke down...*bad*. Her knees stayed on the cold tile.

"Believe me," the Abyss Girl said softly. "Just don't let them get away with this."

"Damn you." Matt's body relaxed, but everything else screamed drowsiness, as his head bobbed around, like he was unsure with which side to go. "God*damn you*."

The nurses cleared out—one of them swiped the syringe that Nurse Olive left behind on the tray. Most of them eyed their boss for approval. But Dr. Brown only held eye contact with his patient, lingering about a foot away from the bed. Her body gave out and sent her down to her side.

The Abyss Girl gave him one last look and turned away. She glided from the beside to the doorway, her shoulders heavy with grief. She solemnly turned back at him, both disappointment and rage on her pink face.

"Believe me," she beseeched, "you'll know the full truth, but maybe not today."

Dr. Brown stepped toward Matt, seeming to purposely block the child from Matt's sight. "Not good, Matthew," he said with the click of the tongue. "I don't like my patients appearing like they've just seen a ghost."

"What HAPPENED to them?" But Matt's tone diminished because he started to cry. "Oh, GOD..." There it was again: the black dots spotted out his vision and worked its way from the exterior and inward. "I *hate* you—"

"Don't," Dr. Brown implored and daubed his hands at his sweaty, glistened forehead. "Just *STOP*—"

"FUCK YOU!"

Riiiinnnnngggg…

It stung the middle of his forehead—almost a fuzzy feeling—and his head rolled to the side and stopped.

"He's bleeding!" One of the nurses turned around.

"*Goddammit*, Matt!" It was all Dr. Brown said before he removed his coat and wrapped the material around his patient' wrist. Red into the white.

The nurse at the door called out, "CODE BLUE!"

"The shit you put yourself through." Dr. Brown applied more pressure to his wrist. "Matt, you do know that in your current condition, it'll only do more harm to you by discussing what Lisa had—"

Matt gave a steep, groggy groan. His eyes opened and closed, opened, and closed every other second. "Just…tell…me." His breathing was at a shallow pace; his chest elevated up and down, down, and up, "I'm…sick…of…everyone…sugarcoating."

The disappointment and sadness washed away his patient's color. Matt was pale again. Dr. Brown sighed and bowed his head to process it for a moment.

"Dr. Brown…Address IT!"

"'A Tragedy in a Family,'" Dr. Brown finally said, all shaky and in between deep breaths. "You want the truth so bad…"

Up…up…and down Matt's chest went.

"I've always known it, Matt. Since day one. The truth."

"What…are…you…saying?"

"There was never a car accident, Matt. It's all a lie."

Matt's eyes stayed open for a few seconds longer. The doc's face appeared in full sight, but not everything around him remained in full focus, since those blurred out fast. He held his breath, the air swimming in his chest. Dr. Brown sniffled and looked up at him in tears.

"They were...shot. Murdered." Dr. Brown looked away from the blood that soaked through his coat and stained all over his hands. "Matt, your mother killed your grandpa and dad."

To Be Continued,
END OF BOOK ONE.

ACKNOWLEDGMENTS

Finishing this novel was always important to me. Someone remarkably close to me had passed a few years ago, just weeks before I finished a draft of *Elephant*. My wonderful Grandma Connie was the biggest reader and until this day, I credit her for my passion growing immensely over the years for literature and storytelling. She used to tell us grandchildren, "Ditto," whenever we told her, "I love you," because the movie, *Ghost*, was one of her favorite movies. So, Ditto forever and ever, Grandma.

Thank you to everyone who was behind this journey of *Elephant*, from earlier readers such as family, friends, and the amazing editorial and publishing team.

Thank you, Sarah Fader, for being the first "yes" and seeing this story through from start to finish and understanding the journey of Matty. THANK YOU!

A HUGE shout out to the editors of this book, including Hilary Jastram for her expertise and notes; Aaron Smith for guiding me through the earlier edits of *Elephant* (he also designed this AWESOME book jacket too); Ben Parris and his wonderful team for additional edits; and lastly, Katie Walsh for coming on board and magically bringing this book home.

And THANK YOU MOM for hearing yap about Matty and his journey for the past years (and crying over rejection letters for the earlier drafts of *Elephant*).

A HUGE shout out to Quail Summit Elementary in Diamond Bar, California, where Matty Smith's story was created for a fifth-grade school project in Mrs. Burke's class <3

Lastly, this is for the voices who go unheard. You MATTER. There are people out there who are waiting to listen. If you or a loved one are in crisis, you can reach out to the National Suicide Hotline 1-800-273-8255 or text HOME to 741741.